tery to solve . . . I highly recommend *Meet Your Baker* and look forward to reading the next book in this new series!" —*Fresh Fiction*

"*Meet Your Baker* is the scrumptious debut novel by Ellie Alexander, which will delight fans of cozy mysteries with culinary delights." —*Night Owl Reviews*

"Alexander weaves a tasty tale of deceit, family ties, delicious pastries, and murder against a backdrop of Shakespeare and Oregon aflame. *Meet Your Baker* starts off a promising new series."
  —Edith Maxwell, author of *A Tine to Live, A Tine to Die*

A Batter of Life and Death

"Clever plots, likable characters, and good food . . . Still hungry? Not to worry, because desserts abound in . . . this delectable series." —*Mystery Scene*

"A finely tuned mystery!" —*Dru's Book Musings*

"A delightful cozy mystery that will keep you turning pages to see what Jules is going to get into next . . . Grab a few napkins, because you'll be drooling all over the pages as you read some of the delicious-sounding recipes these chefs are cooking up." —*Fresh Fiction*

Fudge and Jury

Ellie Alexander

St. Martin's Paperbacks

This is a work of fiction. All of the characters, organizations, and events portrayed in this novel are either products of the author's imagination or are used fictitiously.

FUDGE AND JURY

Copyright © 2017 by Kate Dyer-Seeley.
Excerpt from *A Crime of Passion Fruit* copyright © 2017 by Kate Dyer-Seeley.

All rights reserved.

For information address St. Martin's Press, 120 Broadway, New York, NY 10271.

ISBN: 978-1-250-08805-5

Our books may be purchased in bulk for promotional, educational, or business use. Please contact your local bookseller or the Macmillan Corporate and Premium Sales Department at 1-800-221-7945, ext. 5442, or by e-mail at MacmillanSpecialMarkets@macmillan.com.

Printed in the United States of America

St. Martin's Paperbacks edition / January 2017

St. Martin's Paperbacks are published by St. Martin's Press, 120 Broadway, New York, NY 10271.

10 9 8 7

Chapter One

They say that chocolate makes everything better; I agree. Torte, our family bakeshop, looked as if it had been dipped in chocolate. Every square inch of counter space was filled with chocolate tarts, chocolate éclairs, chocolate cakes, chocolate cookies, and chocolate truffles. Whimsical chocolate posters promoting Ashland's annual Chocolate Festival hung on the bakeshop's front windows and the scent of chocolate simmering on the stove permeated the cozy kitchen.

Every March in Ashland, Oregon, my hometown hosts one of the largest chocolate festivals in the Pacific Northwest. This year Torte had been chosen as one of the showcase vendors, which meant we would have a prominent booth in the center of all the delicious action and have an opportunity to showcase our chocolate artistry. Being recognized as a showcase vendor was a huge accolade, but also meant that we had to prepare double—if not triple—the amount of chocolate samples. Our staff had been working around the clock.

I surveyed the kitchen. It looked like a scene from

Charlie and the Chocolate Factory. Chocolate bubbled on the stove and cooled in long thin sheets on the butcher-block island. Stephanie drizzled white, dark, and milk chocolate over marzipan. Mom dipped short-bread cookies in vats of molten chocolate. I twisted the lid onto an industrial-sized container of cocoa powder and brushed dust from my hands.

In addition to the bakeshop being taken over by chocolate, we were in the middle of a remodel. After months of skimping and saving, Mom and I had finally managed to amass enough cash to purchase the new ovens we desperately needed. Since the Chocolate Festival would take place over four days, we decided to close Torte for the duration of the fest. Andy, Stephanie, and Sterling, our small but mighty staff, would focus on the kitchen upgrade while Mom and I dazzled guests with our chocolate confections at the festival.

I moved canisters of sugar and flour to the side and gave the whiteboard a final glance. I had worked out a schedule that would allow enough time to clean and prep the kitchen, paint, reorganize and inventory our stock, upgrade our ordering and payment system, and— fingers crossed that everything went as planned—to in-stall the new ovens just in time to reopen for business on Monday. The Chocolate Festival kicked off tomor-row, which meant that the team had two and half days to complete everything on our to-do list before the in-stallers arrived with our ovens on Sunday afternoon. It was going to be tight, but I was confident we could pull it off.

No one at Torte was afraid of hard work or a little el-bow grease. I knew that was due to Mom's incredible work ethic. I smiled as I watched her dunk a shortbread cookie in dark chocolate and banter with Stephanie. She set an example for our young staff; despite the fact that she was in her mid-fifties she was still one of the first people to arrive at the bakeshop every morning and last to leave.

She had been at Torte's helm since my dad died, and thanks to her tireless effort, kind listening ear, and delicious bread and pastries, Torte was thriving. I wanted her to thrive too. As the thought passed she turned and caught my eye. Her face was bright. "What is it, honey?"

"Oh, nothing," I replied, sliding the canisters back into place. "Just going over the schedule one more time."

Mom chuckled and winked at Stephanie. "Is that the hundredth time so far this morning?"

Stephanie poured white chocolate onto parchment paper. "At least."

I ignored their teasing, and walked to the sink to rinse cocoa powder from my hands. As much as I knew that Mom loved the bakeshop, I also knew that she was due for a vacation. She and the Professor, Ashland's resident detective and Shakespeare buff, had been getting serious. The Professor wanted to travel, but Mom had been reluctant to commit and I had a sneaking suspicion I knew why—me.

When I returned to Ashland last summer my heart was broken. I'd left everything I knew, including my husband, at sea. Being back in Ashland, surrounded by warm and welcoming familiar faces and Torte's bright cherry-red and teal walls was exactly what the doctor ordered. My heart had finally started to mend. It helped that Carlos, my semi-estranged husband, had made a surprise visit to southern Oregon last month. When we had parted ways we agreed that we would take a hiatus. He was the last person I expected to show up in Ashland.

At first the distraction of having him back in my life and back in my kitchen had been overwhelming, but after a few days we fell into our old easy rhythm. I guess in some ways it was inevitable. Food was our love language. We didn't even need to speak when we were in the kitchen together, our bodies remembered. We moved in a comfortable easy cadence just like we had on the ship. But things were different now. Carlos had lied to me. He had hidden the fact that he had a son for the duration of our marriage. I hadn't been sure that I could forgive him for that.

When he first arrived I was angry, but that had begun to dissipate. Of course I was sad and disappointed that he had kept something so important from me, but I began to understand why. He was trying to protect his son, Ramiro. I couldn't blame him for that.

It would have been so much easier if I could have stayed angry with him. When Carlos was oceans away I had been able to concentrate my time and energy on Torte and let thoughts of us slip into the recesses of my brain. He became more like a fuzzy dream—until he showed up in real life and flipped everything upside down again. His sultry dark eyes and playful personality had sucked me back in, and I found myself not only forgiving him, but falling for him again.

Then, as quickly as he had appeared, he was gone. My heart hurt, but not like it had when I left him. Things were healing between us and, for the first time, I knew that Carlos loved me and would do anything for me. But that didn't change the fact that we were worlds apart. My life on the ship was a distant memory. My future was at Torte, and only time would tell if Carlos was part of that future. For the moment, he was back on the ship and sailing under sunny Caribbean skies, and I was due at a meeting on the other side of the plaza.

I shook myself free from my thoughts and concentrated on my immediate surroundings. Mom and Dad used to tease me about living in my head too much when I was growing up. I blame them; after all, they named me Juliet Montague Capshaw. A name like Juliet requires time spent in your head.

The clock on the far wall signaled that it was a few minutes before noon. I needed to get moving. I dried my hands, untied my apron and folded it on the island. "Back in a few," I called to Stephanie and Mom and headed for the front door.

The sky dripped like a leaky faucet as I stepped onto Main Street. It had been raining for five days, which was a rarity in Ashland. Many tourists are surprised to learn that we get very little rain in this corner of the state. People tend to think that Oregon is one giant mud puddle. While there's some truth to that—Portland and the surrounding valleys west of the Cascade Mountains tend to get waterlogged—Ashland has a much more Mediterranean climate. It's one of the sunniest cities in the Pacific Northwest, another reason I was happy to call it home.

I pulled my rain jacket over my head and ducked under the red and white striped awning at Puck's Pub. In addition to boasting a serene climate, Ashland is also known around the world as being home to the Oregon Shakespeare Festival. Our quaint downtown plaza could be mistaken for an old English village. Most of the buildings are Shakespeare–themed, with ornate façades and gables, and many of the shops have witty Bard-inspired names, like Puck's. Right now I was on my way to meet with Rosalind Gates, the president of the downtown business association. Rosalind had been working with the city to preserve Ashland's old-world charm. The city (thanks to Rosalind's persistence) had recently passed new design ordinances in order to ensure that businesses in the busy plaza adhered to the Elizabethan aesthetic.

Rosalind was spearheading a grant program to help small businesses, like Torte, expand. That's why I was meeting with her today. I tucked a white paper bag with our Torte logo stamped on the front into the inside pocket of my jacket and hurried along the wet sidewalk.

Hearth & Home, the brokerage firm where I was meeting Rosalind, was located just outside the plaza. I headed toward Lithia Park and took a right at the end of Main Street. Rain spattered on my jeans and soaked through my tennis shoes.

When I arrived at the homey, wood-framed building, I pushed open the glass door and stepped inside. Rosalind was waiting for me near the reception desk. Her silver hair was tucked behind her ears, revealing plastic earrings in the silhouette of Shakespeare's bust. She wore a purple T-shirt that read ASHLAND: SUCH STUFF AS DREAMS ARE MADE ON. The last time I'd seen Rosalind she had been sporting a SAVE OUR SHAKESPEARE shirt when a chain restaurant threatened to move into the plaza.

"New shirt?" I asked, taking off my raincoat and hanging it on a rack by the door.

She glanced at her chest. "Do you like it? I'm testing out a new tagline for the plaza. I'm not sure if this one is going to stick."

"But you made a shirt."

"My son bought me a screen press for Christmas and I figured I'd give it a whirl."

"That's great." I walked toward her and handed her the bag. "Sorry I'm a little late, but I come bearing chocolate."

"Lateness is completely excusable if it involves chocolate." Her eyes lit up as she removed a dark-chocolate-covered cherry from the bag. When she smiled deep crevasses formed on her aging cheeks. "Oh my, talent does run in your family, doesn't it? Your mother and then that romantic husband of yours. I can't wait for another Sunday supper at Torte. Everyone is in a twitter about how delicious your husband's tapas were. He enchanted the entire town, you know."

"He has that effect on people." I smiled. Carlos's tapas were irresistibly succulent and full of Spanish flavor. They were one of the reasons I fell for him—hard—on the ship. I understood why Rosalind and everyone else in Ashland had fallen under his spell.

"Will he be back in Ashland anytime soon?" Rosalind asked.

The truth was I had no idea. We had left things open-ended when Carlos went back to the ship. I wasn't sure when I would see him again, and I was trying my best to be okay with that. The distraction of preparing for the Chocolate Festival and cleaning out the kitchen had been helpful. It felt symbolic to clean and reorganize things at Torte as I was reprioritizing my personal life. To Rosalind, I said, "Hopefully."

"Yes, let's hope." She gave me an understanding smile. "Come on back. I have the paperwork for you to look over." She led me to an empty office near the back of the building. Blueprints and maps were tacked to the walls along with old photos of Ashland from the early nineteen hundreds, and a plan for a railroad terminal and station. "Is this for a railroad?" I pointed to the far wall.

Rosalind's smile broadened. "Yes. It's not public knowledge yet, so let's keep that between us."

I studied the sketch. "But the railroad tracks have been abandoned for years."

"Exactly." Rosalind walked behind the oak desk and took a seat. She motioned for me to sit too. "Do you remember the sound of the train whistle when you were a girl?"

I nodded.

"We've been cut off from the rail line for too long and I intend to change that. Not only will freight deliveries return, but with my plan we're also negotiating with Amtrak to bring passenger trains to Ashland again." She nodded toward the wall. "The Siskiyou Summit Railroad Revitalization Project is set to resume train traffic early next year. I can't wait to hear those lovely whistles again."

Rosalind explained that the railroad had abandoned

service to Ashland in 2008. Since then freight had to be hauled by big-rig trucks. In the winter when the mountain passes were snowed in that meant that goods and supplies often couldn't be delivered until the roads were cleared.

"I didn't know there were any plans to reopen the rail lines," I said to Rosalind.

She nodded. "It's been a long time coming, and a vital step for our local economy. Per-mile costs are much less by rail, and that's a very good thing for you as a business owner."

"Right," I agreed. If anyone could handle a project of this magnitude it was Rosalind Gates. Most of her peers had retired and spent their days knitting and volunteering to hand out seat cushions at the theater. Not Rosalind. She was a powerful force in Ashland's downtown community, constantly petitioning the city council on behalf of business owners.

Pushing a stack of blueprints rolled up with rubber bands to the side of the desk, Rosalind picked up a file folder and handed it to me. "Here are the loan papers. You'll need to fill them out and return them to me no later than tomorrow at noon. That deadline is firm. The city council will be making all of their decisions on granting funding. I've already submitted your preliminary application. This is the final paperwork—and Juliet, I do think you're a sure thing. Would you and your mother like to do a walk-through this afternoon?"

"I think that's probably a good idea." I could hear the hesitation in my voice. Everything was moving so fast. It had only been a couple of weeks since Rosalind approached me about the city's grant program. The space below Torte had come available for lease, and we were seriously considering an expansion. It was rare for property on the plaza to open up, and when it did there were usually multiple offers from businesses vying for a spot in Ashland's prime retail market.

Mom and I had discussed expanding Torte *someday*, and suddenly that dream was within reach. We both had reservations about more than doubling our square footage, though, especially as Mom was starting to think about scaling back. At the same time, we knew that opportunities like this didn't come very often.

Having help from the city would be paramount. Renovating the basement space was a much bigger project than our kitchen remodel and new ovens. We couldn't afford that kind of undertaking on our own, but with grant money or a low-interest loan from the city, the idea was one step closer to reality. The only problem was that this was a temporary offer.

"Juliet, I can't stress this enough. If you're serious about moving forward, you have to be ready to go. This is unprecedented. Thanks to Lance we have secured an art development grant, but that money has to be spent before the first of July. If Torte is awarded a grant, construction must start immediately."

"I understand." I nodded.

"The city is also planning to roll out a new loan program for businesses in the plaza that are directly in the flood zone." She paused and studied me for a minute. "Torte hasn't had many issues with flooding, has it?"

"Not as far as I know."

"I'll ask your mother." She made a note on a yellow pad. "In any event, we have to do something about this ongoing flooding issue. It's critical to the plaza's con-tinued success, so the city is going to offer low-interest loans. Those funds must be used specifically for build-ing upgrades."

"Got it." I took the final loan papers, thanked Rosa-lind for her time, and left. The loan papers felt heavy in my hands as I made my way outside into the dripping sky. I took a different route back to the bakeshop, along the Calle Guanjuato, a brick path complete with antique street lamps and deciduous trees that paralleled Lithia Creek. Tiny green buds bent the tips of the tree branches, revealing the first signs of spring. I tightened my rain-coat and smiled at the thought of cherry blossoms and fresh cut grass.

Many of the shops and restaurants with storefronts facing the plaza also had outdoor space and seating on the Calle Guanjuato. During the height of the season theatergoers would dine creekside on second-story decks under the stars. For now, patio furniture and tables had been stacked away and sandbags barricaded the back entrances.

The entrance to the basement was on the opposite side of the street from Torte's front doors at the far end of the Calle Guanjuato. Steep concrete steps with a black iron railing led down to the shop. I couldn't resist peek-ing in the window for the hundredth time. The steps were slippery. I held tight to the railing as I made my way down the slick moss-covered steps. Water had pooled in a large puddle about two inches deep in front of the door. That wasn't a good sign.

I bent down to see if it was spilling under the rusted old door. Power had been cut off to the empty space months ago so it was too dark to tell. I'd have to mention that to Mom and add potential flooding to our "con" list.

Ashland's plaza sits in the middle of a flash-flood zone. When heavy rains fall (which, fortunately, doesn't happen very often) they spill down the city's surrounding hills and funnel straight into the plaza and Lithia Creek. One summer, when I was in high school, a thunderstorm erupted over the city and three inches of rain fell in less than an hour. Every business on the plaza, including Torte, was inundated with water. In some places the water came as high as the second story. We fared better than most, with only a few inches of water flooding Torte's dining room, but it took weeks to pump all of the water out of town, and for business to return to normal on the plaza.

Was this a sign? I pressed my face to the wet glass and peered inside. As far as I could tell the basement looked dry—at least for the moment. But I could hear Lithia Creek raging only a few feet away. If it spilled over its bank the basement property would definitely be underwater.

I sighed and walked back up the stairs. There was nothing I could do for now. A contractor would know what to do about potential flooding and, fortunately, we were scheduled to meet with the city's building inspector soon. At the moment, I had to get back to my chocolate.

Chapter Two

Two preschoolers wearing bright yellow rain boots splashed in a puddle in front of Torte as I rounded the corner. Their mom shot me an apologetic smile when I ducked to avoid their spray. I grinned and waved. "Looks like fun."

She held up a paper coffee cup and scooted under the awning. "At least I have one of your warm coffees to keep me company while these two do their rain dance."

I wondered what she was drinking. Andy, our head barista and college student, had earned a reputation around town as a coffee mixologist. His drink creations were unique and craveworthy. The bell hanging above the front door jingled as I stepped inside. A line snaked past the pastry case to the espresso bar where Andy was pulling shots and chatting with customers. Mom cut between the line with a tray of panini in her arms.

"Hey, boss," Andy said as I squeezed past the espresso machine. "It's heating up in here. Everyone wants to escape the rain."

"What are you making this afternoon?" I asked.

He carefully poured steamed milk into a mug using a silver spoon to create a leaf pattern out of the foam on top. "I'm going old-school for lunch today. A classic. Double latte with extra foam and a just a dash of brown sugar."

Usually, Andy's coffee drinks were unique flavor combinations. I was surprised that he was going for such a simple drink. Not that I was complaining. There's nothing better than a smooth latte with rich espresso in my opinion.

I leaned close to him and whispered. "Is this because we've already started to pack everything up?"

He grinned and winked. "Maybe."

"Nice." I gave him a half salute of approval and headed for the back. Part of running a small business is knowing how to market, and Andy had that down. I grabbed a clean apron from the rack and tugged off my rain jacket, then I washed my hands and checked on our chocolate progress.

Stephanie stood at the stove stirring melted chocolate in a double boiler.

"How's it going?" I asked, dipping my pinkie into the pan to check the consistency of the chocolate. It had a gorgeous, lovely sheen. "This looks ready."

"Cool. I was going to ask your mom if I should start dipping." Stephanie wore her jet-black hair streaked with violet in two shoulder-length braids.

"Yeah, it looks good to me." I motioned to the stack of marzipan squares assembled on the counter. "You've got the technique down, right?"

Stephanie nodded and demonstrated the chocolate-dipping technique I had showed her yesterday. Once the marzipan was coated in a thick layer of shiny chocolate she placed it on parchment paper. "Good?"

"Perfect." I gave her a thumbs-up. "Only—what? Five hundred more to go."

"Great." She rolled her eyes and scowled. I knew that she wasn't serious.

"It could be worse," I said as I rolled up my sleeves. "I could put you on fondant duty."

Chocolate dripped from Stephanie's hand as she plunged another marzipan square into the creamy mixture. "No way. Never again. I loathe that stuff."

"I promise it's not that bad once you get used to it."

Stephanie shook her head. "Maybe for you, but that stuff kills me. No, thanks. I'll stick with dipping chocolate."

"Don't fear the fondant," I teased, reaching under the island and grabbing a bucket of white fondant.

Stephanie pretended to jump. "Don't bring that any closer to me."

"Bring what?" Mom interrupted our conversation.

"Mom, we have failed our young staff."

"How?" Mom placed an empty tray in the sink. Her brown eyes held a look of concern.

"Stephanie is afraid of fondant."

A look of relief washed over Mom's face. "Oh, whew, you had me worried for a moment." She walked to Stephanie and wrapped her arm around her shoulder. "I'm with you, Stephanie. I have nightmares about fondant."

"Hey!" I plopped a mound of fondant on the countertop. "Don't encourage her fear. Fondant is a cake artist's canvas."

Mom wrinkled her brow. "And it's a nightmare to work with. You are professionally trained, Juliet. You have to remember that all of us novice bakers learned to decorate cakes the old-fashioned way, with generous layers of buttercream and pastry bags."

I sprinkled the countertop with cornstarch and then coated my hands with Crisco. Over the years I've experimented with different combinations when rolling out and cutting fondant, from using powdered sugar to clear vinyl mats. Cornstarch and Crisco are my secret weapons when it comes to fondant work. The cornstarch magically disappears into the fondant, and the Crisco acts as a barrier so my hands don't stick to it. I use a rolling pin so the fondant doesn't clump together. Many professional bakeries have fondant sheeter machines that automatically roll the dough into thin pliable sheets. We don't use enough fondant at Torte to warrant the cost of a professional dough roller. Plus, it's a great arm workout.

"You know I love working with buttercream too, but there's no need to be afraid of fondant. There are some pretty amazing designs that you just can't create structurally with frosting," I said, starting to roll out a long sheet. Fondant has a tendency to dry out and crack easily, so it's important to work quickly and continually lift and rotate the sheet as you go.

The fondant began to stretch as I rolled it in alternating directions and smoothed it with my hands.

"How did you do that so fast?" Mom's brown eyes widened as she watched me.

"I'm telling you, it's so easy to use. You both just have to get over your fondant phobia."

"Or we give all the fondant work to her, right Stephanie?" Mom grinned.

Stephanie nodded in agreement. "Yeah, that."

"You two are no fun." I brushed cornstarch from my hands. In reality it didn't matter if Mom and Stephanie mastered the art of fondant work. Most of the cakes and pastries we crafted at Torte were designed with buttercream. We didn't drape our cakes in fondant like some bakeries. Fondant doesn't add any flavor to the cake. I always recommend that clients remove the fondant before eating a slice of one of our many rich and moist cakes. However, I did want to add some three-dimensional accents to our showpiece cakes at the Chocolate Fest and fondant was my best option.

I dusted the entire sheet with gold powder and waited for it to dry. Then I planned to hand-cut a delicate leaf pattern from the fondant. I would frost our triple-layer chocolate cake with chocolate buttercream frosting and dark chocolate ganache and adorn it with the gold leaves. If the vision I had for the cake in my head was executed properly it should be a stunning centerpiece for the Chocolate Fest and hopefully attract some new wedding accounts.

Mom watched over my shoulder as I ran the tip of a carving knife over the gold sheet of fondant. I wanted to trace the pattern before I made any cuts.

"That is amazing, honey. You really are skilled." Her thin hands ran across the dough.

"It's my way of making art. I don't do it enough, but I'm hoping that's all going to change if we can pull in some more wedding business."

Mom wiped down the far side of the island and began

assembling butter, sugar, eggs, and vanilla. "If all of your cakes look as beautiful as these we'll probably end up with more cake orders than we can manage." She motioned to the cakes that I had finished yesterday. One was a five-layer square chocolate cake. I had frosted each layer by alternating chocolate buttercream with white lace piping and French vanilla buttercream with dark chocolate lace piping. The piping work had taken hours and left my fingers numb, but the result was dramatic. I was pleased with the elegant design and glad that Mom was too. The second cake was "naked," as we call it in the business. The sides of the cake are the star of the show in naked designs. Instead of covering the entire cake with buttercream, naked cakes expose each layer. My naked cake would be a three-tiered round chocolate spice cake with mocha spice buttercream filling. I planned to roughly frost it with vanilla icing in order to let each layer shine. I would use it to demonstrate a variety of piping techniques during our vendor showcase.

In addition to the five-layer square and the three-layer gold leaf design, I was also going to create a more modern look with multiple smaller tiered chocolate cakes displayed on log slices and enhanced with fresh pine boughs and edible Oregon berries. We were also bringing tasting samples of our family recipe for chocolate cake, the marzipans that Stephanie was dipping, and chocolate pasta. The Chocolate Festival opened to the public tomorrow afternoon, and we had to be there early to set up. We had hours of work to finish, and if we didn't pick up the pace we might be here all night.

"Speaking of more business, how did the meeting

with Rosalind go?" Mom asked. She tucked her brown bob behind her ears. I might be biased, but she is one of the most beautiful women I know. She prefers clogs and comfortable clothing to high fashion or heels, but somehow manages to exude a simple elegance in whatever she wears.

"Good." I concentrated on my leaf design. "She thinks we have a really good shot at one of the grants."

"And?" Mom raised her brow as she creamed butter and sugar in a large mixing bowl by hand.

"And." I looked up and met her gaze. "If we decide to move forward it will mean starting demolition right away. Remodeling must be completed by July."

"July!" Mom almost shouted.

"Yeah." I frowned. "I don't know. What do you think? I'm so torn. I don't know that we'll get a financial opportunity like this again, but are we ready?"

Mom paused and looked thoughtful for a minute. She tasted her butter and sugar mixture then smiled at me. "We're always ready for anything."

Chapter Three

I wasn't sure if we really were ready for anything. At the moment we certainly weren't ready for the Chocolate Fest or our upcoming kitchen remodel, but Mom had an all-knowing look in her eyes. I was familiar with the look. Her ability to listen and ask just the right question at exactly the right time has often led to moments of great insight. Mom has always been more of a guide than director. But there have been a handful of times throughout my life when she voiced her opinion and didn't back down. Like encouraging me to go to culinary school and take my first job on the cruise ship. This felt like one of those times.

"So you think we should do it?" I asked.

She measured vanilla extract. "You already know you want to. It's written in every muscle in your body, Juliet."

"But . . ." I started to protest. In response I twisted my ponytail and felt my cheeks warm. Was I that transparent?

Holding a long dainty finger to her lips, she smiled. "Honey, how excited have you been about the possibility? How much time do you think you've spent reimagining the space below us? How much sleep have you lost these past couple of weeks?"

"I, uh . . ."

"Exactly. I knew when you raced in here after that first conversation with Rosalind that we were going to do this. It reminded me of the day that you got accepted to culinary school. You couldn't contain your joy. That's the way life is supposed to be."

"But are we really ready? Are we jumping in too fast? What about this rain?" I nodded to the windows, which were spattered with fat wet drops. "What if it floods?"

Mom held up her wooden spoon in protest. "How many pro and con lists have we made? Twenty? Juliet, at some point you have to make a decision and stick with it. I know you want to do this. Is there risk involved? Of course. But that's also called life."

My hands sparkled with gold dust, and my body felt equally invigorated. "Mom, are you sure this is what you want? If we do it, you have to promise to let me take the lead. I know that you and the Professor want to travel and I don't want an expansion to change that for you."

"It won't." She shook her head. "And I fully intend to let you take charge of the expansion. I think having a positive distraction will be good for you." She raised one eyebrow.

I didn't have to ask her what she meant. Her words gave me pause. Was I excited about expanding Torte to keep my mind off Carlos? Maybe. But honestly, I hadn't been this happy in years. Ashland was my home and I wanted to do everything I could to make Torte the most successful bakeshop in town.

Stephanie cleared her throat. I'd almost forgotten she was in the room with us. "I'm running out of parchment. Could one of you lay down more for me?" Rows and rows of neatly lined marzipan squares filled the entire section of the countertop next to the stove.

Mom rested her wooden spoon in the mixing bowl and sprang into action. "Of course." She lined the opposite counter with parchment. Stephanie had done a nice job with the chocolate. The squares were uniform and the chocolate held its sheen. I had to resist biting into one.

We spent the next few hours focused on our individual tasks. The gold leaf design on my chocolate wedding cake matched my original sketches. That was two wedding cakes complete and one to go. Mom had finished baking the cakes for my third modern Northwest-inspired cake design. They cooled on the countertop and made the entire kitchen smell like the holidays. Even if people didn't like my designs I knew that they would fall in love with Mom's signature chocolate cake. It was an old family recipe passed down from my great-grandmother. Mom would bake the cake every Christmas and layer it with peppermint frosting and then again in the springtime for my birthday and layer it with custard and raspberries. It was an extremely versatile recipe.

After we closed the shop to customers Andy, Sterling, and Stephanie helped pack the marzipans and gather tasting supplies. Mom sent them home sometime after five with bags of extra chocolate bark.

Andy ran his fingers through his shaggy auburn hair and tucked earbuds in. "Thanks, Mrs. C. This will be gone by the time I'm halfway home." He clicked on his tunes and gave us a wave.

Sterling covered his head with his hoodie and waited by the front door for Stephanie. I couldn't tell if she was intentionally making him wait or moving at a snail's pace because she was tired after a long day of delicate chocolate work. They left together without making eye contact or conversation. For the last few months they had had an on-again, off-again relationship. I knew that Sterling had feelings for Stephanie, but she was a tough nut to crack. I couldn't figure out if she returned his affections and wore her aloofness as a mask of protection. Or maybe she just wasn't that into him.

"What's next on our list for the Chocolate Fest?" Mom asked as she loaded coffee mugs into the dishwasher.

"I think we're at a good place. I need to decorate this last wedding cake, but I wasn't planning on baking the tasting cakes until tomorrow. We want them to be as fresh as possible, right?"

Mom looped her hands together and stretched her fingers. "Right. Tomorrow we divide and conquer. Marzipans and the wedding cake showpieces. That will leave us with the chocolate pasta and tasting cake?"

"Can you think of anything else?"

"Nope. I think we've got it under control." She tossed her apron into the basket near the office.

I noticed her shuffle a bit as she walked. She was

tired, not that she would ever admit it. "Why don't you head home then? I'll finish the wedding cake and we can tackle the rest tomorrow?" I suggested.

"Are you sure you don't need any help?"

"I'm sure. Go."

Mom hesitated. "I'll look over the paperwork. Don't stay too late."

"Me? Never." I tried to wink, which usually meant my face scrunched up and tilted to one side.

"Yeah, right." Mom tossed a dish towel at me on her way to the front door. "Get some sleep tonight, honey."

"I will," I called after her. She locked the front door and turned off the dining room lights. With the bake-shop quiet I could concentrate on my design work. Like any other art form, cake artistry requires focus and attention to detail. I popped a CD of classical music into the player and poured myself a glass of red wine. Then I began carving each cake. For the final wedding show-piece I wanted the cakes to have a natural and almost woodsy construction. As I tossed cake scraps into the waste bin, my vision began to take shape. Once I had formed the cakes I covered the log slices in parchment. I would frost each cake with Swiss mocha buttercream and remove the parchment when I was done.

The Swiss buttercream had a bright coffee finish and just the right balance of bitterness to sweetness. It spread on the cakes like butter. Next, I filled a piping bag with more buttercream and started the painstaking task of piping a delicate trim around the border of each cake. Then I used a closed star tip to hand-pipe individual tiny stars on the sides of the cakes. The look was both rustic and chic. When we transported them to the Chocolate

Fest I would decorate the tops with Oregon berries and greenery. It should give them a pop of color and tie in with my forest theme.

By the time I finished, it was after nine. I gave the island a quick wipe-down, started the dishwasher, and organized all of the supplies we would need for the fest. Tomorrow we would bake the tasting samples. It looked like we were in good shape, so I turned off the heat and lights and made my way out into the dark rainy night.

Ashland is relatively sleepy in the winter months. With the Oregon Shakespeare Festival closed for the season, tourism dies off, but not completely. Many restaurants and pubs offer specials and discounts to locals and travelers during the off-season. In the peak of the summer season hotels and bed-and-breakfasts can charge triple the rates they charge in January and February. Despite OSF being a huge international draw, there is still plenty to do in town when the theater is dark, and it's nice to have things move at slower pace for a couple months.

I smiled to myself as I passed a group of Southern Oregon college students on a pub crawl. They were dressed for the elements in raincoats and knee-high boots, but didn't appear to be deterred by the rain as they sang a song I didn't recognize at the top of their lungs and headed into Puck's Pub. Things were exactly as they were supposed to be. Torte was thriving, we were going to expand, we were prepped and ready for the Chocolate Fest, and about to install new ovens. Life was sweet. What could possibly go wrong?

Chapter Four

The next day was a blur. Mom, Stephanie, and Andy managed the morning coffee rush. Sterling, our newest staff member, worked the front counter and stove while I began baking chocolate sheet cakes for our tasting. Our old family recipe involved beating egg whites and folding them into a melted chocolate mixture to create a light chocolate sponge. We would frost the sheets with mocha buttercream and cut them into two-inch tasting squares. Torte hummed to life with customers chatting in the dining room and the comforting smell of pastries baking in the oven and coffee brewing in the front.

Mom came into the kitchen a little after eleven to snag the last tray of croissants. "I've told everyone that we're closing at noon. Hopefully that's going to give us enough time. How are the cakes coming?"

I placed the last sheet cake in a delivery box. "I have four. I think that should get us through this afternoon and evening. I'll make more tonight so that they are as fresh as possible when people taste them."

"We're cutting the samples on-site?" Mom asked.

"Yep. That's the plan. Sterling's going to make the sauces for the chocolate pasta and I'm starting on the noodles now. I think we're in good shape."

Mom reached over and knocked on the butcher block. "Knock on wood."

"Mom, you're not superstitious."

"Usually I'm not, but we have so much going on that I don't want to lose sight of anything."

"Agreed." I wiped buttercream from my hands. "As soon as you usher the last customer out the door, let's have a quick staff meeting and make sure everyone is on the same page."

Mom positioned the tray of croissants and gave me a thumbs-up. "Good plan." She scooted past Sterling who came to the back with several coffee mugs.

Sterling had become like a younger brother to me. All of our staff and customers were family at Torte, but Sterling and I had a special bond due in part to our hopelessly romantic hearts, and the fact that we'd both lost parents at a young age. Mom called Sterling an "old soul." He had a wisdom about him that most people in their twenties didn't develop for years. He was also a hit with the teenage girls, thanks to his mysterious dark looks and unsettling blue eyes that pierced your soul.

"I hear you're ready for me," Sterling said as he rolled up the sleeves of his gray hoodie and joined me at the island. "Put me to work."

"Great. You are going to be on sauce."

"Jules, I think the term these days is 'saucy.' Get with the times."

"Funny."

"I do what I can." He leaned closer to study the list of ingredients I had written up earlier.

"We're going to top the chocolate pasta with fresh berries, pistachios, and a sweet cream sauce."

"How are you going to serve them?" Sterling asked, picking up the recipe for the creamy white-chocolate sauce.

"We're actually going to serve the pasta cold in individual containers."

"Got it." Sterling held up the recipe card. "This sounds good—crème fraîche and white chocolate."

"Right? I hope it turns out. I've been playing around with different combinations. Flavor harmony is striking the right balance between bitterness and acidity, so hopefully the sweet and tangy sauce will complement the dark chocolate noodles. Plus, the pistachios will add a crunchy texture and the berries should give it a nice bite."

"Sounds good to me," Sterling said, pushing the sleeves on his hoodie up to his elbow, revealing his tattooed forearms. "Don't hate me for saying this, but I miss Carlos."

"Really?" I was pleased to hear that. Carlos had taken Sterling under his wing and helped mentor him while he was here. Carlos was at his best when nurturing young chefs, so I wasn't surprised that he had made an impression on Sterling.

"Yeah, I mean he cares about the food. Now when I'm working I can hear his accent telling me that I have to 'infuse my cooking with love, no?' "

I laughed. "You've got his accent down."

Sterling motioned with his hands, mimicking Carlos's animated speech. *"Sí, Julieta."*

"No! No way, we are *not* going there. Don't even think about it," I protested, and gave him my best evil eye. It had been embarrassing enough to have Carlos try to seduce me in my own kitchen. I wasn't about to open the door for Sterling's teasing, even though I knew it was all in good fun. Carlos was gone and I was back in control of the kitchen—and hopefully my emotions too.

Sterling cracked up. "Fine, no Spanish accents, but you can't hold me accountable for pulling any pranks. Carlos told me that humor is the life force of the kitchen."

"I'm sure he did." I rolled my eyes and made room on the butcher-block island to begin making the chocolate noodles. I started by sifting together flour, dark chocolate cocoa powder, and sugar. They piled high on the island like a chocolate volcano. Next I hollowed out the center of my mound and cracked in whole eggs. Then I poured in our homemade chocolate syrup and vanilla extract. Carefully working the mixture with a fork, I slowly began incorporating the flour and cocoa powder into the liquid. Soon the dough began to take shape. Once it had formed into a ball I cleared the surface and dusted it with cocoa powder. I wanted to roll the dough out in cocoa powder instead of flour so that it retained its deep chocolate color.

"Let me know if you need help," I said to Sterling as I rolled the dough into thin sheets. "As soon as they close up, it's all hands on deck."

"Yeah, right." Sterling laughed.

"What?" I reached for a pizza cutter and began slicing the dough into long strips.

He nodded to the front of the bakeshop where almost

every table and booth was occupied by customers. "No one is leaving anytime soon."

"Don't count on that. You haven't seen my mom in action."

"Helen? She's like the sweetest woman on the planet."

"Just wait." I gave him a knowing look. "She'll kill them with kindness and kick them out the door with a bag of snickerdoodles."

Sterling shrugged and walked to the stove to melt white chocolate for the cream sauce.

While Sterling worked on the sauce I finished cutting the noodles. I felt like I was in an Italian pasta shop as I shook cocoa powder from the pasta and gathered the delicate noodles into tidy clumps on the island. Their rich color reminded me of one of Carlos's most famous savory pasta dishes—squid-ink noodles. The dish was visually impressive with spaghetti noodles the color of midnight drizzled with olive oil, chunky plum tomatoes, roasted garlic, marinated red peppers, and fresh shrimp. In addition to stunning guests with a vibrant plate, the squid ink in the noodles gave the pasta a briny flavor perfect for warm nights on the sea. I drank in the memory and then glanced out the window to the dismal gray sky.

"Hey, Jules, your water is boiling," Sterling called from the stove.

I pushed away memories of the brilliant aqua Caribbean and gathered a handful of noodles. Before I dropped them into the boiling water I salted it. I'm a big believer in the philosophy that every sweet dish needs a touch of salt. The noodles needed to boil for three minutes, just until they had been cooked al dente. Then I would drain and cool them, and pile them into mini cardboard to-go boxes. Stephanie had hand-stamped the shiny white Chinese-style takeout boxes with our Torte logo. We ordered plastic forks that we would insert into each box so that people could nosh on the pasta as they strolled between vendor booths at the Chocolate Festival. I was fairly confident that people would appreciate the unique offering, but I was also starting to worry that we had bitten off more than we could chew. Assembling hundreds of boxes of chocolate pasta was going to take time and extra effort.

When the clock struck noon Torte immediately began to empty. Mom walked each customer to the door, thanking them for understanding and offering them a parting bag of her signature snickerdoodles. Sterling gave me an incredulous look. "She did it."

"I told you she would."

He stirred chunks of white chocolate into a double boiler. "A side of Helen I've never seen."

"Don't let her sweet face fool you. She can be ruthless." I wiped steam from my brow. Working near boiling water was like giving myself a warm facial.

"Did someone call me ruthless?" Mom's walnut eyes sparkled as she danced into the kitchen. Andy followed behind her, balancing a tray of coffee.

Stephanie cleared a space on the island for him.

I practically drooled at the smell of the rich espresso.

"How did you do that, Helen?" Sterling asked.

"Do what?"

"Clear the dining room. Everyone looked like they were settled in for the afternoon." He stirred molten chocolate as he spoke.

Mom threw her head back and laughed. "Oh, I have my ways, but if I told you I'd have to kill you."

Sterling shook his head. Andy handed us all coffees. "Hey, Mrs. C., we all know that you couldn't kill a fly."

"Don't be so sure," Mom teased as she swatted at an imaginary fly in the air.

I breathed in the scent of Andy's coffee. "Another double latte?"

"How did you guess?" Andy's boyish face lit up when I took a sip and savored the milky drink. "You like it?"

"Love it."

"That's good, because I literally used the last drop of syrup a few minutes ago in a woman's vanilla mocha. Everything else is packed. It's a plain latte or straight-up espresso for the next three days."

"Works for me." I took another sip.

"What do you want this in, Jules?" Sterling asked. He scooped the white creamy sauce on a wooden spoon and let it drip over the pan. "This is the consistency you were looking for, right?"

I rested my latte on the counter and walked to the stove. "Did you taste it?" I'd been trying to impart the importance of taste to our young staff. Nothing that comes out of Torte's kitchen gets served to customers before it's tasted. No exceptions.

Sterling nodded, and held out the spoon to me. I dipped my pinkie in the sauce. The warm tangy sauce had a smooth texture and a sweet finish. Achieving the right texture can be difficult, since white chocolate has a tendency to become grainy if you don't watch it. "Great job," I said to Sterling, handing him a stack of plastic lidded containers. "Let's put it in these."

"You want us to get started with cleaning now, boss?" Andy asked. He had removed his apron and wore a black and red Southern Oregon University football sweatshirt with the Raiders' mascot on the front. In some ways it was a miracle that our young staff worked so well together. Their personal styles couldn't have been more contrasting—Stephanie with her alternative anti-establishment vibe, Sterling's laid-back skater style, and Andy's obsession with football and collegiate sports. But somehow, they meshed in the kitchen.

The professional kitchen was a great equalizer. People from all walks of life found common ground and connection through food. Language barriers and petty arguments faded away when chefs banded together in the quest to create a memorable and palate-pleasing meal. I fantasized for a moment about bringing world leaders together at a communal table. Maybe we could solve some of the planet's most pressing problems with platters of fresh baked scones and cinnamon bread.

Mom cleared her throat and brought me out of my daydream. I asked Sterling to turn the heat on low as everyone gathered around the center island. We walked through the kitchen renovation plan one last time. The first task was taking inventory of all of our products. Mom had suggested the idea, since we had to take everything out of the pantry and cupboards anyway. After we finished taking stock of our supplies then we could begin priming and painting the walls, and taking turns learning the new point-of-sale system.

"Make sure you keep everything in the nut-free cup-board separate," Mom said, pointing to a cupboard la-beled NUT FREE next to the sink. We often got requests for nut-free cakes and pastries for customers who have nut allergies. Although we do have to specify that we're not a nut-free bakery, we keep our nut-free products—from flour to the pans that we bake in—self-contained so that we minimize the chance that any trace amount of nuts could get into the products.

Mom reached under the island and removed stacks of plastic tubs and containers. "Stephanie, you can start organizing and labeling all the spices in these. Andy, you are going to be responsible for inventorying the walk-in and freezer, and Sterling, you can help us de-liver everything to Ashland Springs Hotel."

I handed each of them inventory sheets. "Once you've completed the inventory checklist, go ahead and move everything to the front of the bakeshop."

"Even the island?" Andy asked.

I shook my head. "I don't think you guys can lift it, can you?"

Sterling flexed his muscles. Andy copied him. "Hey, my coach at SOU will make me lift double if he hears you talking like that."

Mom patted Andy's arm. "Tell your coach that we all agree that you're strong, but I don't want you boys mov-ing the island. You can push it all the way against the back counter if you want, but it's way too heavy to lift. It won't fit between the office and espresso bar. You'd have to lift it over."

"We can do that." Andy flexed again.

Sterling didn't look as enthusiastic.

Stephanie shook her head. She'd undone the braids she'd worn yesterday, so her hair was crimped and wavy. "What is it with guys and having to prove how strong they are?" she asked as she began removing spices from the far cupboard.

Mom furrowed her brow and pursed her lips. I was familiar with her "mom" look. She meant business. "Listen, you two are not to lift this. Is that understood? I am not running the risk of either of you getting injured. You're way too valuable to Torte and to me."

Andy looked disappointed, but nodded and lumbered off to begin taking stock of the inventory in the fridge.

Sterling looked relieved. "We won't touch it, Helen."

"Good. I'm serious. I don't want either of you hurt."

"We'll be safe. Steph is here to keep us in line, right, Steph?"

Stephanie rolled her eyes and ignored him.

"And about getting on the ladder," Mom continued. "I want you to be very careful when you're climbing it. One person should always be at the bottom making sure it's stable. And don't use the top step."

Sterling laughed, but I could tell that he appreciated her concern. Once a mom, always a mom. "You don't need to worry, Helen. We'll all be responsible. We shouldn't really need the ladder much, except to paint the edge between the ceiling and wall."

"Well, you just be careful. I worry about you all." Her voice caught. "You're my family."

Sterling's eyes became especially bright. I saw him blink back a tear and turn to the stove. We were so lucky to have such a great team. My eyes felt misty too. We had built something special together and there was so much more in store. If I had known that trouble was right around the bend, I might have held on to the moment a little longer.

Chapter Five

We loaded Mom's car with the cakes, pasta, marzipan, and all of our supplies. The Chocolate Festival was taking place at the iconic Ashland Springs Hotel, just a short walk up Main Street from Torte. The hotel had hosted celebrities and visitors from all over the world since it opened in 1925. It's one of my favorite buildings. At nine stories, it's also the tallest building in town and the most regal.

Walking into the hotel's inviting lobby always made me feel like I was stepping onto the set of an Agatha Christie movie, with its warm yellow walls, iron veranda, giant potted palms, white ceiling fans, and sparkling chandeliers. When I was a kid we would go to the hotel on special occasions for high tea or a celebratory dinner. I used to love sitting in the lobby in front of the large marble fireplace and imagining that I was in a faraway and exotic corner of the world like Morocco or Bath.

Today we entered the hotel through the back entrance, which had a long covered walkway to shield us from the rain. Mom parked the car in front of the walkway while I wheeled our boxes to the ballroom.

The ballroom was as magnificent as I remembered. It had been transformed into a chocolate wonderland. Chocolate-colored tulle and gold twinkle lights had been strung from the ceiling. Six-foot tables ran the length of the room on all sides. Each table had been draped with a dark chocolate-colored tablecloth. A stage and demo kitchen sat in the center of the ballroom with four large booths surrounding it. Overhead a massive crystal chandelier rained drops of shimmering light down onto the plush patterned carpet. Huge silver-framed mirrors reflected the light and made the room look twice its size.

A musical trio was warming up on stage. The sound of their strings mingling together warmed the space and made me feel like I was in Paris. Signs directed guests upstairs to the conservatory for spirits, wine, beer, and outdoor dining, and to the Grand Ballroom to see chocolate sculptures, the dessert contest, and the silent auction.

I couldn't believe how many things were going on as part of the festival. The entire hotel had been made over in chocolate.

After I paused to listen to the trio for a moment and take everything in, I wheeled our supplies to our booth. The four showcase vendors, including Torte, had three six-foot tables arranged in an L-shape. Mom and I had sketched out our design for the festival. We planned to use one of the tables to display our wedding cakes and brochures. The other two would be our tasting tables. Vendors were allowed to decorate their booths in any chocolate design that they could imagine.

After much discussion, Mom and I had agreed that we wanted our products to be the star of the show. We decided to order floral arrangements from A Rose By Any Other Name, my high school friend Thomas's family's flower shop. Otherwise, our chocolate could speak for itself.

Mom arrived and shook off her raincoat. "Wow, this is really something. They've outdone themselves this year."

"It's amazing," I agreed as we began unloading and organizing our supplies.

I had second thoughts about our choice of decorations as I watched a professional decorating crew assemble the booth next to ours. It belonged to Confections Couture, a high-end chocolate company that was owned by Evan Rowe. His truffles had been featured in every national magazine and were revered by chefs throughout the world. He'd won every award, graced the cover of every foodie magazine, and had exclusive deals with three major retail chains. I'd never met Evan, but his name was synonymous with chocolate not only in southern Oregon but in boutiques and five-star restaurants everywhere. A two-piece box of Confections Couture truffles would set you back a whooping twelve dollars.

Evan's profit margin must be high, I thought as I watched his team transform his booth. There were strings of white lilies cascading from the sky to the floor. Giant iron candelabras glowed in the center of each table. They were accented with glittering crystals and beads of gold. Life-sized cutouts of Evan in various stages of the truffle-making process were displayed along the back of his booth. A chocolate fountain with shimmering gold napkins and skewers was set up at the end of the booth closest to ours. Suddenly, my wedding cakes seemed quaint and homemade. How were we going to compete with Confections Couture?

Mom caught my eye and grimaced. "It looks pretty amazing, doesn't it? There's a reason that Evan has been named People's Choice and Best in Show for five years running."

"Have you met him?" I arranged a stack of brochures that we'd had printed. It had been an additional cost, but Mom hadn't spent any money on marketing and advertising. She had never needed to. Torte was an institution when it came to pastries and baked goods on the plaza. If we wanted to expand our business, particularly our specialty and wedding cake business, we would have to spend some dough getting the word out.

"A few times." Mom handed me a tightly bundled package of business cards. "He's much shorter in real life." She pointed behind us at the cardboard cutouts of Evan Rowe. "Much shorter."

As if on cue, Evan Rowe strolled in at that moment. The life-sized cutouts made him appear larger than life, almost superhuman. In reality, Evan probably came up to my shoulder and looked almost sickly. Granted, I'm tall, but still.

Evan sauntered toward us, surrounded by an entourage. Three women, wearing custom chefs' uniforms with "Confections Couture" embroidered on the breast pocket, flanked Evan on each side. A younger guy in his early twenties tagged after them with a notebook and two coffee mugs.

Evan stopped in front of the Confections Couture booth. The crew working on assembling the masterpiece paused. One of them jumped off a stepladder and hurried over to Evan. "What do you think, Mr. Rowe?"

Evan didn't respond. He snapped his fingers in the direction of the guy holding his coffee. "Make a note, Carter. This has got to go. I said classic elegance. Not gaudy Vegas strip." He waved his arm over the chocolate cloths being draped over the back of the booth.

Carter balanced the coffees in one hand and tried to pull a pencil from the top of the spiral notebook he held in the other hand. "Got it." His face was spotted with acne and two cowlicks at the top of his forehead twisted in opposite directions.

"You didn't even write that down." Evan glared at him and ignored the designer who asked him three more questions. He continued over to our booth. Mom kicked me under the table.

"Ouch," I whispered.

"Sorry. I didn't mean to hurt you, but put your best face forward. It looks like you are going to have the pleasure of meeting Evan Rowe."

I nudged her to be quiet as Evan approached our booth.

He gave Mom a forced smile. "Ellen, right? You have that quaint family shop on that plaza, what's it called again? Cake? Layer? Something like that, right?" His skin had a slightly yellowish tint. It didn't blend well with his dark hair and scruffy dark beard.

"It's Torte." Mom handed him a business card. "And I'm Helen."

"Helen, Ellen, I was close." Evan tossed the business card at one of his female chefs. Then he turned to me. "And who might you be?"

Before I could respond, Mom reached her arm in front of me as if she were trying to block Evan from coming any closer. "This is my daughter, Juliet, she's just returned home from working as the head pastry chef for a world-renowned luxury ship."

Mom never bragged. It wasn't her nature. She must really not like Evan Rowe.

If Evan was impressed, he didn't let it show. "Buffet lines." He shuddered. "That is humanity and cooking at its worst."

I thought Mom might punch him in the face. Instead she smiled broadly and handed Evan a marzipan. "You should taste Juliet's marzipan. It will make you think twice about buffet cooking."

Evan reeled back as if Mom had tried to take a swing at him. "Get that away from me."

Mom stared at the marzipan and then at Evan.

"I do not want that." He turned and stormed to his booth without another word. His entourage followed.

"What was that all about?" Mom popped the marzipan into her mouth.

"Who knows?" I shrugged. "Napoleon complex?"

"I guess. He can say whatever he wants about Torte, but he does not get to belittle your culinary talent. I'm not going to stand for that, and I don't care that he's been on *Oprah*. She would not approve of his superior attitude."

"Mom." I placed my hand on her shoulder. "It's fine. I'm used to working with and around guys like Evan. They have to prove their power. It's not worth it."

She swallowed the marzipan and stared at his booth. His young staff member, Carter, was scrambling to write down all the orders that Evan barked out. "Why did he have to be at the booth next to us? We're going to have to see him for three days."

I returned to displaying our marketing materials. "It could be worse."

Mom scowled. "How?"

"Richard Lord could be here."

"Oh, you're right, honey. That would be much worse."

Chapter Six

It took us another hour to put the finishing touches on Torte's booth. As Mom placed the last marzipan in a neat row on a silver tray, a voice sounded behind us. "Delivery."

We turned to find Thomas carrying a giant box of flowers. Their fragrant scent filled the air. "Where do you want these?" He shifted his feet. Thomas covers the downtown beat for the Ashland police and was outfitted in his standard blue uniform. His blond hair was cut short and his freshly shaven face made him look more like an all-American football player than an intimidating cop.

"These are lovely," Mom said, clearing a space on the floor for Thomas to put the flowers. "Your mom outdid herself this time. Be sure to send her my thanks."

"Anything for you, Mrs. Capshaw." Thomas gave her a half bow and handed her the first bouquet of flowers. Each bundle of flowers was tied with a satin chocolate ribbon. There were white peonies, cream roses, curly long-stemmed willow branches, and delicate cherry blossoms. The bouquets blended seamlessly with our booth.

Mom positioned the vases next to the trays of marzipan and alongside our wedding cake display. "Beautiful." She stood back and surveyed her work.

"When does all the chocolate action start?" Thomas asked.

I checked my phone. "Soon. We have about thirty minutes before the vendor meeting and then the doors open to the public." I pointed to a fading bruise on his temple. "Hey, how's your head by now?" Thomas had been involved in a car accident while on the hunt for a killer and ended up with a concussion. The bruise appeared to be healing well, but I hadn't seen him since he'd been discharged from the hospital.

He squeezed one hand into a fist and knocked on his forehead. "Solid as rock."

Mom shook her finger at him. "Be careful. You don't want to injure yourself more."

"Not to worry, Mrs. Capshaw. I can't feel a thing. My head is as good as new." Thomas tucked the empty delivery box under one arm and scrutinized our booth. The police badge pinned to his chest reflected the light from the chandelier overhead. "Torte gets my vote! You guys did a great job. Do you need any help before I go?"

"Thanks, Thomas." Mom squeezed his free arm. "I think we're about done. Let me write a check for the flowers before you go though."

While Mom wrote the check Thomas stared longingly at our display.

"Do you want a taste?" I handed him a marzipan.

"I don't want to ruin your setup." He gave me a sheepish

look and popped the marzipan in his mouth. "But if you insist."

"Right. Since when do you turn down chocolate?"

"I've changed my ways, you know. I'm an upstanding member of this community. Sworn to serve and protect." He stood with his shoulders squared and saluted.

"Of course, Officer. I meant no offense."

Thomas pretended to be offended. "I tell you, we get no respect around here." He helped himself to another marzipan. "Just for that I'm taking my payment in chocolate."

Mom handed Thomas a check. "You know that we will always pay you in chocolate. Don't listen to her."

"What is this, gang-up-on-Jules day?" I joked.

Thomas winked at Mom. "She's such an easy target."

"Hey!" I protested.

"I'm kidding." He swiped one more marzipan. "And I'm getting out of here before I get in more trouble. Good luck with the fest. I'll be rooting for Torte."

With a final wink to Mom he headed for the doors. I was going to say something to her about not encouraging him, but at that moment an announcement sounded overhead that vendors should gather in front of the stage.

We made our way to the stage. Evan Rowe and his chocolate entourage held court near the center. Chef Garrison, who was at the helm of Ashland Springs' award-winning restaurant, took the stage. Mom and Garrison had been friends for years. He caught her eye and waved.

"Welcome to the Chocolate Festival!" His jovial voice boomed into the microphone. He wore his black chef's coat like a regal cape.

A young woman standing next to us wearing a pink

T-shirt that read THE UNBEATABLE BROWNIE. #GET IN MY BELLY, let out a little yelp. She blushed and threw her hand over her mouth. "Sorry," she said to me. "I'm so excited to really be here."

"Me too." I returned her smile.

Chef Garrison explained the timeline for the demonstrations and how judging would work for both the People's Choice and Best in Show awards. There were three official judges: a food writer, a culinary instructor, and a corporate chef. He introduced each of them. I was shocked when he announced the name Sandi Kramer, and a woman wearing a black pantsuit and thick-framed oversized glasses joined him on the stage.

"Is that the Sandi Kramer of *Sweetened* magazine?" I asked Mom, as excited as the young woman next to me.

Mom nodded. "I heard a rumor that she was coming."

Sandi Kramer was notorious in the foodie world. She was the editor of my all-time favorite pastry magazine, *Sweetened,* and had a reputation for making and breaking careers.

"Oh my gosh!" the woman standing next to me squealed. "That's Sandi Kramer! She's so stylish, isn't she?"

I agreed. Sandi's shockingly white hair was cut tight above her ears. Chunky black pearls dangled from her lobes and hung around her neck. She moved with graceful confidence as if she were walking the catwalk.

"Happy to be here," she said in a posh East Coast accent as Chef Garrison introduced her. "Charming little town you have here. I've been hearing about Ashland for years, thanks to your very own Evan Rowe." She gave a curt nod to Evan.

I watched as he glared at her and then intentionally turned to ignore her steely gaze. "That was an icy reception," I whispered to Mom.

"What did you say, honey?"

I spoke louder and repeated what I had said.

Mom glanced in Evan's direction. "I don't think that Evan likes having someone with so much clout here."

After the judges had been introduced, Chef Garrison went through the weekend's agenda and invited the four showcase vendors to join him on the stage. I nudged Mom. "You go."

She frowned. "I hope I don't have to say anything."

"You'll be great." I pushed her forward.

The four showcase vendors included Torte, Confections Couture, Melted Masterpieces, a drinkable chocolate company from Medford, and Howard's Sea Salts. Chef Garrison raved about each of our businesses and encouraged everyone to make time to attend our demonstrations and to taste our fellow chocolatiers' offerings. He sounded like he was done with his introductions, but Evan Rowe jumped forward and tried to grab the mic from his hands.

Chef Garrison looked unsure what to do. "Let me introduce Evan Rowe of Confections Couture."

Evan addressed the audience. "What you're not being told is the real history behind the Chocolate Fest. Many years ago when Confections Couture was a boutique chocolate shop—of course, even back then we were receiving accolades for our extraordinary work—I recognized that there was a need, a hole, in the chocolate community, if you will, which this festival has filled. I started the Chocolate Fest to shed light on the confectionery culture here in southern Oregon. Over the years, as my company has expanded and been named one of the world's best chocolate producers, I haven't had time to commit to running this kind of show, but I am committed to making sure that only the most exclusive and high-end chocolatiers are invited to participate. I'll be taking it upon myself as a favor to the organizers to taste your creations."

Chef Garrison's mouth hung open.

Evan cleared his throat. "If your chocolate doesn't meet my refined standards then I'm afraid you may be asked to pack up your things and leave."

"Can he do that?" the young woman standing next to me asked.

"No," I replied. "Look at Chef Garrison."

The chef took the mic from Evan's hands. "Thank you, Evan. We're honored to have Confections Couture here with us again this year. If you've attended the Chocolate Fest in years past you may know that Confections Couture has been named People's Choice and Best in Show many years running."

"Five." Evan pulled the mic back to his face. "And I have an exciting announcement that I'll be making later today." He glanced behind him. "Stick around, it's going to get quite interesting around here."

Chef Garrison took control of the mic. "Has it been five years, Evan?" As Evan returned to his entourage, he looked relieved and tried to reassure the crowd. "There's no need to worry about packing up or being judged. I assure you our team here has procured some of the finest chocolatiers in the Pacific Northwest. We're looking forward to a great show. Have fun, everyone."

"Wow, someone has an ego," I said to Mom when she returned.

"That's nothing."

We walked back to our booth. "Really?"

"The problem is that his ego isn't exactly unfounded. He has built Confections Couture into one of the most famous chocolate companies in the entire world."

"That doesn't excuse his attitude, though."

Mom rearranged a stack of brochures next to our chocolate pasta boxes. "Agreed. My point is simply that he has a reason for his attitude. Don't get me wrong, I don't approve of his approach, but he does produce some amazing chocolate."

I had a feeling his chocolate would leave me with a bitter taste in my mouth. I'm a believer in the theory that our emotions come out in the food. Evan's superior attitude had to have a negative effect on his chocolate. There was no doubt that he wasn't going to win the fan favorite vote with the vendors.

While we put the finishing touches on our booth, I noticed Evan and Howard, of Howard's Sea Salt, arguing at the Confections Couture booth. Howard reminded me of a fisherman, with his weathered skin and knee-high waders, which weren't exactly necessary inside the ballroom. Although, if the rain continued, I might be changing my tune and asking Howard to borrow his boots. Howard caught my eye as he stormed away from Evan's booth and gave me a half nod.

A few minutes later, Evan walked to the booth across from us—the Unbeatable Brownie. The table was completely covered in pink polka dots and chocolate stripes. An assortment of baskets with handwritten place cards were arranged in a whimsical pattern. There were cute pink signs tied with pink ribbon on each basket with hashtags like #GetInMyBelly, #TreatYoSelf, #EEEE ATS, and #BrownieBatter.

"Are you familiar with the Unbeatable Brownie?" I asked Mom as we watched Evan stop in front of her table.

"Her name is Bethany. She's a recent college graduate who has a food blog that's been a big hit. She's recently started delivering her brownies around town, but I believe she's working out of her home kitchen."

Sandi Kramer watched from the stage. She typed ferociously on a tablet and directed the photographer who was with her to take snapshots of Evan and Bethany.

"Get in my belly?" Evan scoffed. "What does that even mean?"

Bethany, the young woman in the pink T-shirt with whom I had been chatting, looked terrified as she replied. "It's a hashtag for my blog."

"You're a food blogger? How did you get an invite?" He puffed out his chest. "You know in the food world, bloggers are considered pond scum."

She gulped and caught my eye across the aisle. I felt terrible for her.

Evan picked up a sample brownie from one of her baskets. He tasted it and then proceeded to spit it into a paper napkin. Making a face of disgust, he spoke intentionally loud so that everyone around could hear. "This is terrible. Grainy and dry. Did you use cocoa powder?"

Bethany's voice cracked as she replied. "Yes, all of our brownies are made with premium cocoa powder."

"Big mistake. I think you might need to change your

tagline to 'Get *out* of my belly,' " Evan bellowed. "The cocoa powder dried them out and gives them a terrible sandy texture. You should have melted your chocolate instead."

Her cheeks turned a bright shade of pink. "Thanks for the advice, Mr. Rowe. I'm a big fan of your work."

"You should be. Let me give you a free piece of advice, learn to bake. Hashtags are not going to sell any brownies if they taste this bad."

For a minute, I thought she might cry. Mom came to her rescue. "Evan, come on over." She held up a box of our chocolate pasta.

Evan tossed his napkin at the young baker and stalked over to us. Great.

"Thanks a lot, Mom," I said under my breath.

"I had to do something. We can handle him. That poor girl looks like she's going to throw up."

"What is this?" Evan scowled when Mom handed him a box of chocolate pasta.

"It's our signature dessert this year." Mom smiled broadly. "Chocolate pasta with cream sauce, pistachios, and fresh raspberries."

Evan shook his head. "I have a nut allergy."

Mom quickly pulled the tasting sample away from him. "Here," she said, reaching for a slice of chocolate cake. "How about our signature chocolate cake instead? Definitely nut-free."

Evan took the sample and stabbed a plastic fork into the cake. I couldn't wait to see what his reaction was. I had dealt with my fair share of nasty customers while at sea. Some people are impossible to please, and I had learned that it was better to let them vent and smile politely. Trying to engage with antagonistic customers always led to disaster.

Mom must have had the same thought. Her smile was plastered on her face like the royal icing we used to construct gingerbread. We stood shoulder to shoulder as Evan chewed for an extended period of time.

"How quaint. An old family recipe," he finally said after a long pause. I could tell that he liked it. He took three more bites in quick succession. Then he turned and motioned to Bethany "You should come try this. It's moist and decadent. Exactly what a chocolate cake should be. If I made cake at Confections Couture, which I don't, since they are much too common, this is the kind of cake I would bake. Tell me, Ellen, do you use cocoa powder in the cake?"

Mom nodded. "We do."

"You must be kidding." Evan looked surprised. Bethany walked from behind her booth and started toward us.

Evan scoffed. "I was speaking metaphorically. I didn't mean you have to taste it right now."

She stopped in mid-stride and looked to Mom and me for guidance.

"It's, it's . . ." Evan's voice trailed off. He started to cough. I thought for a minute that he was choking on our cake. His face turned at least three shades darker than Bethany's pink tablecloth. He dropped the cake sample on the ballroom floor and threw his hands to his throat.

I'd been trained in first aid and CPR. The kitchen can be a dangerous place and accidents are known to happen. It's a required skill set when managing a kitchen.

I recognized the signs of an allergic reaction right away. Evan wasn't choking. His airway was closing.

"Call 911!" I yelled to Mom and raced toward Evan.

His lips were swelling so quickly they looked like balloons inflating. His hands puffed like red marshmallows. This was bad.

"Does anyone have an EpiPen?" I yelled to the crowd that had begun to circle around us. I grabbed Evan's arm as he started to sway. His eyes were wide with panic and his cheeks were tinged with blue. He needed help immediately.

Someone hollered from the back of the crowd. It was Evan's young assistant, Carter.

"He has an EpiPen. I'll go find it."

"Run!" I commanded.

Carter sprinted to the Confections Couture booth. Evan started slipping from my grasp. One of my fellow chocolate vendors grabbed his other arm. "Let's get him to the floor," he said.

We got Evan to the floor and rested him on his back just as he lost consciousness. "Benadryl! Does anyone have Benadryl?" I yelled. A woman in a white chef's hat nodded. "I might."

"Go check."

Where was Carter? Why was it taking him so long? I scanned the crowd. Sandi and her photographer had pushed to the front of the growing crowd. I couldn't see Carter. Where had he gone? Evan's booth was only a few feet away.

The guy who helped me get Evan to the floor looked up at me. "He's not breathing."

I returned my gaze to Evan's face and nearly lost

consciousness myself. His face had expanded to the size of a pumpkin. His cheeks were turning a horrible purplish blue.

He clasped his hand around my wrist so tightly I lurched back in pain. Struggling for air, he tried to mouth something, but nothing came out.

"It's okay, don't try to talk. Just stay calm. Help is on the way."

Evan's head tossed from side to side. He squeezed my wrist tighter and yanked me toward his ballooning face. I could feel his urgent breath and see his pulse in his forehead.

He wheezed and tried to speak again.

"Try to relax," I repeated in the calmest tone I could muster.

Evan shook his head violently and in one raspy final attempt whispered, "Murder."

"What?" Had he said murder? "Evan, stay with me," I cried.

The next thing I knew Evan released my hand, clasped his throat, and stopped breathing.

"What do we do?" the guy asked.

Without thinking I plugged Evan's nose and started rescue breathing. My training and adrenaline kicked in. I didn't even hear the EMS workers when they arrived. Finally, someone pulled me away from Evan's body, and the paramedics took over. I watched with everyone else as they administered a shot in Evan's thigh and warmed up the defibrillator. A sick feeling rose in my stomach. Their efforts were futile. Evan Rowe was dead.

Chapter Seven

My ears started to ring, and the ballroom began to blur. What just happened? Was the floor swaying or was that just me? The EMS team barked out orders and pushed everyone back. One of them covered Evan's body with a silver emergency blanket.

His last words haunted me. Murder—he had whispered "murder." Why? Had someone poisoned him? Had I heard him wrong?

Carter, Evan's assistant, appeared with an EpiPen in his hand. "I found it . . ." He trailed off. "I'm too late?"

An EMS worker nodded. Carter dropped the EpiPen on the floor and fell to his knees. "How?" He scanned the crowd. "Who gave him nuts?"

No one spoke. Carter was obviously distraught. He looked even younger than he had earlier as he rocked on his knees and glanced wildly from person to person. His blotchy red skin made the pimples on his face more pronounced.

"Everyone knew that Evan had a nut allergy. Someone must have done this. Someone must have slipped in some nuts." Carter's voice sounded accusatory. "Someone did this. Someone killed Evan."

I inhaled through my nose, trying to steady my breathing. Why had he immediately jumped to the conclusion that Evan had been killed?

Something about his reaction seemed off. If Evan had had such a deadly allergy to nuts why didn't he carry his EpiPen on his body, especially in a conference room with tables full of nuts? As vendors, we were required to label anything that contained nuts. From the looks of my fellow chocolatiers' displays, almost everyone had at least one offering with nuts. Chocolate and nuts are such a traditional pairing. Evan had to know that. Confections Couture produced a variety of nut truffles. He must have taken special precautions in his own bakery. Why hadn't he done that here?

And why had it taken Carter so long to get the medication?

Questions swirled in my mind. Carter stood and focused his gaze on Bethany. "Did you give Evan nuts?"

She shook her head and backed away.

Carter lunged at her. "Did you?" he repeated.

She looked like she was going to cry. "No. I swear the brownie he tasted is my signature double fudge. It doesn't have nuts in it."

I thought he might keep going after her, but instead he swiveled around and locked his eyes on me. "Then it had to be you! Evan was at your booth. Did you give him nuts?"

"Easy." I held my hands up to try and calm Carter down. His show of emotion surprised me, since Evan had been so condescending to him. I'd seen that happen before. Aspiring chefs tend to idolize their mentors, even when their mentors treat them like errand boys. "Take it easy. We're all in shock. Let's calm down and wait for the authorities to get here."

A paramedic joined me in my attempt to get Carter under control. He took a firm hold of the young chef's scrawny arm and pulled him away. "Take some deep breaths, man." The paramedic modeled slow easy breaths through his nose.

Mom hurried over to Bethany, whose face looked as white as the piping on my wedding cakes. People began to murmur. The EMS workers asked us to disperse back to our booths.

"Are you all right?" Mom asked Bethany.

She nodded, but her light green eyes bulged from her freckled face and her hands quivered.

Mom motioned to me. "How about a nice hot cup of coffee. Decaf, I think, Juliet."

"Good idea," I replied as I reached for a paper cup and filled it to the brim with our dark brewed decaf. A Torte booth wouldn't be complete without carafes of our coffee. "Cream or sugar?"

"No, black is good." She gave me a timid smile when I handed her the cup.

"I don't think we've officially met, but I've heard absolutely wonderful things about your brownies. I'm Helen and this is my daughter Juliet—Jules." She nodded at me.

"Wow, it's so great to meet you both. I'm Bethany, and I'm a huge fan of Torte. I can't believe you've even heard of me—or the Unbeatable Brownie. I hope you don't think I'm competition or anything. I mean, I love

Torte and I would never want to take away business or anything from you."

Mom placed her arm around Bethany's shoulder and gave her a half hug. "There is always room in the market for other bakeries. We all have our own niche, and from what I've heard yours is brownies."

Color returned to Bethany's pale cheeks. I wasn't sure if it was from the warmth of the coffee or from Mom's compliment.

"Thanks, that's a relief." Bethany took a sip of the coffee. "This is amazing."

"You look better." Mom removed her arm from Bethany's shoulder and offered her a box of chocolate pasta. "Do you think you can eat?"

Bethany shook her head. "No, thank you. Coffee is fine for the moment. That was awful." She glanced in the direction of Evan's body and shuddered. "I've never seen anyone collapse like that before."

Mom took a bite of the chocolate pasta. "I know, dear. We're all upset."

"I swear my brownie didn't have nuts." Bethany looked to me and then Mom. "I'm really careful about that. I mean I know that nut allergies can be dangerous, but I had no idea they could be that dangerous. Now I'm going to have to rethink my entire kitchen strategy."

I wondered if she'd been professionally trained, but I decided it was probably best not to mention safety precautions at this moment, given how upset she was.

I didn't have time to educate her anyway because Thomas and the Professor, Ashland's resident detective and Mom's beau, arrived on the scene. The Professor acknowledged Mom and me with a slight nod of his head, but went straight to work. He removed his tweed jacket and reading glasses and listened intently as the EMS workers filled him in. Thomas stood by his side taking notes on his iPad. They were quite a contrasting team. The Professor looked like he belonged in front of a college classroom with his houndstooth scarf, Dockers, and loafers. Thomas, on the other hand, wore a belt that held a flashlight, walkie-talkie, and gun. I'd never seen the Professor with a weapon, although he must carry one. I'd have to ask Mom about that.

"What are the police going to do?" Bethany asked. She had finished her coffee and smashed the empty cup between her hands.

"Can I take that for you?" I asked.

Bethany glanced at the mangled cup in her hands. "Oh, yeah. Sure."

I tossed the cup in the garbage can hidden behind our display. "Do you want another cup?"

"Oh, no. That's okay. I'm already kind of shaky." She held her hands out to demonstrate.

I guessed that her jitters were from the shock of seeing Evan's body and not the decaf that I'd given her.

Mom gave me a knowing smile. "Don't worry, dear. Ashland police are absolutely the best. They'll take care of everything."

"What about our booths and the festival?"

"That I don't know about," Mom replied. "I would guess that everything will be postponed. If not canceled entirely."

Bethany let out a moan. "Oh, no. But what about all of the samples and tastings? I've spent so many hours and so much money getting ready for this. They can't cancel it."

Mom rested her hand on Bethany's shoulder. "It's too early to know what will happen, but try not to worry. It's out of our control now. If the festival is canceled, I'm sure we'll find another use for all this chocolate. For the moment the police have to focus on Evan."

"That sounded really cruel, didn't it?" Bethany put her hand to her mouth. "I didn't mean it like that."

"We know you didn't," Mom reassured her.

Bethany apologized again and thanked us for the coffee before returning to her booth. It felt like hours before Thomas and the Professor finished speaking with the paramedics and assessing the scene. I wondered if anyone had informed the crowd that had to be gathered outside by now. The doors were supposed to have opened thirty minutes ago. Like Bethany, I couldn't help but wonder if the fest was going to continue as planned this evening or whether we should pack up our chocolate.

I was about to say as much to Mom when the Professor strolled over.

"Helen, Juliet." He gave us a slight bow. Then he stood back and studied our booth, running his fingers through his auburn beard that had begun to streak with gray. "You've outdone yourselves once again."

"Doug." Mom reached for his hand. "I know what you're trying to do and it's not going to work. Don't bother with the small talk."

He massaged her fingers, which looked small in his hand. "Always the voice of reason, Helen, always."

"How are you holding up?" Mom removed her hand

from his grasp and poured him a cup of coffee without asking whether or not he was thirsty. She added a splash of cream, two teaspoons of sugar and dusted the top with cinnamon and nutmeg.

The Professor took the coffee and turned to me. "Your mother knows me too well, Juliet."

"Do they know what happened?" I asked. "It looked like he was having an allergic reaction to something."

"Indeed." The Professor ran his fingers through his beard. "It does appear that way."

I'd come to expect vague responses from him. He was known to quote Shakespeare and speak in some sort of cerebral code that no one else seemed to understand.

"His assistant told us he had a nut allergy," I continued.

"Yes, yes. That also appears to be true." He paused and sipped his coffee, as if considering his words.

"So do you think it was just an accident?"

Mom gave me a disapproving look.

The Professor took another sip of coffee. "Time will tell."

"He whispered something to me right before he died." The words sounded muffled and distant as if they weren't coming from my own lips.

Thomas, Mom, and the Professor all locked their eyes on me. I exhaled. "Murder. He said, murder."

"Juliet!" Mom's hand flew to her heart.

The Professor removed a pair of wire-framed reading glasses from his jacket, placed them on the tip of his nose, and then took out a Moleskin notebook. "Murder?" the Professor asked, making a note.

"I think so."

"Think? Or know?"

Everything was muddled. My brain felt like molasses. "I think so. It all happened so fast. Maybe I misheard him."

"Do you know what Lucio says in *Measure for Measure*?"

I shook my head.

"He says that our doubts are traitors." The Professor's kind eyes bored into me from behind his glasses.

I had no idea what the Professor meant by that. Did he mean that he had doubts that Evan's death was an accident? The Professor didn't expand his thought. Instead he picked up a tasting sample of our chocolate cake. "Is this the cake the victim consumed before going into anaphylactic shock?"

Mom nodded. "Yes."

"How much did he eat?" The Professor waved Thomas over. Thomas immediately began typing on his iPad.

Mom looked to me for confirmation. "Maybe two or three bites. Not much."

The Professor pointed to the rows of marzipan. "And these? Did he consume one of your chocolate candies?"

Mom shook her head. "No. Those are marzipan and definitely contain nuts. See the sign."

Thomas stopped typing and clicked photos of our display. There were two prominent table signs in the front and back of the marzipan that informed people they contained nuts.

"You are quite sure that the victim didn't consume the marzipan?"

Mom nodded again. "Positive. He told us that he was

allergic to nuts. You know, the funny thing is that's the first time I'd ever heard that. I'm surprised because many of his products are nut based. He must have had strict protocols in place if he reacted that quickly."

"We'll have to determine the cause of death. The medical examiner will do that later. We don't know that the victim consumed nuts. There are many possibilities. It's quite possible he reacted to something else. However, it's also quite possible that one of the products Mr. Rowe tasted contained nuts."

"You don't mean Torte?" Mom's walnut eyes brightened.

"Of course I do not have any doubts that either of you could have made such an error. However, protocol must be followed. We're going to need to test your samples for nuts. Thomas, please go ahead and bag these up." The Professor motioned to the table. He kissed Mom's hand. "Parting is such sweet sorrow. Alas, I must continue my work."

"Have you talked to Carter yet?" I interrupted.

The Professor tucked his notebook back into his tawny tweed jacket. "Why do you ask?"

"Right after Evan died, Carter assumed that he had been killed."

Pursing his lips, the Professor tapped his fingers on his well-groomed scruff. "Hmm. We'll consider that."

Mom caught my eye. I could tell that she was worried.

"What about the festival?" I asked.

The Professor cleared his throat. "Thank you for jogging my memory, Juliet. Indeed, there is a mob of chocolate lovers amassed outside. I don't see any reason why they can't have their appetites satiated once we've finished our investigation and the medical examiner releases the body. We'll let you know when we've made a decision."

"What about Evan?" I nodded in the direction of his body but kept my gaze focused on the Professor.

"Ah, yes, that might put a damper on the festivities." He gave me a sheepish smile. "Sorry, a lame attempt at trying to lighten the mood. The body should be released to the coroner's office soon."

The Professor and Thomas continued on. I was left wondering whether I was relieved or not that the festival would continue as planned.

Chapter Eight

The sound of Mom's voice brought me back into the present moment. "Juliet, did you hear me?"

"What? Sorry." I gave my body a little shake, trying to break myself free from the horrid memory of Evan collapsing.

"Are you okay?" She looked concerned.

"I'm fine."

Her eyes narrowed. "Juliet."

I recognized the tone in her voice. "Really, I'm fine." I made eye contact. "I needed a minute to focus, that's all."

"Honey." She placed her petite hand over mine. Her fingers were cold and instantly calming. "Are you sure that Evan said *murder*?"

It was impossible to keep my tone neutral. I could hear the apprehension in my voice. "I don't know, Mom. Maybe I misheard him, but I swear that's what he said."

Giving my hand a firm squeeze she furrowed her gently lined brow. "Juliet, Doug will figure it out. He always does. I don't want you to worry right now."

Goose bumps ran up my arm. "I know. I'm okay, Mom, really."

She frowned and released my hand. "We don't have to do this, you know."

"Of course we do. We're doing this." I grabbed two aprons from a large plastic tub and tossed one to her. "I'm with Bethany on this. We've done so much work to prepare for the festival, and according to what the Professor said the show must go on, as they say, so we might as well be part of it." What I didn't tell her was that I couldn't stop replaying Evan's last words in my head. I needed a distraction and something else to focus on in the short term.

Mom wrapped the brown apron around her petite waist. Our aprons are chocolate brown with the Torte logo stitched on the front. Like our pastries they are simple and elegant. As always, Mom looked lovely in her apron with her warm olive skin. We made quite the pair. I definitely took after my father. He was tall and lanky whereas Mom is short and petite. I also inherited his pale skin and blond hair.

"We're basically ready to go, right?" I asked, securing my apron.

"Yep." Mom turned up the heat on the burners and gave the molten chocolate sauce a stir. "Everything looks good."

"I wonder what they're going to tell everyone waiting to come in."

Mom shrugged. "I would guess the truth." She paused. "You know, I hope that there's not nuts in one of the tastings. What if one of the vendors' products accidentally contains nuts, and someone else attending has a nut allergy?"

"Good point." I appreciated her logic.

She held up her index finger. "Wait right here. I'm going to go find Doug."

The Professor was extremely meticulous, and Ashland's most revered detective. Mom was right, I needed to focus on chocolate and try to let go of Evan's distended face and final words.

Sandi Kramer strolled over to the booth. She extended her expertly manicured hand. "You must be Juliet, the pastry queen I've heard so much about. Sandi Kramer, editor of *Sweetened* magazine."

I wiped my hand on a dish towel and shook hers. "Nice to meet you. I love the magazine."

Reaching into a black clutch, she found a cream embossed business card and pressed it into my hand. "Excellent. I'm glad that you are familiar with the publication. We're in our fortieth year of producing the nation's best-selling dessert magazine."

"That's impressive."

She closed the silver clasp on her clutch and walked to the table that held our wedding cakes. "As are these. I was admiring your work from afar earlier. I had to come get a closer look for myself. Your piping is flawless."

"Thank you. That means a lot coming from you." I was pleased that Sandi had taken note. Piping is a skill that takes years of practice. I hadn't spent much time doing it in recent years, since the volume of desserts we produced on the cruise ship didn't lend itself to detailed design work.

Sandi leaned to the side to get a better angle. "It should. I don't dish out compliments unless they are warranted. This is excellent work. Some of the best I've seen. We should talk."

Her purse started ringing. "That'll be my assistant in New York calling. Again. I swear I cannot leave for five minutes. I need to take this but I'll be back."

I did a little dance as she strolled away on four-inch heels. Sandi Kramer was impressed with my cakes! By "talk" did she mean talk about featuring Torte in *Sweetened*? We couldn't pay for that kind of exposure. Having a story or photos in *Sweetened* would basically ensure that our wedding cake business would skyrocket.

"Nice moves, Jules." Thomas snuck up behind me.

I jumped.

Thomas grinned. "You've got rhythm. I didn't peg you for a dancer."

"It's not nice to sneak up on someone."

"I didn't sneak. You were too wrapped up in your dance moves." He swayed his hips from side to side.

I punched him in the shoulder. "I don't look like that when I dance."

He raised an eyebrow. "Yeah. Actually, you do."

Glaring at him, I folded my arms across my chest. "Did you need something other than making fun of me?"

"But making fun of you is so easy." Thomas smiled. "Okay, okay, back to business. I'm letting everyone know that there's been a change of plans. We are not going to open the festival to the public tonight."

"Why?"

"Your mom raised a valid concern, and the Professor

agreed. If someone's chocolate has accidentally been tainted with nuts we can't put the public at risk. I need to gather samples of every product here that is labeled nut-free. The Professor is having me drive them up to the lab in Medford right away. We'll get them tested immediately in hopes of being able to open the doors tomorrow."

Good thing Mom followed up, I thought.

"And speaking of nuts, you're sure that there's no way nuts got into your cake?"

"Yeah, why?"

Thomas glanced around the ballroom. "Everyone has given their statement now, and everyone agrees that Evan had a reaction after tasting your cake."

"We already went over this. There's no possible way that my cake contained nuts."

I could tell that Thomas was nervous. He stared at his feet as he spoke and fiddled with his holster.

"No one is accusing you of intentionally putting nuts in your cake, Jules, but I know that Torte is going through a fairly substantial renovation right now. Maybe things accidentally got mixed up. Don't you use a variety of flours? What if in the middle of the remodel your cake and almond flour got swapped or something?"

My heart rate picked up, and I could feel heat rising in my cheeks. "Thomas, come on. It's me. You know me better than half the people in this town. There is no way—no way—that our almond and cake flour got mixed up. It's not possible."

"I know you wouldn't make a mistake like that, but what about one of your team?"

"I don't understand why you're pressing on this. I

have hammered kitchen safety into my staff. We have practices in place to ensure that this sort of thing doesn't happen. All of our products are labeled, and we have an entirely separate cupboard for storing nuts."

Thomas clicked on his iPad. He sighed. "Yeah, I believe you, but I still have to test everything you brought."

"That's fine. Go ahead. You're not going to find nuts in anything except for the marzipan, which is clearly labeled."

He took a random sampling of cake slices and chocolate pasta boxes. "All right, I'm off to gather more chocolate. Too bad I can't sample it all myself." He chuckled.

I exhaled after he left. I wasn't sure why I was so angry that everyone assumed that Torte had been responsible for Evan's death, but I was fuming. Safety was my number one priority in the kitchen not only for our customers, but also for my staff. I wondered why Thomas was so convinced. Was someone intentionally trying to throw suspicion at me? I thought back again to Evan, gasping for breath, wheezing out his final words. I was feeling more convinced that someone had done this on purpose.

Mom returned a few minutes later. We packed everything back into the tubs. Most of it should do fine overnight with the exception of the chocolate sauce. Someone would be in for a treat tonight. Mom always made a point of delivering any of our overstock or test pastries to our neighboring businesses on the plaza.

"What are you thinking about this?" Mom asked as she scraped gooey sauce into a container.

"I was kind of thinking we might as well go help the

team with painting. We could grab some pizzas on the way back. I think we have ice cream in the walk-in. What if we bring the sauce and treat them to ice-cream sundaes and pizza?"

"Great idea." Mom clicked the lid on the top. "I hope the pasta and cake slices don't dry out too much tonight."

"Me too. I think they'll be okay. I used plastic wrap between each layer and made sure the lid was on tight, but we'll see. I don't know what else to do. I don't know if the Professor will even let us serve these."

"Good point." Mom sighed. "I'm worried about him."

"Do you think something's wrong?"

"I'm not sure." She shook her head. "He's been distracted lately and I can't pin down why."

I took off my apron, folded it neatly, and put my arm around her. "I'm sure he's fine," I said as we walked out together.

In reality I had a feeling that I knew why he was distracted. He had told me that he wanted to propose to Mom, but had yet to make a move. I wondered if he was finally ready to pop the question.

Chapter Nine

Fortunately, things at Torte were nowhere near as dramatic as they had been at the Ashland Springs Hotel. When Mom and I showed up with two large pizza boxes, Andy and Sterling both cheered.

"Pizza!" Andy hopped from a step stool and wiped his hands on a rag. "Awesome."

Sterling stopped stacking plastic tubs of spices and walked to the front to help us. "Awesome is right, but what are you doing here?"

Mom handed him a cardboard box with the sweet sauce. "Come take a dinner break and we'll fill you in."

We gathered around the island. Mom opened a bottle of wine and I grabbed sparkling sodas from the walk-in. The team had made great progress in the short time that we'd been gone. All of the kitchen cupboards were emptied and I could tell by the way the white paint popped that they'd been wiped down as well. Baking supplies, dishes, coffee mugs, wine glasses, and utensils were piled around the countertops. Stephanie folded an inventory sheet and tucked it into a box filled with champagne flutes.

"You guys are rolling," I said, offering her a blackberry soda.

She shrugged. "Yeah, I guess."

Andy raised his hands in front of him. "Toss me a soda, boss."

I threw a soda at him. He caught it in one easy motion. "I still got it. Even in the off-season I have to keep my skills fresh."

Andy played college football for Southern Oregon University. He took the sport seriously. It always surprised me that his athletic hands could produce such delicate latte art.

Mom lifted the lid on the first pizza box and the smell of pepperoni and sausage quickly filled the kitchen. My stomach rumbled in response. "Who wants a slice of the meat combo?"

Sterling and Andy both reached for slices.

"Stephanie, we got a vegetarian option too," Mom said as she opened the second pizza box revealing a Greek-style pizza with olive oil, sundried tomatoes, feta, artichokes, and three kinds of olives.

"Thanks." Stephanie almost smiled as she took the paper plate from Mom.

"Jules?" Mom waved her hands over both boxes. "Do you have a preference?"

"I think I'll go Greek." I poured two glasses of red wine and traded Mom a glass for a slice.

"What's the deal, Mrs. C.?" Andy asked. He had already scarfed the first piece of pizza down and was going in for number two.

Mom swirled her wineglass. "I'm afraid we have some bad news. There was an accident at the Chocolate Festival and they had to cancel it for tonight."

"What kind of accident?" Sterling asked. He folded his pizza in half and ate it like a taco.

"One of the vendors, Evan Rowe, had an allergic reaction to something he ate."

"You mean Evan Rowe of Confections Couture?" Stephanie asked. Last fall, when the Pastry Channel had come to town to film Take the Cake, a pastry competition, I had learned that Stephanie was a huge fan of cooking shows. Yet somehow I was still surprised at how much she knew about the world of pastry.

Mom nodded. "Yes, that Evan."

"Is he okay?" Andy reached for another slice of pizza. Then he looked around. "Is it cool if I have another?"

"Of course. We bought extra-larges for that reason." Mom slid the box closer to him. "Unfortunately, no. Evan died at the scene."

"What?" Sterling almost choked on his pizza. His startling blue eyes locked on mine. "Jules."

I shook my head. "I know. It was terrible."

Sterling looked concerned. "So what's the deal? Is the festival canceled?"

Mom cut a slice of the Greek pizza in half. "I don't think so. Doug made it sound like we should be able to continue with the Chocolate Festival tomorrow, but we'll have to wait and see what happens."

"Speaking of that," I said, putting my plate on the island. "The police think that Evan had a reaction to nuts. They are taking samples of everyone's chocolate tastings to be tested tonight, but I need you guys to be honest with me. Is there a chance that any of you may have moved the flour canisters around?"

Andy shook his head. "No, boss. We follow your instructions. All of the nut products are over there."

Sterling grabbed my arm and pulled me to the sink. "See. We were super careful. Just like you told us." Indeed, there was a large cardboard box labeled "Nuts" on each side. It was packed with almonds, cashews, peanuts, walnuts, and canisters of nut flour.

"Nice work." I gave them a thumbs-up. "But what about before today? I know things have been moved around as we were prepping. Could almond flour have accidentally gotten tossed into the wrong canister?"

Stephanie pointed to the flour canisters lined on the opposite countertop. "Jules, they are individually labeled. We know better."

I felt validated that my staff agreed. We had labeled each canister with the type of flour since we use different flours in our baking. The canisters were lined up in neat rows with two-inch chalkboard stickers on the front reading whole wheat, cake, unbleached, corn meal and so on. The nut-based flours had the same labels but were contained in the box with the other nut products. Nut flour has a different consistency and color than cake flour. I knew that there was no way I had made that kind of mistake, but I felt relieved seeing that, even in the chaos of rearranging and painting, our safety procedures were intact.

"Good." I sighed. "Thanks, you guys. That makes me feel better. Not that I doubted you. I was starting to doubt myself."

Sterling laughed and caught Mom's eye. "Yeah, right.

We all know you run a tight ship, Jules. You may seem sweet to all of our customers, but all of us fear the wrath of Juliet Montague Capshaw in the kitchen."

"Excellent." I grabbed a spatula and waved it at them. "I've got you all exactly where I want you."

Kidding around with the team helped relieve my internal tension, as did the two slices of pizza and glass of wine. After we had finished our gourmet dinner, Mom tossed the empty pizza boxes in the recycling bin. It was a good thing that we decided on two extra-large pizzas. There was nothing left by the time Sterling and Andy pushed back their barstools and tossed their paper plates in the trash. It was as if a swarm of locusts had devoured the pizza.

"Who's ready for an ice-cream sundae?" Mom asked.

Everyone groaned. "Sorry, Mrs. C.," Andy said, rubbing his belly. "I've got to take an eating break. I can't fit anything else in yet."

Mom laughed. "Well, put us to work then. Jules and I are here, so you might as well use us."

"No way, Mrs. C." Andy pushed her toward the front door. "My mom always says that the young ones should work while our elders rest. You go home. We've got this."

"An elder?" Mom put her hand to her heart. "Am I an elder now? I don't want to be an elder. I thought age was nothing more than a state of mind, and I assure you, in my mind I'm still quite young."

Andy grinned. "You are, Mrs. C., but you do so much for us. Let us paint. We've got a plan. We're going to blast our tunes and turn this place into a paint mosh pit."

Mom frowned.

"He's kidding." I helped Andy move her toward the door. "But he's right. You should go home. We'll take it from here."

"You're going to stay?" Mom asked.

"You can't hear when the music is loud anyway."

She pretended to be hurt. "Fine, I know when I'm not wanted, but I'll have you know that I'm going to go out on the town now that I have a night free." She grinned. "Or maybe I'll go home and take a long bubble bath."

"I like the sound of that."

"Just wait, Mrs. C., when you see the space tomorrow it will be a brand-new Torte." Andy held the door open for her.

"Okay. You kids have fun." She squeezed my arm. "I'll call you when I hear from Doug, and don't stay too late, Juliet."

"You got it, Mom." I kissed her cheek and locked the door behind her. Time to get to work. I couldn't wait to help transform Torte.

Chapter Ten

I started to return to the kitchen, but Andy held his hand out to stop me. "Where do you think you're going, boss?"

"To help you."

"Ha! No way. You're banned too." He nodded toward the door and kept his hand in place.

"What? I'm not an elder. I'm closer to your age than Mom's."

Andy ignored me and hollered to Sterling. "Can I get a little help up here?"

Sterling jumped over the front counter. He was an avid skateboarder and I had a feeling that his spry moves were the result of years of launching his board down flights of stairs and hurdling obstacles. "I'm on it," he said to Andy, and then unlocked the front door. "Out, Jules."

"You guys, come on. It's me. I'm cool. I can paint."

Andy and Sterling exchanged a look. I started to plead my case but they each gently grabbed my elbows and practically tossed me out the front door. Before I had a chance to react, Sterling locked the door and smirked. Andy waved. I banged on the glass, but they both turned and walked toward the kitchen.

I would have unlocked the door and let myself back in but my keys and my purse were inside. I knocked on the front windows. They pretended not to notice me.

"Juliet, darling, whatever is the big production about?" Lance's voice sounded behind me. Lance was OSF's artistic director. Our relationship was complicated. Not anywhere near as complicated as my relationship with Carlos, but he was known around town by locals and theater lovers alike as Ashland's resident diva, and it was nearly impossible to crack through Lance's persona. I knew that there was a deeper and more sincere side to him—I'd even seen it once or twice—but Lance was a pro at keeping his guard up.

"I smell desperation in the air. Do tell, why are we banging on the windows, darling?" Lance leaned next to me and peered in the window.

"They locked me out."

Lance cackled. "Brilliant. Absolutely brilliant."

"Don't laugh. I need to get back in there. My purse, my keys, everything is in there."

"It sounds to me like what you need is a stiff drink." He carefully rolled up the sleeve of his tailored navy suit. No one else in Ashland could pull off a three-piece suit, but Lance wore it well. The crisp dark suit matched his slicked hair and black-framed glasses. Looking at the leather-banded watch around his wrist, he continued, "Indeed, it's long past cocktail hour. Come, come. Let's get you a drink."

Lance looped his arm through mine. "But my stuff."
I looked longingly at Torte's cheery window display. We
had redesigned the front window display to feature our
appearance at the Chocolate Festival. Mom and I had
strung vanilla and chocolate macarons on twine and
hung them from the ceiling. They reminded me of a
sweeter, more upscale version of the popcorn and cranberry strings we used to make for Christmas.

"We'll come back for it later, darling. You look positively parched." He scowled and stared at my face.
"You've lost all the color in your cheeks. Something's
wrong." He stopped in mid-stride. "What's happened?"

I had to give Lance credit for being so astute. "Nothing."

Lance removed his arm from mine and placed both
of his hands on my cheeks. He has a tendency to invade
my personal space. If it was anyone other than Lance I
would have slapped his hands away, but I knew it was
his way of being dramatic. "Juliet, do not play coy with
me. I heard a wailing siren earlier. Something's happened, hasn't it?"

There was no way Lance was going to drop it, so I
figured it was better to come clean now versus drag-
ging it out. "There was an accident at the Chocolate
Festival."

"Accident?" Lance let his hands drop from my face.

I nodded. "Do you know Evan Rowe from Confections Couture?"

Lance rolled his eyes. "Please."

"He had an allergic reaction to something he ate.
The police assume it was nuts. Apparently, he had a very
serious allergy."

"Had?"

I swallowed twice. Talking about Evan's death made it that much more real. "He's dead."

Lance gasped and fanned his face with his hand. "Dead? As in dead?"

"He died right there on the ballroom floor. It was horrible."

"Don't say another word. Come with me. You really do need a drink, darling." Lance ushered me down the sidewalk and around the corner to the Green Goblin, one of Ashland's most popular bars. He entered the forest-themed bar the same way an actor enters the stage. People gathered around the crowded bar squeezed closer together making room for us to pass. There wasn't an empty table inside, but without a word a couple sitting at a high-top near the back of the room waved us over. I recognized them as young actors in the company. "We were just leaving. Here, take our table."

There was no doubt that Lance knew how to make an entrance. However, I didn't like the feeling that all eyes were on us. Lance might enjoy the spotlight, but I tend to hide from it.

"Sit, sit, Juliet," Lance commanded. "I'll get us some cocktails. You rest your pretty face and plaster on a smile. We don't want to make the masses think something is amiss."

He paid no attention to the line snaking around the bar. I chuckled in disbelief as everyone moved to let Lance cut to the front of the line. In a matter of seconds, he was back with two martinis and a devilish grin.

"Lance, you can't cut the line like that."

Rolling his eyes, he placed a martini in front of me.

"Juliet, please. The people love me. They want to feel like they are part of the inner circle."

"Inner circle?"

Motioning between us, he gave me an exasperated look. "Yes, us. We are the inner circle, darling. You have to make the little people feel important. I know this is a difficult concept for you to grasp, because, my dear naïve friend, you don't even realize the power you exude, but we are the inner circle and every so often I like to throw people a bone. Make them feel like they're in the know."

"By cutting in line?" Sometimes Lance was too much for me.

"Of course." He waved his hand over the martini. "Drink up. And then dish. I want all the gory details—all of them."

I took a sip of the martini and coughed. Lance wasn't kidding about bringing us strong drinks. The martini was heavy on gin and vermouth and light on any lemon flavor despite the fact that a fresh lemon slice adorned the side of the chilled glass.

"Easy," Lance cautioned. "I knew that you needed a drink but I didn't know that the refined Juliet was going to knock one back like a barstool regular."

"It's strong." I cleared my throat and stuck out my tongue.

"Exactly what the doctor ordered." Lance held his pinkie in the air as he drank his martini. "Now, on to this ghastly accident. Do tell, what happened?"

I filled him in on everything that had happened. When I got to the part about Evan clutching me and whispering "murder," I took a long drink.

Lance popped an olive into his mouth. "Well, well, this changes everything, doesn't it?"

"I don't know. Maybe I didn't hear what he said correctly. He was struggling for air. He could have said anything."

"Nonsense." He loosened his silver and navy striped tie. "You are one of the most astute women I know."

He was right. I didn't think that I had misheard Evan, and I couldn't escape the feeling that he had been murdered. There were too many loose ends—like Carter claiming Evan had been killed, and the fact that everyone seemed to have an issue with the deceased chocolatier. I explained how Evan had made it clear that he intended to be the star of the show again and how cruel he'd been to Bethany.

"You mean that young timid thing who runs around town with her basket of brownies like she's Little Red Riding Hood on her way to grandma's house?"

"Well, I never thought of it quite like that, but yes, Bethany recently started a brownie delivery service, the Unbeatable Brownie."

Lance finished his martini, but before he'd even placed his empty glass back on the table a new one was delivered. "I make it a point to know everything that goes on in town. I've already ordered from the poor little thing. Her blog is quite divine, actually. Gorgeous photos. She has a nice aesthetic and a way with words, but you would have thought that I was the big bad wolf by the way she cowered when she delivered her brownies. You know, if you're going to have the guts to use the word 'unbeatable' in the name of your business, you had better have some confidence in your product."

"I think the name is kind of a pun on beating brownies. You don't want to overbeat the mixture, otherwise they'll turn out dry and cakey."

"Spare me the cooking lesson. We're talking about a potential motive for murder here."

I threw my hands in the air. "Wait, we don't know that it's murder. The only thing we know for sure right now is that Evan had an accident."

Lance leaned forward. He scanned the room before he whispered, "Juliet, you are the worst liar on the planet. I know exactly what you're thinking and I assure you that I'm thinking the same thing. Evan was clearly hunted down and killed by a crafty baker. Don't try to pretend that you're not as delighted as I am that we have another case to solve."

"Lance! You are terrible. You can't be happy that someone is dead." Still, I had to admit that being the last person to talk to Evan made me feel responsible for finding out what had happened to him.

"Darling, don't be crass. Of course I'm completely shaken up that Ashland has lost such an important member of our community, but that's all the more reason to work together to figure out who could have done something so horrific." Lance dabbed the corner of his mouth with a cocktail napkin. "Talk me through what happened step by step. Go back to the part about Evan and Bethany."

"What part?" I asked.

"The part where he spit out her brownie and called her the scum of the food community. Don't you think that's suspicious? What if he tasted nuts in her brownie? Think about it, darling. What if that was for show? Let's imagine that he got a bite of nuts, realized it, and then spit it out. He wanted to save face so he proceeded to hurl insults at Bethany."

"Yeah, but if he knew there were nuts in her brownies why would he have come over to our booth? He would have gone straight to his booth to get his EpiPen."

"But you mentioned that his assistant, what's his name again?"

"Carter."

"Yes, Carter. Where was Carter when this was happening? Maybe Evan sent Carter for the EpiPen. If he was the egomaniac I remember him to be he wouldn't have taken any chance letting on that he was in need of help."

"I guess." I wasn't convinced. It seemed highly unlikely that if Evan knew his allergy was so deadly, he would have risked waiting to inject himself with the epinephrine.

"You don't look convinced."

"It's a stretch, Lance." My martini glass was half full and even so I felt like the room was starting to spin.

"Play along for a moment before you dismiss me." Lance shook his head in disdain. "Now, let's imagine our Little Red Riding Hood, where does she bake her unbeatable brownies? I'm guessing in grandma's kitchen?"

"I think she does bake everything out of her home kitchen, but that doesn't necessarily mean anything. She would have had to obtain her food handler's permit and they would have inspected her kitchen. There are pretty stringent laws in place to protect consumers."

"But what if she didn't?" Lance removed his glasses

and placed his index finger on the side of his mouth. "What if she's been running an illegal brownie operation?"

Part of me wanted to laugh. Lance was so ridiculously over the top sometimes that it was hard to tell when he was being serious and when he was being funny. "Running an illegal brownie business sounds like you're saying that she has an underground drug trade going on or something."

Lance narrowed his catlike eyes. "Juliet, you of all people should know that chocolate is as addictive as any street drug."

"How have we gotten this far off topic?"

Clapping his hands together, Lance arched his back. "You're right. We must focus. As I was saying, there are two possibilities here. The most straightforward is that our Little Red Riding Hood made a fatal mistake and accidentally contaminated her unbeatable brownies with nuts. Evan had a taste and let his pride get in the way. Instead of calling for help, he pretended to spit out the brownie and proceeded on to your booth. It was too late. The nuts were already pulsing through his veins."

"A highly dramatic scenario, but I will give you that it's a possibility I hadn't considered."

"Excellent, darling. Now, let's dive into the second and much juicier possibility."

I knew there was no point in trying to stop him. Lance was on a roll and he wasn't going to let me leave until he finished.

"Now, imagine this. Our victim Evan was known to have an extremely large head when it came to chocolate, right?"

It took every ounce of my self-control not to laugh. I pursed my lips and nodded. Lance commenting on anyone's ego was more than slightly ironic.

He tapped his chin. "He made fun of our young starlet and her hashtags. He embarrassed her in front of the entire chocolate community. What if she decided to take revenge? Maybe in the heat of the moment she grabbed a nut brownie instead. Think about it, it's a genius, and possibly foolproof, murder weapon. Evan consumes her product. Drops dead and worst-case scenario she gets a little slap on the wrist for the oversight. How could anyone possibly prove the intention to kill even if they do discover nuts in Bethany's brownies? Or for that matter anyone's products?"

He had a point there.

"You're coming around to my theory. It makes logical sense, doesn't it?"

"Yes, but how did she know he was allergic to nuts? I wouldn't have known if he hadn't mentioned it when Mom offered him pistachios."

Lance scowled.

Between the martini, the stress over Evan's death, and the long hours I'd been pulling to prepare for the Chocolate Fest, my eyes were starting to feel heavy.

"Am I losing you?" Lance snapped his fingers. "Don't let those gorgeous lids of yours droop. We have so much more to discuss and we haven't even begun to formulate a plan of attack."

I yawned. "I can't, Lance. I've got to go to bed. You've given me plenty to think about, though."

"Fair enough." Lance rested his chin in his hands and

gave me his best sad face. "I suppose you've had a long day. We'll part ways, but you must promise to observe Little Red Riding Hood as closely as possible tomorrow. I'll start doing some digging and see what I can find about her background and history."

"Thanks for the drink." I stood.

Lance reached out and kissed both of my cheeks. "Anytime, darling. Get some beauty sleep and we'll re-group tomorrow. Ta-ta!"

I hurried through the crowd before Lance had a chance to change his mind. I did note that no one moved for me the way they had for Lance. He might think that we were part of some sort of inner circle, but that was all in his head.

As I stepped out into the dark night, all of Lance's theories played back in my head. Could he be onto something, or was this another case of his flair for the dramatic running wild? I wasn't sure, but I was going to watch Bethany more closely tomorrow. I'd been fortu-nate to have a number of chefs mentor me throughout the years, I could do the same for Bethany. It could be a case of pure innocence. Maybe she needed someone with some real-world experience to help her grow and protect her new business. Lance's theory that Bethany could have intentionally contaminated her brownies with nuts seemed too far-fetched to me. What possible motive could she have?

I started toward my apartment when I realized that my keys and purse were still at Torte. Hopefully, the team would let me in. I pulled the sleeves of my jacket down and scrunched my hands inside. When I arrived at Torte it was completely lit up. I could hear music pulsing from outside. Andy, Stephanie, and Sterling were all painting. I tapped on the window.

Sterling looked up and motioned for me to go away with his paintbrush.

"My keys!" I yelled, pointing to the office. "My keys and purse are in there."

It took a minute for them to figure out what I was saying. Finally, Stephanie climbed down from the stepladder and headed to the office. A minute later she met me at the front door with my purse. Her hands were spattered with paint. "Here." She thrust my purse at me and shut the door.

I guess that was a clear sign that I still wasn't wanted. Honestly, I felt relieved. My bed was calling, and I had a feeling that it wasn't going to take long for me to fall asleep.

Chapter Eleven

Sure enough, I crashed on the couch when I got home and didn't wake up until I heard my cell phone ringing the next morning.

Who would call this early? I thought as I reached for the phone and glanced at the clock. It was just after five. My heart skipped a beat. Could it be Carlos? We hadn't spoken since he'd returned to the ship. Maybe he'd gotten his times mixed up. A twinge of regret swept over my body as I picked up my phone and saw that it was Mom calling.

"You're up early," I said, swiping to answer. "Especially since Torte is closed today. For once, we don't have to be up before the sun."

"I'm sorry, honey. I thought you would be up. You're always up early."

"It's okay. I was starting to stir, and I had fallen asleep on the couch, so my back thanks you." That part was true, my lower back felt like it had been hammered with a rolling pin. One of the cons of being tall is that I don't fit on couches very well. Last night, I'd slept with my legs hanging off the end.

"I just heard from Doug. The Chocolate Festival is going to continue as planned today with two changes."

"Okay." I stretched from side to side trying to loosen the knot in my back. "What kind of changes?"

"Do you want the good news or bad news first?"

"Uh-oh. I guess I'll take the good."

"The good news is that they've pushed back the opening time to eleven this morning."

"And the bad news?"

"They haven't heard back from the lab yet, which means that we can't serve our chocolate cake."

"Oh, no! What are we going to do with all those squares we cut?"

"Doug said that he'll let us all know as soon as he receives the lab report. We might be able to serve them later today or tomorrow. If not, we can donate them. I'm sure Ashland's police and firefighters would be happy to take some cake samples off our hands."

"I guess this means we'll be baking this morning after all."

Mom sighed. "That's why I'm calling. If we get to the bakeshop in the next hour or so that should give us time to bake new tasting cakes."

"Right." My back loosened as I swayed my hips in small circles. "Let me take a quick shower. I can be there in thirty or forty minutes."

"Great. Me too. I'll see you soon."

After we hung up I continued stretching and then hurried to the kitchen to get coffee brewing while I took a shower. Waking early has never really bothered me.

Some of my friends in culinary school struggled with the insane hours required of a pastry chef, but not me. I like the feeling of rising early with the bread, but only, only if I have coffee. My mornings don't start without a healthy jolt of caffeine.

With the coffee brewing and my back feeling more normal, I took a long hot shower, pulled on my favorite pair of well-worn jeans and a honey-colored cable-knit sweater that brought out the natural highlights in my light hair. Since I was going to be on my feet all day, I opted to wear a comfortable pair of fleece-lined knee-high boots. I dried my hair and pulled it back in a pony-tail and dusted my cheeks and forehead with some powder. There's not much point in wearing a lot of makeup in the bakeshop, since between the steaming water and constantly opening hot ovens, makeup tends to run and get sticky. I did apply a pale pink lip gloss and put on a pair of small gold hoop earrings. Dangly jewelry doesn't lend itself well to baking, but since Mom and I would spend the majority of the day talking to potential customers at the Chocolate Fest, I wanted to look polished.

Before heading to Torte I guzzled two cups of coffee and ate a banana. I prefer to start my mornings with coffee and work my way up to breakfast later in the morning. My stomach has never adjusted to eating a big breakfast when it's still pitch-black outside.

I grabbed my winter jacket from the coatrack by the front door and walked downstairs to Main Street. My apartment is above an outdoor store, Elevation. Like most of the buildings on the plaza, Elevation is modeled in Elizabethan design. The contrast struck me because the outdoor store was showcasing spring gear—kayaks, paddle boards, and swimsuits. It looked out of place with the old-world scroll of its logo and the antique iron design around the window frame, but that was Ashland— Shakespeare mashed up with the twenty-first century.

Torte was a few stores down and about a two- or three-minute walk from my apartment. Being so close to the bakeshop and in the heart of all the action on the plaza had made my transition to being home easier. Mom lived outside of town in the hills surrounding Ashland where deer roam free and snack on neighborhood apple trees and backyard gardens. Growing up in the wooded hills made for a magical childhood. I remember one summer when my friends and I discovered a hollowed-out log in my backyard. We transformed it into our secret hideout with blankets, dolls, and a stash of Mom's homemade chocolate chip cookies. The deer, or some other creature, discovered the box of cookies and devoured them. When I lamented to Mom that an animal ate our secret treats, Mom laughed and said, "I'll take that as a compliment. Even four-legged friends love Torte's sweets."

It was true. I smiled at the memory as I unlocked the front door to the bakeshop. The smell of paint assaulted my nostrils. I flipped on the lights and opened the front windows a few inches. Cold air rushed inside. It was a good thing that we had decided to close while working on renovations. The strong scent of fresh paint would overwhelm customers and our pastries. Smell is an extremely important element in taste, and the thought of our sourdough bread infused with the essence of chemical paint was less than appetizing.

I walked to the kitchen to see how much progress the team had made last night. From the look of things, they had primed each wall and all the cabinets in the kitchen. Everything glowed shiny white. When Mom and I were deciding on paint color for the kitchen, the owner of the hardware store had recommended that we prime the walls with a high-gloss white before painting. The kitchen was subjected to constant heat, steam from boiling water, and the cabinets got heavy usage. Priming would take an extra day, but would give us another layer of protection. I ran my finger along the far wall to test the paint. My fingers came back dry, which meant that by the time Andy, Sterling, and Stephanie arrived later this morning they could paint the finish coat. We were right on schedule, just as I had mapped it out. Thank goodness something was going according to plan.

The smell of paint was even stronger in the kitchen. Before I got to work on creating a new batch of chocolate tastings, I needed air flow. Torte's kitchen windows are the old crank style. I twisted the vintage glass pane windows open and welcomed the cool air. Next, I assessed the space. Everything had been carefully boxed and packed away exactly as Mom and I had spelled out. The only problem was going to be finding everything and clearing off a space to work.

Mom arrived as I began moving around boxes and plastic tubs. "Good morning," she called, pausing by the front door and fanning her hand over her face. "Whew, the fumes are pretty strong, aren't they?"

She closed the door behind her, making sure to keep the CLOSED sign facing out. Normally at this hour the bakeshop would be buzzing with energy and the smell of coffee brewing. We open at six every weekday morning and a ton of customers often pop in before work for a cherry turnover and to-go cup of Andy's rich brews. Even though we'd let all of our regulars know that we were closing for a few days, I had a feeling that if anyone noticed Mom and me baking in the kitchen we'd get a knock on the door.

"I know, and I've had the windows open for the last fifteen minutes," I replied. "I probably should have told them to crack them last night. I didn't even think about it."

Mom hung her wool coat on the rack and joined me in the kitchen. "Oh, my, where do we even start?"

"That's what I was trying to figure out." I handed her a box of crystalized decorator's sugar. "At the moment I'm trying to make a space for us to work. Do you have any thoughts on what we should bake?"

She rolled up the sleeves of her thin cream-colored turtleneck and glanced at her watch. "We have at least four hours. There's going to be a vendor meeting at ten and then they will open the doors to the public at eleven, so we have plenty of time to make the cake again, but I don't know, what do you think? It almost feels tainted."

"I'm with you. I think we should do something different. Plus, baking in here isn't going to be easy. What if we hand-dip chocolate truffles? That way we don't have to use the oven. We can melt the chocolate on the stove and they won't require using the mixers or anything."

"See, that's why you get the big bucks." Mom winked. Her eyes held a brightness and a hint of mischievousness. It was one of the many reasons that people were drawn to her. She was an excellent listener, but she also had a playful side that helped lighten everyone around her.

"Yeah, right. Big bucks and family bakeshop don't exactly go hand in hand, do they?" I found a tub of baker's chocolate.

"Juliet Montague Capshaw, how can you say such a thing? You know as well as I do that we're only in this for the money."

I laughed. "Right. The money."

"What if I whip up a batch of your grandmother's marble fudge? We can cut it into tiny tasting squares."

"Fudge and truffles. That works for me. Let's do it."

Mom unzipped the forest-green vest she was wearing and took off the creamy wool scarf wrapped around her neck. Her tone shifted. "Speaking of money, I reviewed all the paperwork last night."

"And?"

"It looks good to me. Basically everyone's application will be submitted for the grant, and as soon as the funds are awarded, the construction begins. It's pretty straightforward from there."

I had cleared a four-foot square on the corner of the island. "They are awarding ten grants, right?"

Mom nodded. "That's right, and we don't have to pay that money back. That would be the ideal outcome, but of course everyone is in the same boat."

"What about a small-business loan?" Rosalind had mentioned that the city was going to offer low-interest loans to help businesses on the plaza retrofit their buildings with proper drainage for flooding. I started looking through a box labeled "Knives" for a chopping knife.

Our chocolate truffles are relatively easy to make. I planned to melt dark chocolate with heavy cream. We would roll the truffles in chopped nuts and dust them in cocoa powder. The thought of nuts made me feel slightly light-headed. Maybe we should ditch the nuts and go for straight chocolate.

"The interest rate is extremely low and we would pay it back over the next twenty years." Mom dug through a box of saucepans.

"That's very doable."

She was quiet for a moment and then handed me a large saucepan. "Yes, but you have to think seriously if that's really what you want to do, Juliet. I don't want you to take on a loan that traps you here."

"Traps me?" I took the pan from her and placed it on the stove. "I don't feel trapped. I want to be here. I'm choosing to be here."

Mom's smile was thin as she measured dark chocolate. "I know that, but I worry that you might feel differently months or even a year or two from now."

"You mean because of Carlos?"

She shifted her head from side to side. "Yes, Carlos but also you. You've only been back for a little while. Ashland is a wonderful place to live and work, but you've had such adventures."

I started to interrupt her. She put a finger in the air. "Let me finish. I know that you're happy to be here now. I can see it in your face. You look lighter, happier. But that could change, and it's okay if it does. I don't want you to feel tied down."

"I don't feel tied down."

She pursed her lips. I could tell that she was considering her words. "You've been through a lot, honey, and they always say that you shouldn't make a major life decision when you're dealing with grief."

"I'm not grieving." I lit the gas burner and took the chocolate that she had measured. We would melt the chocolate on low heat, slowly incorporating heavy cream and flavored extracts.

"I know that this is different than when your father died, but loss is loss."

"Mom, come on, I'm fine." I caught her eye. "Really."

She looked like she wanted to say something else, but instead she squeezed my elbow and said, "Okay, but promise me that you'll really think about it."

"Promise."

She smiled. "I guess I need to go dig out some butter and cream for our new chocolate offerings."

I stirred the satiny chocolate with a wooden spoon. "That would be great."

We worked on the fudge and truffles for the next few hours but kept the conversation light. Mom didn't mention Carlos or expanding Torte again, but I kept replaying what she'd said. Was I grieving? I hadn't ever thought of leaving him as a loss to be grieved, but maybe she was right. Mom had a way of knowing things about me that I didn't know myself. I didn't want to make a rash decision that I would regret, but I also had to make a decision before the ship sailed on getting financial help from the city.

As expected, throughout the early morning hours, a handful of customers knocked on the front door. Each time Mom or I would wipe chocolate from our hands and have to break the news that their Torte fix would have to wait for two more days. We encouraged everyone to come join us at the Chocolate Fest. Andy, Sterling, and Stephanie arrived in paint gear a little after nine. We praised them for their efforts and enlisted their help to finish our chocolate assembly line. I instructed Stephanie on how to cut the marble fudge into tiny squares. Mom had swirled white and dark chocolate together to create the fudge. The cooled fudge had a beautiful sheen and could have been mistaken for an expensive marble countertop.

The truffles turned out even better than I expected. We hand-rolled them into perfect one-inch balls and dusted them with cocoa powder, crystallized sugar, sprinkles, and gold sheen. They looked decadent and fit for a king. Once they had set we boxed them up and returned everything to its original place so that painting could continue.

"Leave the windows open," I cautioned, as Mom and I headed for the Ashland Springs Hotel. "We'll check in tonight, but if you finish before we're done, lock the front door."

Andy gave me a salute. "You got it, boss."

Mom waved and added, "Be warned that customers will probably knock when they see you in here. You don't have to answer, but if you do, let them know we have samples at the Chocolate Fest and that we'll be back open on Monday."

"Don't worry, Mrs. C." Andy nudged Sterling. "You've got the dream team here. We're totally all over it."

"They really are a dream team," I said to Mom as we walked toward the hotel. "I can't believe how much they got done last night. Honestly, I never thought they would get all of the cabinets primed too. We're actually ahead of schedule at the moment."

Mom tapped on the cardboard box of fudge she was carrying. "Knock on wood or something. You might jinx us."

"You're not superstitious."

"I am now. Think of everything that's happened in the last few weeks."

"Good point." I couldn't exactly blame her, especially as we entered the hotel.

Mom paused in front of the doors leading to the ballroom. "Are you okay, honey?"

I gave her my best brave face. "I'm good."

She raised one brow. "I know you're not. I'm not either, but let's do this together, okay?"

"Okay." How did I get so lucky to have a mother like her? I squared my shoulders, shifted the box of truffles in my arms, and braced myself.

Chapter Twelve

There was a palpable feeling of tension in the ball-room. The first people we met as we stepped inside were Thomas and the Professor. They flanked each side of the doorway like guards.

"Hey." Thomas smiled. "You want a hand with that?"

"No, I'm fine." I was surprised to see them here.

As if reading my mind, Mom greeted the Professor with a light peck on the cheek. "I didn't expect to see you this morning."

The Professor took the box of fudge from her arms. "That makes two of us."

We waited for him to expand, but as usual he didn't. Instead he motioned with one arm for us to follow him. "Let me escort you to your table, ladies."

I looked to Thomas for an explanation. He shrugged and shook his head. There had to be a reason that they were here, and I quickly realized they weren't the only police on-site. As the Professor walked us to our booth

I noticed three uniformed officers strategically stationed throughout the ballroom.

Mom whispered to the Professor. "Is something wrong?"

He gave a quick nod and then said, "I assure you that you are both completely safe. We've added extra security as a precaution."

"What kind of precaution?" I asked, setting the box of truffles on our table.

He scanned the area around us. "I have found over the years, Juliet, that sometimes the mere show of force leads to suspects behaving in unusual ways."

"Suspects?" Mom and I said in unison.

The Professor gave us a small bow. "I've said enough. Rest assured that we have eyes everywhere. Continue with your chocolate tasting as planned." With that he walked away and resumed his post at the front door.

I had a feeling that the Professor thought the idea of having eyes on us would be a relief, but in reality there was something unsettling about feeling like we were being watched.

"What do you think that was all about?" I asked Mom, who had begun placing dainty bites of fudge with individual toothpicks on silver serving trays.

"If I was a betting woman, I would place my money on the fact that they're proceeding with the assumption that Evan's death wasn't accidental."

"My thoughts exactly." I couldn't resist biting into one of the round truffles. An intense chocolate flavor hit my palate followed by a creamy finish. It was a disappointment not to be able to serve our chocolate cake, but

I had a feeling chocolate lovers were going to swoon over our truffles.

Mom brushed gold dust and cocoa from her hands. "Let's follow Doug's advice and proceed like normal. I trust him and I'm sure that he has a plan."

Before we could strategize, an announcement sounded asking all vendors to gather in front of the main stage. I ended up standing next to Bethany from the Unbeatable Brownie. She appeared jumpy as we waited for the update. She wore a pink apron with the same #GET IN MY BELLY hashtag. Her apron strings were undone and she fiddled with them as she bounced her feet on the carpeted floor. She reminded me of a writer who was a regular at Torte. He brings his laptop and plants himself by the front windows while he writes and drinks coffee by the gallon. Andy once asked if we should cut him off because customers around him were complaining that the floor was shaking so much that they thought there was an earthquake.

"How's it going?" I couldn't help but place my hand on her shoulder to try to calm her down.

She stopped bouncing. "Good, I mean not exactly good. It's weird seeing all these cops here, isn't it? Do you know why they're here? I mean I know that Mr. Rowe died, but it was an accident, right? It's almost like they're watching us or something. One of them stood over me while I unpacked my brownies. I tried to talk to him. I even tried to offer him a brownie, but he didn't say a word. He just watched me like I was a criminal or something."

I was exhausted listening to her rapid-fire speech. The Professor's words sounded in my head; could this be what he meant by suspects behaving strangely? The Professor took the stage at that moment. He held an index card in one hand and pushed his reading glasses to the base of his nose as he spoke.

"Thank you all for arriving early. As I'm sure you've noticed we have extra police on hand for today's festivities. I assure you this is standard procedure after yesterday's accident."

"That's good to hear," Bethany whispered to me.

"Additionally," the Professor continued. "The organizers have asked us to support them with extra safety precautions for the weekend. If you haven't received new labels and signage an officer will be coming to your booth to give you one. We had a meeting of the minds and determined that in the vein of being extra cautious, everything will be labeled as potentially containing nuts."

In all my years working in professional kitchens I'd never witnessed anything like this.

"When the festival comes to a conclusion on Sunday, the organizers will be meeting to determine new protocols for next year." The Professor turned to one of the women standing next to him onstage wearing a staff T-shirt. "Is there anything else I should add?"

She shook her head.

"In that case, I will bid you adieu. My team is here and will be informing all the guests who walk through the doors about our nut procedures. If you need any assistance, please do not hesitate to ask. I know that often officers of the law are regarded negatively. I assure you that we are here to serve and protect as we have sworn to do."

As everyone returned to their booths I watched Bethany dart toward hers. She was definitely skittish, which could be due to the fact that she was young and not used to having the police around, but part of me wondered if she was playing right into the Professor's hand. I was going to have to try and find a way to talk to her alone at some point, but for the moment it was time to focus on the chocolate.

Mom tossed me an apron. "Are you ready to meet the masses?"

"Hungry chocolate masses?" I tightened the apron around my waist. When I left the ship and Carlos last summer, I had dropped weight that I didn't exactly have to lose. I've always been naturally thin thanks to my dad's lanky genetics, but for a while, I worried every time I looked in the mirror and saw how hollow my cheeks had become. Fortunately, I'd been slowly gaining back the weight that I'd lost. Mom had made a point of trying to fatten me up, offering me buttery scones with clotted cream and strawberry jam and sausage rolls. She claimed that having a pastry chef who looked like a skeleton was bad for business. Her technique was working. My apron felt a tad snugger around my waist and I had noticed that my cheekbones weren't as prominent of late.

"We are here to serve and chocolate?" Mom scowled. "That doesn't really work, does it?"

"I don't know. That has a certain ring to it. If the Professor and Thomas have been sworn to serve and protect, we can swear ourselves in to serve and chocolate."

"Some would say that chocolate is a form of protection. I read a study in the *Journal of Medicine* that eating an ounce of chocolate a day can prevent everything from cancer to Alzheimer's."

I stepped back and took one final look at our display. The white floral bouquets in contrast to the dark chocolate delicacies was striking. I was proud of what Mom and I had accomplished and eager for customers to weigh in with their feedback and favorites. Watching someone experience our creations is one of the reasons I became a pastry chef. There's nothing like observing someone bite into a decadent truffle and watching as the flavor transforms their face—a slow smile spreading up to their eyes. I hadn't had much of a chance to experience that on the cruise ship, but sometimes when I'm working at Torte I'll sneak up to the front counter and pretend to stock the pastry case. In reality, I use the opportunity to watch as customers nosh on our pastries and sip our coffees. Food is an expression of art and love. I remember my mentor in culinary school had a poster in his office with a quote from George Bernard Shaw that read: "There is no sincerer love than the love of food." It was a philosophy that I had learned watching Mom serve customers for years—a pastry with a side of love.

"What do you think?" Mom nudged my hip. She stood parallel with my shoulders.

"Not half bad."

"And maybe even a winner. Maybe." She smoothed her apron. "Let's do this, as the kids say."

The words "the kids" made me wonder how things were going at Torte. If there was a lull in the action, I would try to run over after lunch and check on their progress. We took our positions behind the table as the doors were opened. Chocolate lovers flooded into the ballroom. The next two hours passed in a blur. Mom managed the tasting tables, constantly restocking our supplies as customers devoured our marzipan, fudge, truffles, and chocolate pasta. I talked through our custom cakes, showing people the variety of designs we could offer for weddings and special events and thrusting brochures into everyone's hands.

We were too busy to think about Evan's death. I was happy for the reprieve and even happier with the feedback about our display wedding cakes. One bride ordered an exact replica of the forest-inspired cakes on log slices. When I asked her if there was anything unique or different she'd like done, she pointed to the display cake and said, "I want this cake—exactly."

I laughed as I took down her information and gave her a quote on price. "You probably don't want this exact cake if your wedding is next month. It might be slightly stale by then."

She wasn't fazed by the cost nor was she deterred in making sure that she was explicitly clear that she wanted a carbon copy of the cake in front of her. I promised that we would re-create the cakes for her wedding and thanked her for her business. The Chocolate Festival was off to a better than expected start. We had hoped to attract new customers, but I didn't think we would actually sell wedding cakes at the event.

Mom appeared to be having equal success with our tasting table. She made sure to encourage everyone who stopped at our booth to vote for their fan favorite, even handing them additional ballots. Sometime after one o'clock there was a gap in the crowd. Mom wiped her brow with the back of her wrist. "Whew, that was a madhouse."

I pointed behind us to a new throng of chocolate-hungry attendees heading our way. "Get ready for wave number two."

She reached under the table and removed a paper bag. Unwrapping two sandwiches tied with string and parchment paper, she handed one to me. "Here. We need to eat."

"When did you pack lunch?" My stomach rumbled in thanks as I opened a peanut butter and marionberry jam sandwich on thick-sliced sourdough bread.

"I have my secrets." Mom held up half of her sandwich to me. "I used your trick, what do you think? How did I do?"

The trick that she was referring to was a simple technique to ensure that the jam doesn't bleed into the bread. There's nothing worse than a soggy jam sandwich. To prevent this from happening, I spread a thin layer of peanut butter on both sides of the bread. The peanut butter is a barrier for the jam which stays exactly where it should—in the middle.

"Nice." I took a bite. Mom handed me a bottle of sparkling water and a bag of salted chips. We ate quickly and silently because we could hear the hum of the crowd coming closer and because neither of us could talk with peanut butter coating our mouths. I only had time to eat half the sandwich and a handful of chips before the next wave of chocolate fans made it to our booth, but it was enough to take the edge off and give me a boost to resume my cake pitch.

When the crowd finally thinned again an hour or so later, Mom sent me off to taste and size up the competition. "Juliet, it's slowed down. Why don't you do a lap and then when you're done, I'll do the same."

"Sounds good, but how about you go first."

Mom pulled out the uneaten half of her sandwich. "I've got a date with a PB&J first."

"Right." I grinned. "I won't be long. Honestly, I'm not sure how much chocolate I can taste. I feel like I'm in a chocolate coma, being surrounded by it all day."

"No, you should sample what other vendors are doing. I'm dying to know what you think of the chocolate slushy machine."

"That will be my first stop." I wasn't sure how I felt about a chocolate slushy, but I've learned that it's important to stay open to trying new ideas and flavor profiles as a chef. Some of the best things I've tasted over the years have been completely unexpected and not something I would have ever paired together.

I made a beeline for the slushy machine, which was on the opposite side of the room. The Professor and Thomas were nowhere to be seen as I weaved my way through the candy land of chocolate. Come to think of it, neither were the other police officers. The heavy police presence from this morning was gone. I wondered if there was any significance to the fact that they'd taken their leave.

The line at the slushy machine wrapped all the way to the next booth—a vendor showcasing chocolate-infused teas. Her space reminded me of a fortune-teller's booth. She had a collection of silver teapots and fragrant tea leaves displayed in clear glass jars. There were antique jars with honey, cinnamon, and chocolate swizzle sticks. She poured scalding hot water into a paper mug and tapped her wrist on one of the glass jars. Her bracelets clicked on the glass as she addressed me. "I see you drinking my chocolate and echinacea blend. Your system is in need of a healing tea."

The thought of chocolate and echinacea paired together sounded less than appetizing, but I was committed to trying some new flavor combinations.

She reached for my palm and turned it faceup. Then she ran her tea-stained fingers along the deep lines in my palms. Closing her eyes, she inhaled and nodded. "Yes, yes, I see there has been a darkness around you, but it's beginning to lift."

Suddenly, I became acutely aware of the people in line in front and in back of me. This was a chocolate festival. I didn't remember reading anything in the promotional materials about a fortune-teller and palm reader. Although this was Ashland, and we're known for attracting a variety of eccentric personalities. It was one of the reasons I had fallen in love with my childhood town all over again.

She released my hand and opened the glass jar. The scent of the earthy tea leaves mingled with a spice and chocolate. I couldn't exactly say that it was a pleasant smell, but I breathed it in anyway. With a silver scoop she shook the tea leaves into a mesh bag and plunged it into the paper cup. "Drink this. It will help."

There was something about her steely eyes that made me believe her. I thanked her and started to move forward toward the slushy booth when she grabbed my wrist. "Be careful. That darkness wants to follow you. You have the power not to let it in."

"Thanks." I held up my paper cup in a toast and inched farther away. She probably said that to everyone, a silly trick to add drama to her tea readings, but an involuntary shudder ran down my spine. Don't be ridiculous, Juliet, I scolded myself. Logically I knew that I had nothing to worry about and that a woman selling chocolate-infused teas could hardly see into my future, but I couldn't help wonder what the darkness was around me and if it had anything to do with Evan's death.

Chapter Thirteen

The chocolate and echinacea tea tasted exactly like it smelled. I couldn't pinpoint what the flavor was, and while I wouldn't say it was something I would want to drink again, there was something slightly comforting about it. The chocolate slushy, on the other hand, was delicious. The chocolatier had blended dark and milk chocolate, heavy cream, and ice, which was blended together until it had a thick consistency. It was sweet and almost like a milkshake but with little pops of ice. I could imagine drinking many a chocolate slushy on a hot summer's day.

As I wound my way back to Torte's booth I stopped at Bethany's display. She was finishing explaining her brownie delivery process to an attendee as I walked up.

"Oh hi, Jules. How's it going? I can't believe how packed it's been all day." Her apron was spattered with chocolate and her hair was disheveled.

"It looks like you've been busy."

She blushed and stared down at her messy apron and equally messy workstation. Granted, she was working the fest solo, but cleanliness is imperative when work-ing in a kitchen or serving the public. Yet again it made me wonder about her training and practices. "I know. I can't seem to keep up with the demand. I've been frost-ing brownies as I go. I guess I should have baked a lot more."

I pointed to a caramel and walnut brownie. "May I?"

"Oh yes, please. I'd love it if you tasted it, and please give me your honest opinion. I can take it. Everyone says that the way you improve as a chef is through criticism, so lay it on me."

"I prefer constructive feedback," I said, tearing a bite of the brownie. "Can I offer a piece of advice?"

She nodded.

"Don't let chefs be cruel or condescending to you. Trust your food. Of course, it's important to be willing to hear feedback that will make you a stronger baker, but not when it tears you down." Her brownie was moist and chewy. The salt from the caramel and walnuts paired nicely with the dense cocoa flavor.

Her eyes drifted over to Evan's booth. "Are you talk-ing about Evan?"

"Trust me, I've worked with dozens of chefs like Evan. You can't let someone else's ego get into your head." I took another bite of brownie. "This is great. I like the combination of the salt with the sweet. Really well done."

She blushed. "Thank you."

"I mean it. Your brownies are fantastic." I'd met a number of aspiring chefs like Bethany in culinary school and during my time on the ship. Head chefs can smell fear miles away. It's a delicate balance when starting out in a career in the world of food. Chefs-in-training have to be respectful and willing to listen to the head chef's advice—or rant, depending on the chef—but they also have to have an innate level of self-respect and trust in their skill. I don't know if I developed my self-assurance from growing up in Torte's warm and welcoming kitchen or from Mom and Dad's gentle guidance. It was probably a combination of both, but either way I learned early on in my training that in order to make it in the culinary world you have to be willing to take charge and own up to your successes and failures. Chefs respect a can-do attitude.

My pep talk to Bethany appeared to be working. A smile spread across her pimpled face. The pockmarks dotting her cheeks were yet another reminder of how young she was.

"Evan was pretty mean about my brownies," she said, looking at her feet. "It makes me feel better that you think they're moist and chewy. Don't get me wrong, I know that I'm just a food blogger, but I have over ten thousand followers on Instagram and a lot of customers around town, and I've never had anyone other than Evan tell me that my brownies were stale and dry."

"That's exactly my point. Chefs like Evan will pounce on your weakness to get under your skin. You're going to have to toughen up a little and let those kinds of comments roll off."

Evan had obviously embarrassed her and shaken her confidence, but I still couldn't picture her intentionally trying to kill him. I studied her brownie display. She was offering samples of eight different brownies—a black and tan, blondies with peanuts and white chocolate chips, chocolate raspberry, chocolate mint, apricot and milk chocolate, a double chocolate, cherry cheesecake, and the caramel and walnut that I had tasted. Eight varieties would be a major undertaking for a professional chef, let alone a food blogger baking out of her home kitchen. Looking at her tasting table made me even more convinced that it must have been one of Bethany's brownies that killed Evan. How could she have kept track of so many flavors in a nonprofessional kitchen?

I chose my words carefully. "You have amassed quite the assortment of combinations here. How do you manage working out of your house?"

Bethany's eyes lit up. "Oh, that's easy. I have a system down." She pointed to the ivory place cards with the name of each brownie written in a cursive scroll. "I start with the batter. I only had to make three kinds of batter—dark chocolate, milk chocolate, and the brown sugar batter for the blondies and black and tans. My friend Carter came over to help me bake. We had an assembly line in my kitchen, and as soon as each pan was layered with the batter we would add each new flavor. Believe it or not it only took a day to bake all of these."

She beamed with pride while I tried to wrap my brain around what she'd just said. Carter? As in Evan's assistant and right-hand man?

I couldn't help but voice my bafflement. There was no way that Evan would have allowed Carter to work for a competing chef, regardless of how little he thought of Bethany. "Carter? You mean Evan's assistant?"

Bethany threw her hand over her mouth. "Oh, my gosh, I can't believe I let that slip. I promised Carter that I wouldn't say anything."

"What do you mean?" I leaned closer to her as I spoke. "Carter was working with you?"

She rubbed her temples and sighed. "I don't know how I said that. Carter and I made a pact not to say a word to anyone. Evan would have killed him if he knew that Carter was helping me."

I thought she might cry for a minute. Walking around the front of her single table, I put my arm on her clammy hand and reassured her. "I won't say a word, I promise. Your secret is safe with me, but I'm surprised. Are you sure that Evan didn't know?"

Bethany gave me a pained smile and shook her head. The sound of a group of chocolate lovers approaching made her hesitate. I thought I'd lost my chance to get her to open up, but fortunately, at the last minute they stopped two booths away to sample drinking chocolate.

"I'm sorry to put you in the middle of this, but I do feel like I can trust you. You're so mature and calm."

"It's okay. I was your age not long ago, and like I said, whatever you tell me won't go any further." I didn't mention that if she revealed anything that might have contributed to Evan's death, I would have to strongly encourage her to go to the police.

She sighed again. "I'm worried that Evan found out that Carter was helping me. It was innocent. He and I are friends. We went to school together and when he heard that I'd gotten a slot here at the festival he offered to help me—on his own time. He would never do anything to jeopardize his job. He only helped me on his time off."

"I don't think it's a crime to help a friend on his own time. That's standard practice in this industry. I've jumped in and fulfilled orders and helped my friends more times than I can count, and they've done the same for me."

Bethany shook her head. Her eyes widened. "No, that's the thing. Evan made Carter sign a noncompete contract. Carter was legally bound not to help me."

She appeared even younger as she spoke. I thought back to my early twenties before I'd learned business lingo. A noncompete might have terrified me as well. "I don't think helping you with brownies for the Chocolate Fest would be a violation of the contract. Chefs put those in place so that their best talent doesn't get poached by the competition."

"Are you sure?"

I didn't have the heart to tell her that Evan wouldn't have even considered her in the same realm as his competitors. He wouldn't have considered Torte one, either, for that matter. "I think you can take that off your list of things to worry about."

She looked relieved. "Oh, good. I was worried that I got him fired or something. I saw them yesterday and Evan was livid."

"Here?"

"No. Before the festival." She tapped her fingertips on the table. "I do deliveries to businesses around town, and yesterday I had an order for a staff meeting at the hospital. I saw Evan and Carter there. They didn't see me, but it was impossible to miss them. They were standing by the outpatient clinic fighting."

"What were they fighting about?"

"I don't know. I couldn't hear and I didn't want to take a chance of them spotting me, especially because

I thought they might be fighting about me. What if Evan found out that Carter helped me?"

"Are you sure they were fighting? Evan had a tendency to be brash with everyone. Maybe you misinterpreted what you saw."

"No. They were definitely fighting. Well, at least Evan was. He was shouting at Carter. Carter looked like he was trying to calm Evan down, but Evan said something and stormed away."

"And you haven't talked to Carter about it?"

"I haven't had a chance. Everything happened so fast when Evan collapsed yesterday."

The group of tasters approached the table. "Brownies!" one of them squealed.

I patted Bethany's shoulder. "You have fans. Don't worry. I'm sure it will all work out."

As I walked back to Torte's booth, I glanced at the Confections Couture showcase where Carter stood behind the elegant chocolate display talking with customers. Bethany's slip had shifted my thinking. Could Carter have done something to harm his boss?

Chapter Fourteen

Mom gave me a funny look when I returned. "You and Bethany were sure chatty."

"I know. She's a bit skittish. I hope I helped calm her down. I tried to give her a pep talk about the business, but I'm not sure how much she actually heard." I intentionally left out the part about Carter. Not only had I made a promise to Bethany, but I didn't want to worry Mom.

"If I know one thing about you, it's that you have an innate gift for making people feel good. I'm sure that whatever you said to Bethany struck a chord, even if she might not realize it yet."

"Thanks, Mom." I smiled and squeezed hand sanitizer on my palms. The alcohol in the sanitizer immediately sucked all the moisture from my hands. "How's it been going?"

"Great. People are devouring our samples. The only negative is that we are definitely going to run out of product. I think it's going to be a late night or another early morning tomorrow."

"That's not a big deal. I can knock out another round of truffles tonight."

Mom frowned. "We'll discuss it later."

A bell sounded overhead. We turned toward the main stage where Howard, of Howard's Salt Company, took control of the microphone. "Hey, folks, I guess I'm here to talk to you all about salt. It's pretty fitting because my wife calls me an old, salty dog."

The crowd chuckled and pushed closer to the stage. A long table with rows of sparkling colorful salts had been set up next to where Howard was speaking.

"How many of you are familiar with Howard's Salts?" he asked, holding up a clear glass of pink salt. He was wearing his waders again and a faded cap, both of which looked like they had survived many hours in the harsh elements.

A few hands were raised in the audience in response to Howard's question.

"Good. Good." He picked up another dish of salt as a large white screen lowered behind him. "I'm not up-to-date on this fancy technology but they assure me that while I talk you all are going to see photos of the process we go through to bring you our sea salts. Can you all see anything behind me?"

The crowd laughed again and shouted yes.

Howard tipped his cap. "Alrighty then. Let's talk about salt. My family has been in the salt business for over forty years. We harvest the salt not far from here, right on the shores of Gold Beach."

On cue, a photo of Oregon's Gold Beach appeared on the screen. The photographer had captured the glowing sunset on the horizon. Light danced on the waves and

made the long sandy beach shimmer like gold. I wondered if that was how the beach town had gotten its
name. Howard went on to explain the process of pro-
curing salt from the sea. Nostalgia welled as I watched
pictures of foamy surf and sun-kissed dunes. My years
on the sea were a part of me. I could almost smell the
brine in the air and feel the cold mist of spray on my
face. I didn't want to return to my vagabond life, but
there was something so restorative about the fresh salty
skies above an endless ocean. Seeing Howard's professional photos made me hungry for the sounds of waves
crashing onshore and seagulls squawking overhead.
Gold Beach was only a three-hour drive from Ashland.
Maybe once things had settled down at Torte I could
plan a little coastal getaway for Mom and me. I couldn't
remember the last time we took a trip together.

Howard captivated the crowd with his presentation
and ornery delivery. He reminded me of a famous painting of the Old Man and the Sea with his weathered skin,
chapped lips, and wiry white hair. When he finished he
told everyone in a gruff voice that sounded as if it had
been exposed to too much smoke over the years, to stop
by the booth if they wanted a taste of his salt and chocolate pairings.

"Evan had to go and croak on me," he said, twisting
the cap on a glass jar of salt. "You better come get a
sample while you can."

"What did he mean by that?" I asked Mom.

"Howard and Evan teamed up two or maybe three
years ago. They launched a sea-salt-and-chocolate line
that has done really well."

"Evan and Howard, wow. I can't imagine those two working together."

Mom smiled. "I know. The diva and the fisherman. They were an odd pair but they've been successful with the line. It's gotten national attention."

Our conversation was interrupted by another bride-to-be who gushed about our wedding cakes and signed a contract for a custom cake and a dessert bar, which was the latest trend in weddings. Brides looked to dazzle their guests with more than just the traditional wedding cake. They wanted dessert displays with macaroons, petits fours, tarts, pies, dainty cakes, and frosted cookies. It was the ideal project for us because we could create a gorgeous cakescape with a variety of our delectable treats.

The Chocolate Fest was turning out to be even more lucrative than I could have imagined. As the afternoon began to wind down, Mom and I took stock of our tasting supplies and what we needed for tomorrow.

She was meeting the Professor for dinner so I volunteered to get a head start on truffle assembly. I wasn't being entirely selfless, because I was dying to see how much progress the team had made and I wondered whether the Professor was finally going to pop the question. Maybe we'd have our own wedding to plan soon. We packed up our booth and I promised not to work too late.

On my way out of the ballroom I noticed Bethany talking to Carter at the Confections Couture booth. I wondered if she was telling him that she'd confessed their secret to me. Neither of them noticed when I passed by.

I was almost to the front door when I heard Lance's singsong voice calling my name. "Juliet, over here." I turned toward the sound of his voice and spotted him at Howard's table. He waved with his long fingers.

"What are you doing here?" I asked.

Lance pretended to be insulted. "How is that for a welcome? I happen to be one of Ashland's most esteemed chocolate aficionados." He licked his pinkie and dipped it into a taster of pink salt.

"Good to know. I wasn't aware of that fact."

He dabbed his pinkie into the corner of his mouth and tasted the salt. "Please, darling. You're not the only one in this town with a refined palate. When they need an expert opinion they call on the best."

One of Howard's staff members held a stack of empty tasters in his hands. "Are you done with that, sir?" he asked Lance.

Lance pursed his lips and made a strange motion with his mouth, like he was swishing it with wine. "Am I tasting something spicy in this salt?"

The worker started to reply, but Howard stepped forward when he realized that Lance was at his booth. "How's that tasting? You still selling out of our chocolates?"

Lance tossed his tasting sample at the kid. "Absolutely divine, Howard. As you know, our patrons demand only the highest-caliber products. I'm happy to report that your chocolate-and-salt pairings are satiating their demands."

Howard gave him a curt nod. "Good."

"Do tell," Lance said in his most dramatic voice.

"With the devastating and untimely death of Evan Rowe, will you continue the line?"

"Don't see why not." Howard shrugged.

"Excellent. Most excellent news. It would be such a travesty to lose such an upscale line."

Howard cracked his knuckles. "Yep."

Lance gave me a conspiratorial look. "Well, I must be off. Looking forward to our continued partnership," he said with a nod to Howard. Lance looped his arm through mine. "Come, come, darling. I'll walk you out."

As we weaved through a handful of stragglers trying to sample as many chocolate offerings as they could before the festival closed for the evening, Lance shot a glance behind him to Howard. "I simply cannot wrap my brain around the fact that someone so rough and gruff can produce such delicate flavors. Have you tried his salts?"

I nodded. "Yes, we use them at Torte."

Lance puckered his lips. "I can't identify that pink salt but there's something so spicy about it. I love it. Absolutely love it. You'll have to get your hands on some of it and work your magic."

I couldn't help but laugh. "I'll put that right on the top of my priority list."

"Don't mock me. I might not be a professionally trained chef, but I know exquisite flavor when I taste it and that salt is absolutely to die for." He held open the door for me. "Poor choice of words in light of yesterday's tragedy, but sometimes I can't contain my wit."

Punching him in the shoulder, I scolded him. "Lance, you are absolutely terrible. Death is no laughing matter."

"Darling, I know. We've had this conversation before. It's my way of dealing with the horror of it all. You do have to admit that Evan and Howard are one of the worst all-time pairings. It's like when Julia Roberts and Lyle Lovett had a fling. I'm still recovering from that one."

"Who cares? That's the food world for you, and trust me, nothing goes better with chocolate than salt, except maybe more chocolate."

The skies had darkened outside. A light rain misted from the sky. The smell of wood-burning fireplaces and damp pavement filled the air. I buttoned my jacket while Lance opened a large black golf umbrella.

He held the umbrella up so that I could duck underneath it and then we both started walking down the sidewalk.

"What are you really doing here?" I asked.

"Tasting chocolate like everyone else, darling."

I couldn't see Lance's eyes in the dark, but I could hear the twinkle in his voice. "And . . ."

"And what?" Lance gasped. "All this time and you still don't trust your most esteemed friend and colleague?"

"How are we colleagues? You're an artistic director and I'm a pastry chef."

"Simply two artists working in different mediums. Mine is the stage and yours is chocolate."

"Fair enough." I moved to my left to avoid a puddle. "But what are you doing here?"

"If you're going to be like this I don't even want to play." Lance shifted the umbrella and stopped at the end of the sidewalk.

"For starters, I don't know what we're playing."

"We're on a case again, Juliet. How quickly you forget. Do you not remember our little tête-à-tête last night when we agreed to share whatever information we discovered."

"Okay, and?"

The rain picked up. Fat, wet drops splattered on the umbrella. We hurried on toward the plaza.

"It so happens that I've heard a juicy bit of gossip that could be related to Evan's mysterious demise."

I waited for him to continue, but he kept his eyes forward and leaped over a storm drain clogged with soggy leaves.

"Lance."

"Very well." He sighed. "It seems that Evan and his assistant, Carter, had a very vocal and nasty disagreement."

"Yeah. I heard that too."

Lance stopped in mid-stride. "What? And you didn't call dear old Lance right away?"

"I was working, Lance."

"And your point is?" He raised his catlike eyes and stared at me.

While I had become accustomed to Lance's over-the-top attitude, sometimes it drove me crazy. "My point is I had a job to do."

"As did I, and I am quite proud of the info I dug up."

"Do you know why they were fighting?" I didn't want to say anything about what Bethany had told me.

"Not exactly. But I have it from a reliable source that this isn't the first time the two of them have had words. Apparently, Confections Couture is no Willy Wonka Oompa-Loompa Land."

"Was Evan fighting with his entire staff or just Carter?"

"My source didn't say, but I got the impression reading between the lines that Evan's attitude toward his staff bore no resemblance to the sweetness of his confections."

"So if—and it's a big if—Evan's death was intentional, all of his staff could be suspects."

Lance scooted to the curb to make way for a passing couple. He gave them a little bow, and when they were still within earshot the woman said to her husband, "That was the artistic director!"

We arrived at Torte and stopped in front of the entrance. The lights inside were off and the CLOSED sign turned outward.

"I'm working my sources. Let's plan to reconnect tomorrow. What do you say, lunchtime, and see what we both discover?"

"Maybe, but I can't promise anything. The fest was a mob scene today. I barely had a chance to scarf down half of a sandwich."

Lance leaned in and kissed both of my cheeks. "Nice try, darling. I know you too well, and I know that once you're on the case there is absolutely no stopping you. You're like a dog with a bone, or better yet a pastry chef with a vat of buttercream. See you tomorrow. Ta-ta."

His black umbrella and suit disappeared into the darkness. I hated to admit it, but Lance was right. I couldn't stop thinking about how Evan had died and whether someone could have done it. As much as I wanted to let it go and focus exclusively on the Chocolate Festival, I felt a strange sense of obligation to Evan—a man I barely knew.

I unlocked the front door and was hit with the smell of paint again. Fortunately, this time the windows had all been left open a few inches so the scent wasn't as overwhelming. I flipped on the lights and caught sight of the kitchen. It looked like a brand-new space. The walls had been coated in a satiny layer of teal, two or three shades lighter than the teal in the dining room. We opted for the lighter shade to help identify the two spaces and make sure the kitchen stayed bright enough to do intensive and delicate design work. Torte's dining room walls are a cheery red and brilliant teal with corrugated metal siding acting as wainscoting and a giant chalkboard menu filling out one of the walls. The color combination matches Torte's warm and inviting vibe and gives the space a regal feel.

Now the kitchen was an extension of the front. I smiled as my fingers skimmed the freshly painted walls. They were dry to the touch and had an opaque sheen. Andy, Sterling, and Stephanie had done a great job once again, although it did look like the walls would need a second coat. There were a few streaks where the primer showed through.

All easy fixes, I thought as I gathered everything I needed to make another batch of truffles. Rain pattered the windows as I melted chocolate and became lost in my thoughts. The sound reminded me of my time on the cruise ship. I used to fall asleep every night to the lulling rhythmic sound of waves lapping against the boat's heavy hull. Was Carlos sleeping now or was he dancing

in the galley kitchen blasting Latin jazz as he orches-
trated dinner service?

I pushed the thought from my mind and concentrated
on the oozing chocolate. It wasn't until I began rolling
the truffles in the cocoa powder that I realized the windows were open and potentially letting in the rain. Grabbing a stack of dishtowels, I hurried to assess whether
any water had gotten in. Unfortunately, it had. Small
pools of water filled the bottom of the windowsills. I
mopped it up and made sure the windows were shut
tight. The paint fumes had dissipated somewhat, and
I was done with the truffles. I was also starving.

It was no wonder. I checked the time and it was after
seven. When I'm baking I tend to lose myself in the
experience. Carlos used to tease me about getting lost
in the dough. He would tell staff that the time to play
pranks on me was when I was up to my elbows in dough.
"Julieta, she does not know what is happening around
her when she bakes." Once, he claimed that he had me
paged on the ship three times before I responded. I knew
it wasn't true. Running the ship's kitchen meant knowing exactly what every member of my staff was doing.
The sheer number of white coats and pastry knives made
it impossible not to focus. However, Carlos was right that
when I had a kitchen to myself I could disappear. My
problems and the world around me would fade away as
I kneaded airy bread dough, activating the bubbles in the
yeast. He had the opposite approach to cooking, in part
because he spent the vast majority of his time teaching.
I could picture him leaning over a line cook's shoulder
while plating rack of lamb with pork belly. Carlos would
direct the cook to adorn each pristine plate with exactly

seven dainty bursts of cranberry sauce and a dusting of fresh chopped mint. He would demonstrate and then lean back against the counter and watch. Young cooks would timidly present their plate for Carlos's feedback.

"No, no, you must not have that look on your face." Carlos spoke with his hands. "Do you like this plate?"

The cook would give a half nod.

Carlos waved his arms in the air. "No, this is no good. You must not fear the food. You must embrace it. This is a beautiful plate and when you come to me next time, you stand tall and you tell me that. Okay?"

Usually, the cooks would nod with relief and scurry away while Carlos maintained his casual commanding position as the kitchen's captain. He was intimidating, but not in a mean way. Staff members respected his palate and ability to bring such artistry to each plate that came out of the kitchen. Many of them assumed that Carlos had always been at the helm of the galley, but nothing could be further from the truth.

He grew up in a small hillside Spanish village. His family wasn't wealthy, but they shared a love of food. Throughout his early years he worked every job he could from scrubbing floors in a three-star Michelin restaurant to washing dishes in a street food cart. Those experiences helped mold him into the chef he is today. I remember one night after dinner service Carlos made us Spanish coffees and we drank them on the upper decks. Carlos stretched out on a lounge chair. The moonlight cast a glow on his bronzed skin.

"Can you believe this is our life, Julieta?" he said, drinking me in. When he looked at me like that with his dark eyes I could barely breathe.

"We're lucky."

"*Sí, sí*. I did not think I would ever get to this point. When I left my village in Spain and took my first job on the ship, my English it was so bad that the chef would point to what I needed to clean in the kitchen. I could have never dreamed to be here now. Every hour I had free I would study English and watch the cooks."

I sipped my boozy coffee, feeling the alcohol rush to my head. "You were determined."

Carlos had a faraway look in his eyes. I wondered if I would have fallen for him as fast if I had known him then. "It is true. It is why I tell these young chefs they must be hungry for it. They must work and study and then work and study more."

Our childhoods had been so very different. It was as if the seas had brought us together from worlds that were oceans apart.

"A month later after I was scrubbing the counters and mopping the floors they made me a prep cook, then a line cook, then I continue on to become a head chef. It is all a distant memory now, but the food knows. The food remembers where I have come from. I will never let it forget."

I reached over and placed my hand on his forearm. He wrapped his arm around mine and we drank our coffees in silence staring up at the stars above and gliding over the waves.

That was a lifetime ago, Jules, I told myself as I grabbed my coat and locked the front door. Ashland is home now, and Carlos, well, who knows.

"Jules!" a voice called out as I stepped onto the soggy sidewalk.

I turned to see Thomas running down the sidewalk.

"Hey." He was breathless as he caught up to me. "You are just the person I was looking for."

"Perfect timing then. What's going on?"

Rain dripped from his brow. His uniform was spattered with water and his shoes looked drenched.

"Where did you come from?" I asked.

Thomas pointed behind him. "The station."

"And you're that wet?" Ashland's police station was right around the corner from Torte. It had a blue and white striped awning that blended in seamlessly with the rest of the plaza. Unless you looked closely at the word "police" etched in the glass windows, you'd never guess the small corner shop served as headquarters for the officers assigned to the downtown beat. Not that there was much of a beat to cover in the plaza. Most days Thomas's responsibilities included giving visitors directions to the Oregon Shakespeare Festival and making sure that Ashland's young hippie community didn't panhandle in the square.

"It was coming down hard." He pointed to Puck's Pub. "Do you have time to grab a beer or a bite to eat?"

"Sure." I waited while he opened the carved wood door. Tourists flocked to Puck's during the season. It was the quintessential Ashland experience themed after Shakespeare's most impish character. Giant kegs served as tables in the old-English pub. A wall of taps with ceramic handles lined the bar, where a friendly bartender served pints in ornamental beer steins. A cauldron of mulled wine sat on the edge of the bar with a sign reading GET IT WHILE IT LASTS. $3 A MUG.

During the off-season locals reclaimed the pub as our own. Thomas and I waved to a number of familiar faces as we passed a guy wearing a rainbow beanie playing the accordion on a small wooden stage. A group of college students with guitars and mandolins waited their turn for open mic night and swayed to the music at wooden booths near the bar.

The hostess showed us to a table in front of the bar and offered us menus. "We're running a rainy day special tonight. Meat loaf and smashed garlic potatoes with a side salad for ten dollars."

Thomas caught my eye. "We'll both take the special, plus a couple pints of whatever your guest tap is tonight, right, Jules?"

"Absolutely." Thomas and I had been friends since middle school. He knew my food preferences as well as anyone, except maybe Carlos. Don't think about Carlos now, Jules, I told myself.

"Were you trying to scrounge chocolate handouts at the hotel or doing official police work?" I asked, unfolding my napkin and placing it on my lap.

Thomas followed suit, but dabbed his wet brow with his napkin. "I tried to pocket some chocolate, but everyone had already packed up. If I had been smart about it, I could have confiscated it all in the name of the law and gorged myself tonight." He grinned and dried his hands on the linen napkin before placing it on his lap.

The waitress arrived with two frothy beers. "You guys having the Caldera pilsners?"

"That's us," Thomas said, taking a golden beer from her. "I'm off duty."

Caldera was a local brewery that was known for their Northwest-inspired ales.

"Have you tried this one yet?" I asked, holding my pint to the light. The beer was crystal clear. I could see Thomas through the glass.

"No, I was at the brewery last week and the head brewer told me they were releasing it this week. Pilsners are my favorite." He tapped his glass to mine and took a drink. I watched him sample the beer. A smile tugged at the corner of his smooth-shaven cheeks and his blue eyes glinted.

"I take it you like it?"

He took another drink. "Oh, yeah. It's good stuff. Aren't you going to try it?"

"I was enjoying watching you."

Thomas's cheeks flamed. I hadn't meant anything by my words, but he had obviously misinterpreted their meaning. I didn't want the conversation to take the wrong direction, so I quickly took a sip and swished the beer around in my mouth. There's nothing romantic about tasting anything—beer, wine, food. I exaggerated, puffing my cheeks out like a fish and making a slurping sound. It broke the moment.

"Not bad," I said after swallowing.

Thomas laughed. "You look ridiculous, Jules."

I folded my arms across my chest and gave him my most serious face. "I'll have you know that I have been professionally trained in the art of tasting. If we were being legitimate about this process, we should have a spit bucket. The most revered chefs in the world taste wine and beer like that. Swirling the liquid stimulates your taste buds. After you spit you should have some residual tingling in your palate."

"Got it, chef." Thomas mimicked my tasting actions. He looked equally ridiculous as he inflated his cheeks and made a goofy face. His ability to poke fun at himself was one of things that I appreciated most about him.

"What's going on with investigation?" I asked, trying to direct the conversation.

He set his beer on the table and leaned closer. "I have to tell you, Jules, that this is one of the weirder cases that the Professor and I have investigated."

"What do you mean?"

At that moment our food arrived. The waitress balanced two steaming plates of meat loaf and potatoes. As she placed them in front of us, the scent of garlic and herbs sent my stomach into a series of rumbles. I was famished.

The second she walked away I picked up my fork and cut into the tender meat loaf. The chef had seared it so that it had a sizzling crust. It was slathered in a hearty red wine and tomato sauce. I didn't care that it burned my tongue as I bit into the juicy meat. The meat loaf was sublime. I was impressed, especially for pub fare. Meat loaf is hard to do well because the beef has a tendency to dry out. I guessed that Puck's chef had used a trio of meats, probably a high-fat beef, pork, and top sirloin.

"Easy there, Jules." Thomas chuckled as I dove into another steaming bite. "You look like you're attacking your plate."

"This is so good," I replied from the side of my

mouth. "Do you know how hard it is to make a good meat loaf?"

Thomas blew on his. "Nope. I just know that your mom's is some of the best I've ever had."

He was right. Mom had an old family recipe for meat loaf that reminded me of this. As soon as our remodel was complete I was going to have to make her famous recipe and serve meat-loaf sandwiches on our home-made buns as a lunch special. I could barely reply because I shoveled another bite of meat loaf and scoop of the garlic potatoes in my mouth.

"What were you going to say about Evan?" I mumbled.

Thomas looked over his shoulder before leaning closer to me and lowering his voice. "I don't know. It's weird. We got the preliminary test results back from the lab in Medford and every single sample came back clear of any trace of nuts."

"Really?" His words made me pause from devouring my plate.

"Yeah. The Professor was convinced that we'd have a pretty clear answer about what happened when we got the results back, but now we're at square one again."

"No one's samples contained nuts?" I repeated. I was as surprised as Thomas was with this news.

He rubbed his temples. "Nope. Not a single one."

"Does the Professor have a new theory?"

"We're working every angle at the moment. The most likely scenario is that Evan ate something that his body reacted to, but because of what you said and a few other witness reports we're looking into the possibility that someone intentionally swapped a sample with nuts or found a way to slip nuts into something that Evan ate. We're waiting for the coroner's analysis of his stomach contents. As soon as we get the results back we should have a definite answer."

Who were the other witnesses? My mind raced as I considered his theory. I took a bite of the salad that accompanied the heavy winter dish. It was composed of a medley of greens and topped with shredded carrots, shallots, thinly sliced tomatoes and cucumbers and dressed with an Italian vinaigrette. My mouth thanked me as I took a bite of the tangy acidic greens. Puck's chef had succeeded in finding the harmony of flavor and textures in this plate. When Thomas and I were finished, I planned to thank him and share my compliments.

"Slipping Evan nuts is a pretty impossible undertaking, don't you think?"

Thomas nodded. "That's what's so weird about the case. One of the Professor's thoughts is if, and that's a big if, someone intentionally killed Evan, they could have made a special brownie, cake, candy—whatever—laced with nuts. They could have stashed it away and brought it out only when he came to their booth to taste. It's a pretty good theory if you think about it, because the rest of their products really would have been nut-free." He pushed his potatoes around his plate with his fork. "But this one might be impossible to prove."

"So the Professor thinks it could be murder?"

He hesitated. "Not for sure. Like I said, we're still waiting for the coroner's final report, but at the scene the coroner said he estimated that Evan had had an immediate and deadly reaction to whatever he consumed."

We paused our conversation when the waitress came

by to ask how our dinners were and whether or not we were ready for another round of drinks. We declined drinks, but we both gushed over the food. "Please tell the chef that this is amazing," I said. "It's one of the best meat loaves I've tasted."

The waitress looked pleased and went off to share our praise with the chef. Whenever I eat a meal that I enjoy I make a concerted effort to pass that on to the staff. Sadly, the loudest customers in the food world tend to be the complainers. I think it's important for servers, cooks, and chefs to hear from diners who love their experience.

"Is there any chance it was a reaction to something else entirely?" I asked Thomas after the waitress was out of earshot.

"Maybe. It's possible, but we won't know until we get the coroner's report to see what was in his system. There's documentation in Evan's medical records of his allergy, and we recovered his EpiPen at the scene, so I'd say the odds are definitely in our favor that nuts were the cause of death."

My brain spun. Nuts were not exactly an easy substance to slip into a product. They were chunky and crunchy, the only way they could have been incorporated without Evan knowing would have been to grind them into a fine powder. I thought back to my training in culinary school—was there a technique I was missing? Could the killer have found another way to taint their chocolate with nuts?

"It's a puzzler, isn't it?" Thomas practically read my mind. "I'm worried, and I think the Professor is too, that this might be the perfect murder weapon if it turns out that he was killed. Unless we can dig up a solid motive, someone may have gotten away with murder and there might not be any way that we can prove it." He sounded dejected.

"I'm guessing that means you haven't uncovered any clear motives?"

He sighed. "No. So far it's a lot of hearsay. As you know, Evan wasn't well liked and there have been some rumors about his kitchen staff at Confections Couture, but none of that is admissible in a court of law."

We finished our meals in silence. The head chef came out a few minutes later to thank me for my kind words. Both Thomas and I shared our rave reviews of the dinner. I told the chef he had inspired me to craft a meat loaf sandwich for our lunch menu, and offered him the first taste. He beamed with pride and agreed to stop by next week to sample my creation.

Thomas walked me to my apartment. "Sorry to burden you with this, Jules. I didn't mean to drop my stress on you. You're such a good listener and I guess it's like old times."

"That's okay." I touched his arm. "I want to find out who did this to Evan as much as you do."

He waited while I unlocked my front door.

"You know, I can ask around a little more tomorrow if you think it would be helpful. I'm going to be at the fest all day."

"Like you haven't already been doing that, Jules. Come on."

"What? Me?" I grinned.

Thomas rolled his eyes.

"Okay, maybe I asked around a little. I couldn't help

it. I watched Evan die." The memory made my stomach lurch. "No one deserves a death like that. If there's anything I can do to help bring his killer to justice, I have to—for myself and for him."

Thomas's face softened. "I know, Jules. Trust me. I know. But I have a bad feeling about this case."

He said good night and left me with a thousand thoughts spinning through my brain. I hoped he was wrong, but I had a sinking feeling that he was right. Had someone pulled off a perfect murder?

Chapter Fifteen

The next morning, I slept past dawn—a rarity in my profession. Lingering over a bold and smoky dark roast coffee, I flipped through cookbooks and decided to make myself a leisurely home-cooked breakfast. My apartment kitchen was nothing like the ship's massive galley kitchen, but it was well stocked and warmed quickly. Rain pounded on the rooftop and spattered on the large bay window at the front of my apartment as I grabbed eggs, heavy cream, Parmesan and Gruyère cheese, and chicken apple sausages from the fridge.

A quiche sounded like the perfect accompaniment to the gloomy weather. Next, I found pastry flour and butter and started on my pie crust by cubing the cold butter. The key to a light and flaky crust is making sure not to overwork the dough. I added the butter, flour, and salt to my food processor and blended it until it resembled coarse crumbs. Then I removed the mixture from the processor, formed it into a rough ball and added a few tablespoons of water. One of the reasons that pie crust can be intimidating to new bakers is because it takes some practice to get the ratio of water right. My philosophy is that it's always better to add as you go. Once the dough had formed into a soft ball with nice chunks of butter I floured my countertop and rolled it out.

Then I beat the eggs and heavy cream until they were a golden yellow color. I grated in two cups of cheese, added a handful of fresh chives and sprinkled in salt and pepper. The chicken apple sausages would cook in the quiche, but I wanted them to have a little char, so gave them a quick grill. While they sizzled on the stove I placed my dough in a pie pan and fluted the edges. Once the sausages had cooked, I chopped them and added them to the egg mixture. Then I poured everything into the pie crust and popped it into the oven.

My kitchen smelled like savory sausage and baking pie dough. I could hardly wait for my quiche to be done. While it baked, I curled up on the couch with a soft fleece blanket and my coffee. Thoughts of Evan's murder invaded my mind as I thumbed through glossy photos of elegant European cakes and sweets. Trying to push the thoughts away seemed to make them all the more determined. Had it all been a terrible accident? Maybe there was some other explanation, but everyone seemed like a suspect to me. What had Evan and Howard been arguing about? Could Bethany have acted on a whim and given Evan a nut brownie? And what about Carter? I sighed and rubbed my temples, trying to silence my head.

The timer dinged on my oven, saving me from my thoughts. I hurried to remove my quiche from the oven. It had baked to a lovely golden-brown color. Breathing in the scent, I almost swooned. Quiche is a dish that can be served any time of the day and made with any ingredients on hand. I poured myself a second cup of coffee and cut into the steamy egg bake.

I sipped my coffee and tucked into my quiche. The tang of the cheese paired with the earthy herbs in the sausage and milky eggs was near perfection. I devoured the first slice and helped myself to seconds. After I finished my breakfast and cleaned up the kitchen my mind returned to Evan. It was no use. Even the distraction of baking wasn't helping, so I gave up. If my mind was going to spin, it might as well spin on something productive.

Twenty minutes later I arrived at Torte to find Mom in the dining room. She and the Professor sat with their heads close together at one of the small tables. They shared a pot of coffee and a plate of muffins sat between them.

"Oh, hey!" I said, wondering if I was interrupting something. "I didn't expect to see you here this morning."

The Professor stood. His intelligent eyes flashed from me to Mom. He removed his tweed jacket from the back of the chair and gave me a slight bow. "Good morning, Juliet. I was just on my way out." Turning to Mom, he caressed her hand and raised it to his lips. "I bid you good day, Helen."

Mom tried to conceal her delight but it was evident on every line on her face. Her cheeks brightened and her eyes sparkled as the two of them shared a gaze that didn't last long but made me feel acutely aware of the fact that I was the third wheel in the room.

"Wait, take these muffins with you," Mom said as she wrapped two muffins in a paper napkin.

The Professor took her offering and gave us both a bow on his way out the door. "I'm sure I'll be seeing you soon," he said with a wink to me.

I walked over to Mom and sat in the chair the Professor had warmed. "Sorry about that. I didn't know you were having a romantic coffee date. You should have warned me."

Mom laughed and pushed the plate of muffins toward me. "Hardly. Doug is getting an early start on the investigation this morning and I made my famous banana-nut muffins at home this morning. He stopped by and I offered him a muffin, that's all."

"That's all?" I bantered back. "It looked like I walked in on a serious conversation."

"No," Mom scoffed. "Muffin?" She held up the plate.

"I already ate, and don't try to change the subject. What's going on with the Professor?"

Color rose from the base of Mom's jaw up her cheeks. "Nothing." She reminded me of a schoolgirl trying to lie and failing miserably.

"Mom! What is going on?"

She scrunched her nose and ran her fingers through her hair. "Nothing." She paused and caught my eye. "At least not yet."

"You are so transparent, Mom."

She blushed even more. "Am I?"

"Mom." I grabbed her wrist and looked into her gorgeous and wise eyes. "We made a deal, remember? We promised that we weren't going to keep secrets from one another—good or bad."

She squeezed my hand in a show of solidarity. "I know, honey. I remember."

We dropped hands and I waited for her to continue.

"There's nothing to tell, at least not yet. Doug has hinted that he is ready to take things to the next level."

I kept my face as neutral as I possibly could. The Professor had confided in me when we were at an alpine lodge earlier in the winter. He told me that he wanted to marry Mom but wouldn't do it without my approval. I told him that he didn't need my approval; the only thing that mattered to me was Mom's happiness—and she was clearly happy with the Professor. He asked me not to say anything and I willingly agreed to break my "no secrets" vow with Mom. Some secrets, like a surprise marriage proposal, were worth keeping and fell outside the bounds of our pact. I had expected the Professor to pop the question when we returned from the lodge, but it had been over two months and he had yet to make a move.

"What did he say?" I asked Mom.

Her smile was contagious. I couldn't help but grin as I watched her beam with excitement. If anyone deserved a second chance at love it was Mom. She and my dad had enjoyed a long and happy marriage built on self-respect and a mutual love of baking. When he got sick a part of her died with him. Seeing the spark reignited in her made my eyes begin to well. I blinked back happy tears as she continued.

"He said he's the happiest he's ever been." She put her hand over her heart. "I told him that I felt the same way."

"Mom, that's wonderful."

She met my eyes and looked concerned for a minute. "I don't mean to take anything away from the relationship your father and I had. Losing him was the hardest thing I've ever gone through. Those were dark days."

We were both quiet for a moment, caught up in our individual memories. "We've been through this before, Mom. I am so happy for you and I know that Dad is too." This time I couldn't fight back the tears. They spilled from my eyes.

Mom grinned and sobbed with me. "Well, we're a blubbering mess, aren't we?" she finally said, handing me a paper napkin.

I wiped my eyes with it and swallowed salty tears. "I'm blaming the town. This Shakespeare thing, it just gets under your skin."

She laughed and dabbed her eyes with a napkin. "Anyway, we haven't gotten any further than that, but it's nice to hear that he's thinking about our future."

"Have you given any more thought to your future?" I knew the question was loaded, but since we were sharing such a tender moment I couldn't help but ask.

"You mean about Torte?" She exhaled and glanced behind and then to the kitchen. "It sure looks good. The kids did a great job yesterday."

"I know and the ovens will be here soon. It's going to be a whole new bakeshop."

She nodded. "Yes, it is."

"You didn't answer my question."

"I know." She sighed. "I want both. I want to build a new life with Doug and I want to be here with you. I think you know a little something about feeling torn and feeling a deep sense of longing for two very different lives."

Her words hit me. "Right." I looked at my hands.

She started to say something—to apologize, which wasn't necessary—but the door jingled and Sterling and Stephanie came inside. "We'll talk later, honey."

I nodded.

"You two just can't stay away, can you?" Sterling's gray hoodie was soaked with rain and plastered to his forehead.

Stephanie wore a black rain jacket to protect her violet hair, which she wore tied with dozens of tiny black rubber bands. Not many people could pull off the look, but somehow it worked on Stephanie.

Mom held out the plate of muffins. "Breakfast, anyone?"

They both took a muffin.

"You did a wonderful job yesterday," Mom said, handing them each a napkin. "Juliet and I were just talking about how great the kitchen looks."

Sterling tried to help Stephanie off with her coat, but she shoved him out of the way. I knew that he was trying to be chivalrous, but she considered herself a woman of the twenty-first century who didn't need a man's assistance for anything. I appreciated her can-do attitude and had dealt with my fair share of chauvinistic chefs over the years, but I also felt sorry for Sterling. It must be hard to be a man in modern times. There was something to be said for the romance of the Elizabethan era. I considered myself a strong woman who could run a tight kitchen and bake a mean pastry, but I appreciated it when Carlos would open a door for me or take my hand when we walked through Paris's busy streets. In my opinion, romantic gestures were an expression of love, not a way to steal someone's power, but I had a feeling that Stephanie would disagree with me, as I watched her struggle to yank off her wet coat.

I caught Sterling's eye. He rolled his and threw his hands in the air.

We all followed Mom into the kitchen. She set the muffins on the only free edge of the butcher-block island. "Help yourself to more, I made them for you."

"What's the plan for today?" Sterling asked. His hoodie dripped onto the floor.

"Do you need a new shirt?" I couldn't believe he wasn't freezing.

"Nah. I'll be cool."

Mom chuckled. "Do you remember when you were in high school and refused to wear a coat to school even in the dead of winter?"

"Me? No, never."

She winked at Sterling. "She refused. Absolutely refused. I gave up the fight and told her if she was wet and cold at school she might reconsider the coat."

"I did, really?" I had no memory of fighting with Mom about wearing a coat. If anything I tend to be cold. Maybe that's why.

"Oh, yes," Mom said, giving me a knowing smile. "For at least a year. Then one of your friends got a stylish snow parka for Christmas and you had to have one. After that you wore the parka every day."

Sterling frowned. "So you're saying that I have the maturity of a high schooler? Uh-oh. Guess I'm going to have to buy a coat."

Mom's smile faded. I knew we were both thinking the same thing. When Sterling arrived in Ashland last summer he was penniless. We'd given him a job and paid him well, and I knew that he was living at one of the co-ops in town. Because Ashland is home to Southern Oregon University, many of the old bungalows near campus had been converted into co-ops that provided cheap housing for college students. Even with an inexpensive place to live and some of his meals coming from Torte, I hoped that it wasn't that he couldn't afford a coat. My mind flashed back to our time at Lake of the Woods together when Sterling had worn his gray hoodie in the blizzard. I thought he was just being a twenty-something guy, but now I felt terrible. What if he'd been freezing that entire weekend because he didn't have the funds to buy a coat? I had shared Lance's generous tip with him at the end of the long weekend. Hopefully that had given him some extra cash.

"You know," Mom said, moving closer to Sterling and extending his left hand. "If you're in the market for a coat I just might have the thing for you, and you'd be doing me a big favor."

"That's okay, Helen." Sterling looked uncomfortable. "I'm not a coat guy."

"Fine, fine, but I'm going to bring in a bag of some of Juliet's dad's winter gear. It's been sitting in my entryway for over a month and I haven't had the heart to donate it. You and Andy should take a look at his ski gear. It's in great shape and it would make me so happy to see it go to you guys instead of a stranger."

She was good. I smiled internally knowing that Sterling was astute enough to know exactly what she was doing, but also too tenderhearted to refuse her offer to take my dad's winter gear.

"Okay, I'll check it out," Sterling agreed.

Mom gave me a satisfied smile and we returned to the day's agenda. Andy arrived a few minutes later.

"Sorry I'm late, Mrs. C. I had to take my grandmother to the grocery store this morning. She had cataract surgery and can't drive."

"You're right on time, don't worry," Mom said. She turned to me. "What is our action plan?"

"First we need to finish the paint. One more quick coat should do it. How is the inventory count coming along?"

Stephanie handed me a file folder. "We're done with the pantry and all the decorating supplies. We still need to finish the walk-in and the wine."

"Great. While the paint is drying you can finish the inventory and then once it's dry you should be able to go ahead and start putting things back together. The ovens will be installed sometime between two and four tomorrow. Either Mom or I will come over when they arrive to make sure that all goes smoothly."

With the plan mapped out, Andy, Sterling, and Stephanie went to stir the paint and cover the floors and counters with drop cloths. Mom and I packed up our tasting samples and braved the downpour on our way to Ashland Springs. I had a feeling that today would be even busier than yesterday, given that it was a Saturday and most people would have the day off. I was looking forward to introducing more people to our products and being too busy to think about murder.

Chapter Sixteen

As anticipated the Chocolate Festival was a zoo. Mom and I barely had a chance to restock trays of marzipan, chocolate pasta, fudge, and truffles before they disappeared into the hands of our chocolate-obsessed guests. In the frenzy of activity yesterday, I had completely forgotten about the fact that we were slotted for the afternoon baking demonstration.

The Chocolate Fest organizer stopped by our booth midway through the morning to remind us. "You're on at two o'clock. Is there anything you need? I have a wireless mic for you to use so that your hands can be free. I don't know if you've had a chance to watch any of the other demonstrations, but we suggest that you spend the first thirty minutes of your allotted hour talking through your technique and then open it up to questions."

"Sure." I nodded and then winced after she walked away. "I totally forgot about the demonstration this afternoon."

Mom lifted a new tray of sweets from beneath the

table and swapped it with an empty platter. "Me too. What can I help with?"

"Nothing." I glanced at my watch. It was almost noon, which gave me ample time to run down to Torte and pick up the cake and my piping supplies. "Can you handle the rush for a few? Or should I call the bakeshop and send Stephanie up?"

"I'll be fine." Mom waved me off. "The crowd will thin as we get closer to lunch. Not that chocolate can't accompany lunch, but I have a feeling all that sugar will have people hungry for something more substantial. You go ahead. I'll call if we get a rush that I can't handle."

"Yeah, right." I gave a knowing look.

"What? I will," she protested.

"Mom, how long have I known you?"

She winked. "I think your whole life."

"Right, and when do you ever ask for help?"

Frowning, she swatted me on the hip. "Go! I'll be fine."

She probably would be fine, but I knew that even if she wasn't she wouldn't call us for help. Her independence is one of the many things that I admire about her, and after my father died that quality became even more entrenched in her. I hoped that if she and the Professor did take their relationship to the next level, she would let the rest of us pick up some of the slack.

The crowd had begun to thin as I made my way outside. Howard tipped his hat to me as I passed by his booth. "Come see me later, I want to talk about a new line of salts for your bakery."

I agreed and continued on. There were still a few

booths that I hadn't had a chance to visit yet. If there was a lull this afternoon, I wanted to try to taste everything on display.

Outside the rain continued, and heavy black clouds hung low in the sky. They closed in on the top story of the hotel, as if they were consuming the building. I hurried down the wet sidewalks hoping to avoid getting completely soaked. As I turned the corner to Torte, I bumped into Rosalind Gates.

"Juliet, what timing. I was hoping to bump into you today. In fact, I was on my way to see if you were at Torte." She was prepared for the weather with a bright yellow rain slicker and matching hat and boots. The tips of her silver hair peeked out from under the rubber hat.

"I'm working the Chocolate Fest this weekend," I reminded her. "I'm just stopping by to pick up a cake and some supplies."

Her gait was unsteady as we continued toward the bakeshop. "Do you have a minute to come downstairs with me? I have the key, and there's something I want to show you that I think will help make your decision about proceeding with the grant applications much more appealing."

I hesitated. I didn't want to abandon Mom for long, but I was also eager to get another look at the basement property. "Maybe for just a couple of minutes," I said to Rosalind. "Then I have to get back to the Chocolate Fest. I'm doing an icing demonstration this afternoon."

"Oh, wonderful, dear. Perhaps I'll come watch. I'm always so impressed with the artistry that you and your mother are able to achieve on cakes and pastries."

She reached into the inside pocket of her rain jacket

and pulled out a dangling set of keys. They looked like they could have been artifacts from Elizabethan times. "Shall we?"

I followed her around the corner and cautioned her as she started down the cement stairway. "Be careful, Rosalind, the steps look slick."

She clutched the iron railing and took the steps one at a time. That could be problematic for our elderly customers, I thought as I watched her navigate the steep stairway.

At the bottom of the stairs water pooled in front of the basement door. "Rosalind, this isn't good." I pointed to the standing water that must have been at least two inches deep.

She scoffed and twisted the key in the lock. "All fixable. Nothing to worry about. That can all be taken care of."

A basement with a flooding problem sounded like a major issue to me, especially if we moved our baking production downstairs—electricity and water don't mix. Doubt began to rise in my mind as Rosalind swung the door open and made way for me to step inside. The basement was dark, the only light coming from the windows aboveground, but even in the dim light I could tell that water had seeped under the door.

"Rosalind, there's water in here!" I couldn't contain the concern in my tone.

"I know, dear. It happens to all the businesses belowground on the plaza, and I assure you that it's an easy fix. They use a sump pump and get all the water out."

"That's fine, but what about when it rains again?"

"No, it's nothing. Trust me, it's not a problem. I have

a wonderful waterproofing contractor who can install a French drain, and even connect it to a permanent sump pump or sometimes they just dig and excavate around the foundation and then firm it up."

"That sounds expensive."

She nodded her head from side to side. "Not too bad. Most of these kinds of expenses will be covered by the grant, and remember, the city is offering loans at very low interest to any business in the flooding zone."

"If we get the grant." The thought of waterproofing the basement made me want to seriously reconsider the space, since regardless of whether we were awarded a grant or loan from the city we would likely have to dump a ton of cash into making sure the space didn't leak.

Sensing my trepidation, Rosalind reached into her other jacket pocket and clicked on a small flashlight. "Don't let your mind go crazy about projects, come with me. Let me show you what the building inspector discovered."

The light illuminated the floor, revealing a half inch of standing water covering the old carpet. I grabbed her arm to stop her. "Wait! I don't think we should be in here. There's water everywhere."

She plunged ahead, ignoring my warning. "Nonsense, it's perfectly safe, dear. The power has been cut off for over a year. Nothing to worry about."

Actually, I had everything to worry about. If Rosalind was trying to entice me to move forward with buying the space, her plan was backfiring; all I could think about was how much money renovations would cost and what a state of disrepair the building was in. Mom and I had toured the space last week on a dry day, and while it had been obvious that the space had sat empty for a while, it hadn't been wet. Water scared me. Sailing over deep seas was no problem, but deep water in a basement was just plain bad for business.

I followed Rosalind's light toward the back of the cold damp room. A shiver ran down my spine along with a feeling of disappointment. I'd been so excited and energized about the idea of expanding Torte, but at what cost? If all of our funds went to drying out the basement we wouldn't be able to make any other upgrades to the space, and I wasn't sure we wanted to take on more debt. It was great that the city was offering low-interest-rate loans, but that was still money we would have to pay back.

"Here!" Rosalind positioned the flashlight so that it was shining on the far wall.

Stepping closer to get a better look, I realized that there was an exposed brick wall. I hadn't noticed that when Mom and I originally toured the space.

"Has that always been here?"

"Yes and no," Rosalind said, moving the light from the wall down to the floor where broken Sheetrock had been piled. "The previous owner put up a number of partition walls like this one. When the building inspector came through here with me yesterday he brought along the original blueprints. We realized that for some reason the previous owner barricaded this wall." She ran a long bony hand along the bricks. "Isn't it beautiful? Why would they cover something like this up with Sheetrock? This is old-world craftsmanship right here, each brick placed by hand."

I admired the brick work with her. It was masterfully

done, and constructed with bricks pressed in Ashland. I recognized the maker's stamp. "You're right," I said to Rosalind. "It's beautiful." I wasn't sure that, however cool or artistic a hidden brick wall might be, it would offset the cost of waterproofing the basement.

Rosalind smiled. "I knew you would like it."

"Yes, but . . ." Before I could finish, Rosalind held a shaky finger in the air.

"No, no, this isn't the surprise, dear. Come this way." She shined the flashlight in the opposite direction. The basement property was designed in an L-shape. From the stairs there was one long room that ended at the newly discovered brick wall. Adjacent was another room about half the size, which was where Mom and I thought the new kitchen could go.

It looked like the brick wall extended into the other room. Rosalind waved me closer and again positioned the flashlight so that it cast a halo on the wall. At first I didn't think that there was anything unique about the wall, until Rosalind circled the light in a clockwise motion, "See!"

I realized that the light was circling a large cutout section of bricks.

"Do you know what that is?" Rosalind asked.

"Is it what I think it is?"

Her voice squeaked with excitement. "It's a wood-fired oven. A bread oven. We discovered that this was originally built as a bakery in the early nineteen twenties. It's divine intervention. You and your mom will be restoring this space to its intended purpose."

Suddenly, the standing water on the floor seemed like a minor problem. I had been dreaming about owning a wood-fired oven for ages. Mom and I had even explored the idea of installing one upstairs, but there was no space and the cost would have been exorbitant. Now I was standing in front of a vintage brick kitchen that could potentially be mine.

Chapter Seventeen

Rosalind's smile was almost smug as she held the flashlight at an angle and stepped to the side so that I could get a better look at the oven. It was in surprisingly good shape, much better than the rest of the damp basement.

"I knew you would love it," she said, positioning the light below the brick oven. "There's even storage for the wood right here."

Sure enough, there were wooden double doors below the oven that opened to a four-foot-long cupboard specifically designed to store firewood.

"This was originally a bakery?" I asked, unable to mask the excitement in my voice.

"Yes, don't you see this is meant to be?" Rosalind sent the light ascending up the brick chimney. "Rumor around town is that you have been angling to put in a brick fireplace at Torte. I think I've solved your problem, haven't I?"

"How did you hear that?" The only person I'd spoken to about installing a brick oven had been Mom.

"You know Ashland, dear. Word gets around."

I couldn't imagine Mom telling anyone that this was something I coveted, but as Rosalind and I moved toward the door I knew exactly who told Rosalind—Lance! He had been at the retreat I had catered for the Oregon Shakespeare Festival board, and he'd raved about the food that Sterling and I made at the lodge. He must have passed that on to Rosalind, and who knows how many other people. The only thing I couldn't figure out is why Rosalind, and Lance for that matter, cared so much about Mom and me taking over the basement property.

Either way my mind raced with recipes and ideas for a wood-fired oven. I could almost smell the bread and hear the crackle of hickory logs. Imagine our customers curled up on comfortable chairs with the intoxicating scent of baked goods in the fire warming the basement and their spirits. We could host our Sunday Suppers down here and offer holiday-themed parties, like an underground dinner on All Hallows' Eve.

You have to stop, Juliet, I chided myself, knowing that I could spend hours and hours fantasizing about Torte's future. For the moment I needed to focus on the Chocolate Fest.

"I should get moving," I said to Rosalind.

"Of course." She shifted the light to point the way back to the door. Rosalind navigated the slick steps slowly. I stayed behind her just in case she happened to slip. Once we were safely back to the street level, she ducked under Torte's side awning and asked, "Well, what do you think, dear?"

"I think it's amazing, but it's also going to be a ton of work."

"Not necessarily. Why don't you meet with my contractor and have a little chat? I think you'll find that he will put your mind at ease."

"I guess, but can I ask you something?"

She nodded. "Of course, dear. Ask me anything. I want you to know everything there is to know about the property before you proceed."

"That's the thing, I mean, please don't take this the wrong way. I'm thrilled that you're helping us with this decision and for everything you've done, but why is it so important to you that Torte take the space?"

She looked flustered for a minute, but quickly recovered her composure. "As you know, I love your bakeshop and your mother has been a pillar of this community for years. I would like to see the space occupied and renovated by a true Ashlandian."

Ashlandian? I hadn't heard that term before, but I caught Rosalind's meaning. She had worked to ensure that the downtown plaza maintained its Shakespearean aesthetic after a chain restaurant tried to move in. However, I still had the sense that she was leaving something unsaid. "That's all?" I asked again.

"I'm not at liberty to say anything about the other applications for the building, but I will say that it's *imperative* that the plaza retain its high standards, and Torte is an exemplary illustration of just that."

Aha! I was right. Someone else wanted the space, someone Rosalind didn't approve of. I wondered who it could be, but I didn't have time to press her or dwell on it since I was due back for an icing demonstration. We parted ways only after I promised to have a meeting with Rosalind's contractor. I hurried into Torte to grab the cake and my piping tools.

"How's it going, boss?" Andy called from a stepladder. He was touching up the trim above the cupboards. I could barely hear him over the blaring rap music.

"Good!" I shouted. "I have to grab my cake."

"What?" he shouted back.

Sterling motioned to Stephanie who was closest to the stereo to cut the music. The deafening beat stopped with one click.

"What did you say, boss?" Andy shouted again before he realized the bakeshop was quiet.

"I said I need my cake." I emphasized each word. "And you are all going to lose years off your hearing with the music that loud. Good thing Mom isn't here," I joked.

Andy blushed. "Sorry, boss. It's mood music, you know." He flashed a grin.

Stephanie rolled her eyes.

"You look like you're making good progress," I noted as I made my way to the walk-in. "Do you need anything before I take off again?"

Sterling pointed to a stack of inventory sheets piled in front of him. "We're working our way through everything step by step, so far so good. Lance stopped by looking for you. He said to tell you if you don't see him at the fest to call him."

Of course he did, I thought as I found the chocolate spice cake where I'd left it in the fridge. It was already boxed and ready for delivery. I figured the box would probably do okay on the walk back to Ashland Springs but there was no reason to risk it—piping a wet cake would be a disaster—so I covered the entire box in plastic wrap.

I hoisted the box and carried it to the front of the bakeshop.

"You want me to take that for you?" Andy asked from the stepladder.

"No," I replied, tucking my tools and premade royal icing under one arm. "It's fine. Keep at it. It's looking great in here."

The cake box was heavier than I expected and the rain was coming down in sheets. Maybe I should have taken Andy up on his offer. Icy drops of water pelted my face. The wind had kicked up, sending my ponytail flying. By the time I had walked four blocks to the hotel my hair was soaking, but the cake box was dry, thanks to the plastic wrap.

"Pretty wet out there?" Mom noted as I unwrapped the wet plastic.

"It's a monsoon and it doesn't look like it's going to stop anytime soon." I wiped water from my forehead and pulled my damp hair free from the ponytail.

Mom helped me remove the cake from the box and set it up on a display stand. "I hope that there isn't any flooding. When we get rain like this, it concerns me. The last time we had a large rainstorm the plaza was inundated with water."

"Funny you should mention that," I said, filling a pastry bag with royal icing and massaging the bag. Royal icing is a thin icing used primarily for piping work and intricate designs. It consists of water, confectioners' sugar, and cream of tartar. I like the taste of buttercream better but when I'm showcasing drapery and lace work, royal icing is much easier to work with. I told Mom about bumping into Rosalind and our spontaneous tour of the basement property. Her face reflected an equal amount of concern as mine when I told her about the standing water. However, she perked up when I told her what was hidden behind old Sheetrock.

"A brick oven, really?" Her eyes sparkled. "Juliet, that could be worth considering. You know how expensive those are to put in. What did the masonry company quote? Twenty thousand dollars?"

"Yes, and that wasn't even for all the accessories, just the basic model and install." I tested the star pastry tip I planned to use for the top layer of the cake. The icing squeezed from the bag into a perfect star on my finger. "But water damage, I don't know about that."

Mom nodded and thought it over for a minute. "I think we should at least go ahead and talk to the contractor. That will give us a better idea of cost and what it would entail to ensure that the space doesn't flood again."

Chef Garrison came to let me know that I was due on the stage in ten minutes. "I didn't know we had a pool," he said with a smile.

"A pool?"

"You look like you've gone for a swim."

I laughed. "Yeah, it's a bit wet out there. Do I have time to go clean up?"

"Absolutely. Swing by the front desk. They'll give you a towel and toiletries."

"Thanks." I hurried to the lobby, not wanting to look like a drowned rat for my presentation. When I explained

my predicament to the woman at the front desk I
think she took pity on me, because she called one of the
housekeepers who arrived with a stack of fresh towels, a
hair dryer, and a bag of travel-sized lotion, hairspray, de-
odorant, and a comb. "You are a lifesaver!" I thanked
them both profusely and headed to the bathroom.

The women's bathroom was more like a spa, with
antique silver-framed mirrors, couches, and seating in
front of a well-lit vanity. I assembled the toiletries on
the marble counter and began drying my hair with a
towel. I was about to comb through it and give it a quick
blow-dry when I heard a high-pitched voice coming
from one of the stalls.

I recognized the New York accent right away—it was
Sandi Kramer. What was she doing having a conversation in the bathroom stall? I leaned back slightly on
the plush stool to get a better listen.

"No, no way," she yelled. "You get him on the phone
now. I'm not losing this now. With Evan dead everything
is . . ." She stopped in mid-sentence. My heart rate
quickened. Had she realized that she wasn't alone?

I returned my attention to the mirror and scooted the
stool closer.

For a minute there was silence. I flipped on the blow-
dryer and ran my fingers through my hair. The house-
keeper had given me mousse and hair gel. I squirted a
dollop of foamy mousse into my hand and worked it
through my hair. Sandi still hadn't emerged from the
stall by the time my hair was dry. Who was she talking
to, and what was she going to say about Evan? My
curiosity was running high, but I had to get on stage so
I twisted my hair into a high ponytail, smoothed a

thin layer of lotion onto my face, and ran some gloss over my lips. The result was much better than the drowned-rat look. My face had a light pinkish glow and my blond hair shimmered under the lights.

Showtime, Jules, I told myself, and headed back to the ballroom.

Chef Garrison helped me carry the cake onto the stage and showed me how to work the headset and wireless mic. After a glowing introduction, he turned the mic over to me. I thought I might be nervous, but talking about design technique was my comfort zone. I felt like I was back on the ship, teaching new chefs shortcuts for piping the company logo on cookies and demonstrating how to drape one of the many onboard wedding cakes that we produced.

My thirty minutes flew by, and soon Chef Garrison signaled that he was about to open the floor for questions. I looked up from the cake for the first time and spotted Sandi Kramer in the front row. She was taking notes and clicking photos of me with her phone. Did she know that I had been in the bathroom with her? When I caught her eye she waved, acted completely natural, and motioned for me to pose. I tried to relax and not force a fake grin as I leaned closer to my nearly finished cake.

A woman about three rows back raised her hand and asked what my thoughts were on 3-D printers and edible pastry paper. Using machine-crafted fondant had been a brewing controversy in the pastry world for the past few years. Like other industries, technology had revolutionized cake design. Images could now be screen-printed and placed on cake tops, giving them a professional, if somewhat sterile look. The top pastry chefs absolutely refused to acknowledge the movement, and I tended to agree with them because to me each cake that I created was an expression of my art. However, I had seen some amazing things done with the technology, like a cake artist who constructed a five-story cathedral that he frosted and piped by hand and embellished with jewel-colored stained-glass windows printed on edible icing sheets. Like most things, the key was striking a balance between using technology to enhance creativity versus allowing technology to eliminate the creative process of cake design.

I answered honestly and whatever I said must have resonated with Sandi Kramer, because she nodded enthusiastically and scribbled in her notebook as I spoke. The questions that people asked were quite sophisticated and I found myself becoming more and more animated and passionate as I talked about my love for the pastry arts.

"Thanks so much, Jules." Chef Garrison joined the crowd in a round of applause when my time was finished. "I know I've learned some great new tips and I'm sure all of you have too. Jules will be at her booth for those of you who didn't have a chance to ask your question. I'm sure she'd be willing to continue the conversation."

I agreed and left the stage.

"Great job!" Mom said, practically gushing. Her voice rose an octave as she spoke. "Is it loud in here or just me?"

Mom had a hard time hearing at Torte on busy days when we were packed with customers and had the mixers churning at high speed. The noise level in the ballroom, between the hum of guests and vendors, was definitely loud.

"It's kind of loud in here," I assured her.

A look of relief washed over her face. "Oh, good. You were a pro up there, so calm and confident. I was impressed. You could teach, you know."

"Thanks, Mom. But I think you might be slightly biased."

She pursed her lips and shook her head. "Not even a little. I'll have you know that you drew the largest crowd of the weekend so far. People are buzzing about how helpful and insightful that was."

The sound of Sandi Kramer clearing her voice interrupted us. "Excellent presentation. I'm convinced that you are going to be our next cover feature. Do you have a few minutes?"

I couldn't tell if she really wanted to talk to me about being featured on the cover, or if she knew that I'd heard her in the bathroom. A line had begun to form at our booth. I frowned. "Could we do it later? I'm free this evening, but I don't want to leave my mom with this line."

She gave the first woman in line a dismissive look through her oversized black glasses. "Fine, fine. I'll meet you here at exactly five o'clock. I have a dinner date and I do not like to be late."

"That's perfect," I replied, handing the woman in line a marzipan. "I'll be ready."

I hoped I would be. Sandi Kramer had a notorious reputation for eating pastry chefs for lunch if she didn't like them. A glowing review in *Sweetened* could vault us to the top of Oregon's foodie culture, but a bad review could hurt business.

Chapter Eighteen

Mom skillfully managed the line while I answered follow-up questions to my talk and handed out tasting samples. People wanted to know more about my training and whether there were any culinary programs in the region that I would recommend, which got me daydreaming about expanding the bakeshop. There would be plenty of space in the renovated basement to host baking classes and pastry workshops. That could be another revenue stream for Torte, and a fun outlet for me to teach some of the tricks of the trade. I'd have to talk to Mom about it later.

Our marzipan tray thinned, as did the stack of brochures that I had on display, as people crowded around our booth.

"Whew," Mom said, brushing cocoa from her hands and letting out a long sigh. "That's the last of it. One more day tomorrow and I think we can officially call this a success."

"They are like locusts." I shook my head in disbelief. Our tables had been decimated. It looked as if a swarm of chocolate-hungry bugs had stripped every morsel of food from our display. Not a single crumb of chocolate remained.

"Be careful what we wish for. I guess it's back to the kitchen again." Mom rubbed her temples. My back ached and my toes were tender even in my sensible shoes. It wasn't just the physical strain either. At Torte, we have an established rhythm to our days. Sure, there were times throughout the day that we would get a rush, like during the lunch hour or right after the matinee ended during the season, but for the most part we had a system down. Being "on" all day was exhausting. Not that we weren't energized and excited about having so many new customers, but it was hard not to feel like our words were rehearsed. How many ways can you describe a piece of chocolate after all?

"Mom, you look tired, why don't you go home. I'll do the interview with Sandi and then head back to Torte."

"No, no, I'm fine." Her tone was insistent, but she moved just a tad slower than normal as she wiped down the trays. Baking is physically demanding and the years had taken a toll on her. It made me all the more convinced that it was time for her to scale back.

I placed my hand over hers. "Mom, really, are you feeling okay?"

She blinked. "I can't hide a single thing from you, can I?"

"Nope." I smiled and folded my arms across my chest.

She wiggled her fingers. "The doctor says it's just a touch of arthritis. Your grandmother had it, you know.

Do you remember her fingers? She had real trouble using them as it progressed."

I did remember my grandmother's disfigured hands
and how she used to struggle with basic tasks like opening a jar or writing. Was that Mom's future?

"Mom, why didn't you say anything?"

"There's nothing to tell. The doctor says that it's the
early stages. He gave me some exercises to try and anti-
inflammatory medication. It's not so bad. The rain
seems to make it worse."

"What made you go to the doctor?" I had a feeling
she was underplaying how much pain she'd been in.
Like not connecting the fact that Sterling might not have
been able to afford a winter coat, I kicked myself for not
pushing her before. One of the very first things that I'd
noticed when I returned home last summer was her
slower pace, but she brushed it off and I figured it was
the stress of running the bakeshop alone. If I had paid
closer attention I should have realized that her pace
hadn't improved since I'd been home.

"Honey, I see that you're concerned, but really it's not
that painful—now the doctor did warn me that it will
eventually get worse—but that could be years from now.
They have no way of knowing. My hands get crampy
sometimes, but the reason I finally went in was because
I was getting a dull, burning sensation. I was actually
relieved to hear that it was arthritis. I thought it might
be something worse."

"Worse like what?"

She looked at her fingers. "Oh, I don't know, but I
didn't remember my mom ever complaining about a
numb or burning feeling."

"I want to know everything that the doctor said. Did you explain how much you use your hands and how physically demanding the bakeshop is?"

"You're being dramatic, which is not like you. Don't worry. I'm fine and the doctor said I was absolutely cleared to continue to work, which is what I intend to do."

"No way. You, young lady, are going home right now and resting your hands and doing the exercises that the doctor prescribed."

She started to protest, but I pushed her out of the booth. "I'm serious, Mom, you have taken care of me and everyone in this town for years. It's time for you to focus on yourself. I think your hands are trying to tell you that. No baking tonight. I've got it all under control."

"But—"

"Nope. Not another word. Go home. Have a glass of wine and rest. I'll see you here tomorrow at ten o'clock and if I see you anywhere near Torte I'm calling the Professor."

"And what?" Mom laughed. "Have me arrested?"

"Yep. Don't think I won't do it either." I paused. "Does the Professor know?"

She shook her head. "You make it sound like I have a something fatal. It's just a touch of arthritis, honey. And yes, Doug knows."

That was a relief. If the Professor knew, I had a feeling that he would agree with my opinion about Mom resting. In fact, it made me wonder if that was part of the reason he was encouraging her to scale back.

"Good. I'm glad we have that all settled then." I blew her a kiss. "See you tomorrow."

She stepped closer and enveloped me in a hug. "Thanks. I'm so lucky to have a daughter like you."

I embraced her back. "I'm so lucky to have a mom like you."

After we parted, I watched her fade into the crowd. I couldn't tell from the way that she walked or the slight swing in her step that anything was wrong, but I was worried. Arthritis had left my grandmother incapable of performing daily tasks; would that happen to Mom? She had always been so vital and full of life, I couldn't imagine her not being able to work in the bakeshop . . . or worse. I stopped myself from thinking what worse might be. When I got back to my apartment later, I intended to research everything I could on the condition and its treatment options.

As promised, Sandi Kramer showed up at exactly five o'clock for our interview. She wasn't kidding about punctuality. "Are you ready." It wasn't a question. She tapped her tablet and launched into an assault of questions before I had a chance to say yes.

"Tell me about your training. School in NYC, right? Culinary internships on two premier cruise lines, yes? Followed by a rapid ascent to head pastry chef?"

I nodded, but Sandi didn't even notice, nor did she pause for a breath. "And you describe your food style how—French, Italian, classic, fusion?"

"Well, I guess I would say that I'm classically trained, but obviously spending so many years on the ship really opened me up to world cuisine."

"Uh-huh, uh-huh," Sandi muttered, not bothering to look up from her tablet. "And what would you say is your signature style?"

My signature style? Did I even have a signature style? "I'm not sure that I have a signature style," I said to Sandi. "I have a soft spot for French pastry, but honestly, I guess if I have a style at all it's just that I love baking with the highest-quality ingredients, especially when they are locally sourced. That's one of our missions at Torte—all of our vendors are local. The flavor profile of a strawberry that's been shipped versus handpicked locally is so different. We want our customers to know that they're tasting the freshest strawberry possible."

Sandi continued to type on her tablet, but I couldn't tell if she was pleased with my answers or not. "Let's talk about cakes."

"Okay."

"What's your signature style when it comes to cake artistry?"

"Uh, again, I don't know that I have a signature style."

She scowled and looked at me from beneath her black-framed glasses. "Everyone has a signature style. Have you read *Sweetened*? This column is titled 'Signature Sweets.' You need a signature style."

"Yes, I'm a fan of the magazine, it's just not something that I've thought about for myself. My cakes and all of my pastries are an expression of my love and my art. When someone hires us at Torte to create a cake for them, I like to think that they are commissioning us for a custom piece of art. My medium just happens to be pastry."

"Brilliant." Sandi threw one hand in the air. "Thank you. That is a signature style. That wasn't so hard, was it?"

She resumed her rapid-fire questioning. It felt like

I was under attack. If I didn't answer fast enough she would sigh loudly and tap her stylus on her tablet. I couldn't tell if my responses were boring her or if she was just impatient.

After about fifteen minutes, she flipped her tablet shut. "I've got what I need for the moment. I'll be back tomorrow for any follow-up questions and my professional photographer will want to get shots of these cakes." She wrinkled her nose and frowned. "I don't know if this lighting will work. We might have to stage the cakes somewhere else. Your bakeshop, perhaps?"

"Maybe. We're in the middle of a remodel."

"If you want an opportunity like this for a cover shot, then I think you'll get it figured out. My photographer will be here at two o'clock sharp. Be ready to shoot. I want you in the shot too."

"Me?" I'm sure my mouth must have dropped open. "You want me in the picture?"

Sandi rolled her eyes. "That's the point. Yes, you're in it or there's no story. Got it?"

I nodded and she strutted away. There hadn't been a chance to ask her about the phone call in the bathroom earlier, and I didn't want to risk irritating her. She wasn't exactly warm and fuzzy, but I'd run into her type many times over the years. Getting on the cover of *Sweetened* was a major deal, and if that meant I had to be in the photo, I knew exactly who to call to ensure I looked stylish for the photo shoot—Lance.

Chapter Nineteen

While I packed up my piping tools and pastry tips, I couldn't shake the feeling that someone was watching me. As I glanced around the ballroom I saw there were a few stragglers in search of chocolate, and a handful of vendors remaining, but otherwise the elegant space was nearly deserted. The feeling was probably lingering from my presentation. Speaking in public wasn't something that I did on a daily basis, so I brushed the feeling off as residual nerves.

With my pastry gear neatly arranged in my satchel, I started for the front door. The feeling that I wasn't alone grew as I passed the Confections Couture booth. Something moved to my right and I could have sworn that I heard heavy breathing. I froze and scanned the stylized booth. Was it my imagination, or had the life-sized cutout of Evan Rowe just moved?

I squinted and stepped closer. The cardboard cutout swayed slightly from side to side. What in the world? My brain tried to make sense of what I was seeing. The tiny blond hairs on my arm stood at attention; someone *was* watching me. A sense of foreboding washed over me, but I didn't run. After all, this was Ashland's most popular and prestigious hotel; it wasn't as if anyone would be dumb enough to try and harm me here, right?

The cutout rocked again. In a flash I made a decision to ignore the fact that my pulse rate had quickened and approached the booth.

"Is someone here?" I stood tall and made a concerted effort to use my most commanding chef's voice.

I heard a squeaking sound followed by a crash as the cutout tilted to one side and smashed into the front of the booth. Carter was crouched on the ground with his knees tucked under his chin. His eyes widened when they met mine. Any fear that I had been feeling dissipated. Carter's frame reminded me of a toothpick. I could definitely hold my own against him.

"What are you doing?" I asked.

Carter gulped and pushed to his feet. "Uh, this isn't what it looks like."

"It looks like you're hiding behind that cutout."

"Yeah, but I mean I wasn't hiding." He bit his thumbnail and seemed to be frantically trying to come up with an excuse. "I was fixing some things back there, that's all."

"Really?" I raised one brow and gave him my best Mom stare.

He hung his head. "Okay, okay, I was kind of hiding, but only because I wanted to get a minute alone with Sandi. But she stormed out of here before I could stop her."

My lie-detection radar was on high alert. Carter's

story didn't make any sense. If he wanted to speak with Sandi why did he need to hide?

Sensing my distrust he threw his hands in the air. "Listen, I swear, I've been trying to get Sandi alone for two days and that woman doesn't stop. She won't even look at me. I thought maybe I could catch her off guard, you know?"

"As in jump out at her?" I frowned. "I think that would have had the opposite effect."

Color drained from Carter's face. He tried to pick up the cutout and put it back in position, but it slipped from his hands and landed with another thud on the table.

"What's really going on?" I asked.

He gulped again. "Honestly, I was trying to get a minute with Sandi, that's all."

"Why do you need to talk to her so desperately that you're willing to hide out behind this?" I helped lift the large piece of cardboard while Carter secured the base back in place.

"I wasn't desperate, it's just that she's been impossible to get alone."

A custodian opened the emergency exit doors and wheeled in a cleaning cart. He began vacuuming the row opposite us, so I decided to press Carter further. "I heard that you and Evan had a pretty public fight."

Carter cleared his throat. "How did you hear that?"

I didn't want to break Bethany's trust. "It's all over town. Everyone is talking about it. I don't know how long you've been in Ashland, but that's how gossip works around here. Once one person talks, the entire town knows."

Rubbing his temples, Carter let out a pained sigh. "Oh, no."

"Do you want to sit down?" I offered, pointing at the padded chairs folded up behind the booth.

He nodded and set out the chairs. "Everyone knows that Evan and I were fighting?"

I felt guilty for exaggerating, but I wanted to know what was going on with Carter and the real reason he was hiding—I suspected it was because he was spying on me, but why?

"Crud. I don't know what to do." Carter hung his head in his lap and massaged his jaw. "That's why I wanted to get Sandi alone."

"Because of your fight with Evan?" I wished I had some leftover chocolate to offer him. Mom always seemed to get people to open up over a slice of cake or a warm scone. I was going to have to rely on staying calm and listening to whatever Carter would be willing to tell me.

"Yeah." He paused when the custodian vacuumed around the booth with a nod to both of us.

Once the sound of the vacuum quieted, he sighed and looked me in the eye. "Can I tell you something in secret?"

"Of course, unless it has something directly to do with Evan's death. Then I would have to tell the police." Hadn't I just had this same conversation with Bethany? I wondered if Carter's secret was going to be that he'd helped her with her brownie production.

"Evan was pompous, as I'm sure you noticed, but he wasn't that bad. Part of that was for show; he said that people had certain expectations of chocolatiers and he liked to live up to those expectations."

I thought of Lance, who also tended to embellish his over-the-top personality for the sake of the show or the audience.

"The truth is that Evan was losing his sense of taste. He was scared. Really scared."

"What?" I couldn't believe what he was saying. Losing your sense of taste as a chef would be devastating—even career ending.

Carter gnawed on his thumbnail. "Yeah. I was the only one who knew except for Evan's doctor. Evan was suffering from a severe form of GERD. Doctors tried everything, medication, surgery, changes to his diet, but nothing worked. He couldn't taste his products anymore. That's why he hired me."

"That's terrible." I felt a new round of empathy for Evan Rowe. "I don't understand though—why were you fighting?"

"When Evan hired me he made me swear that I wouldn't tell anyone. He was freaking out. In fact, he told me he was backing out of old deals and only taking on new deals and partnerships because he didn't want to risk anyone realizing that there might be a difference in his product."

"That's crazy. Isn't everything automated?"

Carter's string-beanlike body twitched as he replied. "Yeah, that was Evan." He sighed and continued. "He wanted to impart as much of his tasting knowledge and memory to me before he lost it completely. We were doing tasting sessions at his place in secret every night.

He believed that I had a natural palate. In fact, I got the job because I passed a blind taste test."

"A blind taste test?"

"I'm still in school at Southern Oregon. A few months ago my professor passed around a flier for a blind taste testing with Confections Couture. All of us thought it was kind of like Willy Wonka. Whoever passed the blind test would be offered a one-year paid internship at the chocolate company. Everyone applied. I didn't think I even had a chance, but Evan told me that not only had I passed but that I had one of the most pristine palates he'd ever seen."

"That's high praise from someone like Evan Rowe." When it comes to food there are many things that can be taught, from technique to preparation and from plating to science, but some things are innate—and the ability to taste was one of them. I'd witnessed chefs develop and train their palates over the years, but for a lucky few, genetics had bestowed pure taste buds with an unparalleled ability to decipher every layer of flavor in whatever they put in their mouths. Carlos could do that with wine. He used to amaze me when he would swirl a sip and pull out every note from a citrusy finish to the soggy soil the grapes were grown in.

"I know. I thought I had won the lottery at first. A paid internship is a big deal, and having Confections Couture on my resume would assure that I could get a job anywhere in the culinary world after I graduated. Then I found out the real reason Evan had hired me and it became a nightmare."

"Why?" I shifted in the chair, stretching my aching calves toward the floor. "It's terrible that Evan was losing his ability to taste, but that still seems like an incredible opportunity for you."

"Oh, it was," Carter said, nodding and cracking his knuckles. "It kind of sucked to have to play errand boy for Evan, but that was all part of his plan. He didn't want to lose face around the rest of the staff or customers, so the story he told everyone was that I was his lackey. In public, I ran around and got him coffee and picked up his dry cleaning. No one knew what was really going on."

"How does Sandi Kramer play into this?"

"She wrote a scathing article about Evan. He had always been the magazine's golden child. She had 'discovered' him before he made a name for himself in the chocolate industry, but she didn't like his new line of chocolates. Evan thought it was because he was losing his touch. Sandi knows her stuff and Evan was convinced that his chocolate was suffering."

I chuckled. "Chocolate suffering. That's something."

He smiled, but then shook his head and looked at his feet. "Evan loved his chocolate more than anything. He really cared about his product, you know? I get that he was a jerk and had a huge ego, but he poured his entire life into Confections Couture. It made an impression on me."

We were both quiet for a minute. I understood what Carter meant; there was something to be said for chefs— or any professionals—who were passionate about their products. I also wondered at what cost, though.

"Sandi didn't like the new line?"

Carter shook his head. "No. Not at all. Her review was awful. It was almost personal or something. She withdrew everything she'd ever said about Confections

Couture that she'd written in the past. She said it was the most uninspired chocolate that she'd tasted in years and that Evan had obviously lost his touch."

"Ouch."

"Yeah. It was bad. She gave Evan a copy and a chance to read it before it hits newsstands next month. I told Evan to tell her the truth. Maybe Sandi would be kinder if she understood what was happening to his taste buds, but Evan refused. That's what we were arguing about. I begged him to come clean with Sandi. He wouldn't do it. He said that he knew his line was good. I think his ego and pride got in the way."

"*Was* it bad?"

"No, I thought it was great. Honestly, it was some of Evan's better work. I have no idea why Sandi didn't like it."

Food is subjective. What brings childlike delight to one person's palate might bring disgust to someone else's. It could have been that Sandi simply didn't like Evan's new line. But then again there could be a connection to her review and his death.

"And that's why you've been trying to talk to Sandi?"

He nodded. "I figured now that Evan is dead, he can't get mad at me for telling her the truth."

"You really cared about him, didn't you?" I was surprised that Carter was so loyal to Evan.

"He was a great chef and a good teacher and he built a chocolate empire. It doesn't matter if he had an ego; he didn't deserve to have it all destroyed by one bitter article." Carter glanced at the digital watch on his wrist. "I've got to get going. Thanks for listening. I've been holding this in for a while. It feels good to get it off my chest. You won't say anything, right?"

I hesitated. "I won't, but you need to tell the police."

"Why?"

"It could be important to their case."

"Do you think so?"

I could hear the insistent tone in my voice. "I don't know. That's up to them, but Evan is dead and any lead they have could help determine what happened to him. But wait, one more thing. Right after he died, you thought that someone killed him. Why?"

Carter wetted the tip of his finger and tried to pat down the cowlicks that curled on top of his forehead. "He thought someone was after him."

"He did?"

"Yeah, he kept mentioning it. Kind of watching over his shoulder, but he was paranoid about everything, so who knows."

"Did you tell the police about that?" Was Carter one of the other witnesses whom the Professor and Thomas had spoken to?

"Yeah, I did. Right after I told them how careful Evan was about nuts, and how he was worried that someone was watching him."

I let that sink in. Carter agreed to talk to the Professor again as we parted ways, and I agreed not to say anything about Evan's condition. My mind spun as I headed for Torte. Had Sandi uncovered the truth about Evan's abilities, or could it be that she had another reason for wanting to discredit him? And was someone really watching the chocolatier, or had his ego just been so inflated that he was convinced that someone was out to get him?

Chapter Twenty

Rain fell horizontally outside thanks to a biting wind that funneled down Main Street. My cell phone rang above the sound of the gushing water.

"Hello?" I ducked under the hotel's red and white striped awning and tried to shelter my phone with my free hand.

"Jules? Where are you?" Thomas's voice broke as the line crackled. I thought I had lost the signal.

"Thomas?"

"Yeah, Jules. Where are you?" he repeated.

"I'm just leaving Ashland Springs."

"It sounds like you're white-rafting on the Umpqua or something."

"It's raining like crazy." I wondered if the basement at Torte was under two feet of water with all the new rain that had fallen.

"I'm picking up some dinner. I thought I could bring it over to your apartment. There are a few things about the investigation that I was hoping to go over with you."

I hesitated. As intrigued as I was about the case, I

didn't want to give Thomas the wrong idea. Carlos had been convinced that Thomas still had lingering feelings for me, and while I wasn't sure whether Thomas really did or whether it was just easy and natural for us to rekindle our friendship, I didn't want to lead him on.

"Actually, I'm heading to Torte. I need to make more samples for tomorrow. We got cleaned out today."

"That's fine, I'll bring dinner to you. See you in twenty." He didn't give me a chance to decline his offer. The line went dead before I could even form a response in my head. I was hungry and I was eager to hear what news he might have about the case. Tucking my phone back in my bag, I sprinted toward the bakeshop. The effort was futile—rain pummeled me and leaked through my jacket. Main Street was in bad shape with at least four inches of water bubbling up from overflowing storm drains.

One of my fellow shop owners, who ran Tricksters, a novelty shop, flagged me down. "Jules! How's Torte? We're getting inundated with water over here. I'm trying to get all of my inventory onto high shelves but it's coming in so fast."

"Hold on," I called. I hurried inside Torte and threw my supplies on the pastry case before quickly assessing the bakeshop to make sure that we weren't taking on water. Fortunately, Torte was as dry as two-day-old stale bread. The painting was complete and everything had been put back in its original space. I breathed a sigh of relief, tightened my coat, and ran across the street to pitch in.

It wasn't just Tricksters, businesses on both sides of the plaza had their front doors open and owners wearing rubber boots were frantically stacking sandbags and throwing buckets of water out their doors.

"What can I do?" I asked Tricksters' owner.

She tossed me a bucket. "We're starting a brigade."

I jumped into line with my fellow business owners and we scooped buckets of icy water as fast as we could. The water was up to my ankles and coming in fast. Outside was a blur of activity. Police lights and sirens filled the plaza as police officers and city workers arrived with trucks of sand and stacks of bags. Business owners left their own shops unattended to help those inundated by water. Diners left restaurants and began filling sandbags.

The entire town rallied around the flooding businesses. I lost track of time and lost feeling in my fingertips as we did our best to keep up with the onslaught of rain. It felt like it was never ending. Heavy bags piled up above the window of the novelty shop. My feet burned with cold and blisters broke on my hands, but I kept sloshing water outside. Industrial pumps chugging to life and people shouting out orders could barely be heard above the sound of the wind and the rain.

After a few hours the rain finally began to subside and the pumps were sucking out more water than we could with our handheld buckets. The owner of Tricksters thanked us profusely and sent us home. There wasn't much more that could be done tonight. Tomorrow, by the light of day, we would have a better sense of how much damage had really been done.

Thomas waved at me from Puck's Pub as I crossed the street to Torte. "Be there in ten minutes, Jules." He scooped sand into a burlap bag with one muscular arm.

Every muscle in my body ached and my fingers and toes burned with cold. I cranked the heat up to its highest setting and checked the walk-in, storage area, and office to make sure that water hadn't found its way inside anywhere. We were lucky that Torte had weathered the storm without so much as a drop of water inside. Thank goodness.

I kicked off my shoes and warmed my feet on the floor vent in the kitchen. The last thing I wanted to do at the moment was bake. I wanted a hot shower, dinner, and my bed. While my toes started to dry out, I considered my options. If I headed for my apartment now, I would have to get up early to prepare our chocolate samples for the last day of the fest. I decided that forgoing an extra hour of sleep in the morning was fine by me. I needed dry clothes and something warm to drink.

As I closed up shop, I bumped into Thomas outside.

"Hey, I was just coming to find you," he said, holding a large brown paper bag in one hand and his golf umbrella in the other.

"Sorry. I have to change." I pointed to my soggy feet.

"Got it. I'll follow you to your apartment. Dinner is cold, but nothing that your microwave can't fix."

I considered saying no, but my stomach rumbled at the thought of food, and I didn't have enough energy to protest. Thomas walked me home with the umbrella positioned above my head. Once inside my tiny apartment, I flipped on the lights and heat. He shook his raincoat on my front landing and left it and the umbrella outside.

"Go change into dry clothes," he said. "I'll nuke this in the microwave. It's my specialty."

"Microwaving does require a lot of skill," I teased.

"I'll have you know that I'm professionally trained in the art of nuking cold food. I do it daily, so I have lots of practice." He grinned.

Any food—microwaved or not—sounded great. I slid down the hallway on my wet socks and tossed them into the hamper in my room. I tugged off my wet clothes and pulled on a thick pair of fleece yoga pants, a cozy pull-over sweater, and a pair of fur-lined slippers that Carlos had given me as a belated Christmas present. Then I towel-dried my damp hair and tied it back into a fresh ponytail.

When I returned to the living room, I stopped in my tracks. A sinking feeling hit my stomach. I had made a mistake in saying yes to having dinner with Thomas again. He had arranged two plates and plastic wine-glasses on the small dining table at the far end of the living room. In the middle of the table was a bouquet of fresh flowers and a bottle of red wine.

"What's all this?" I asked, taking a seat.

Thomas smiled from the kitchen where he was scooping stir-fried rice and Chinese noodles onto two serving dishes. "Just a little something I brought over."

"In that paper bag?"

He nodded. "Yep. It's like I'm a regular old Mary Poppins or something. Surprise." He placed the steaming Chinese noodles in front of me. "Your favorite—beef and broccoli with extra sauce."

"Thanks." I tried to keep my tone appreciative. Did Thomas have a different idea of what going over the case meant?

"Go ahead, don't wait for me." He motioned for me

to serve myself as he returned to the kitchen for fried rice and a plate of pot stickers.

Once the food had been assembled he poured us both glasses of wine and held his glass in a toast. "To you, Jules."

I swallowed and gave him a hesitant grin. "Thanks, but we don't need to toast to me."

He tapped his glass to mine and held my gaze. I could feel the intensity in his blue eyes. "We can always toast to you."

My foot bounced nervously under the table. "What's going on with the investigation?" I bit into a juicy pot sticker.

Disappointment clouded his face, but he stabbed at his noodles and tried to mask his emotions. "Right, the investigation." Before he continued he took a bite of his noodles. "We're not sure, to be honest. This one has the Professor stumped. I've never seen him like this."

"What do you mean?" I scarfed down two helpings of noodles and fried rice.

"I don't know. I think he's really worried that we're not going to solve this case."

I told Thomas what I had learned from Carter. He leaned back in his chair and tapped his fingers on his lips. "Evan couldn't taste his chocolate. Hmm. That means he probably couldn't taste nuts either."

"You're right! I didn't even think about that. It makes so much more sense now. If he consumed something that he thought was chocolate he wouldn't have known that he had been exposed to nuts."

"Right." Thomas's demeanor had shifted, and now he was fully invested in talking about Evan's murder. "We couldn't figure out how someone could have slipped a professional chef nuts, but if Evan couldn't taste them, that changes everything."

We both reached for a pot sticker at the same time and our hands touched. Thomas tried to let his hand linger over mine. I pulled my hand away and popped the pot sticker into my mouth.

"This Carter kid claims that no one else was aware of Evan's condition?" Thomas asked.

"He was insistent. He said that Evan hired him specifically for his tasting abilities and made him swear not to tell anyone."

"But maybe he did."

"Or maybe someone else on his staff wised up to what was going on. It would be hard to hide that, especially as a head chef."

Thomas looked thoughtful. "Yes, but from my interviews with his staff it sounds like he scaled back in the last few years. He was rarely on-site. He spent most of his time doing press appearances and working in his test lab which no one had access to except for him."

I bit into another pot sticker. The tender and juicy julienned vegetables and spicy pork had been sautéed in a soy sauce, retaining a slight crunch. "Okay, so what if one of his staff members found out that he couldn't taste and spread that rumor around town? If our killer knew that Evan couldn't taste nuts, maybe they recognized a genius way to bump him off."

"Bump him off," Thomas repeated. "I've got to call the Professor right now and tell him about this. You go ahead and finish your dinner. I'll be right back."

He stepped outside onto the landing to call the Professor while I leisurely finished my wine and debated whether or not to eat the last pot sticker. I knew that Thomas wouldn't care, but my belly was full and I didn't want to wake up in the middle of the night with a stomachache from gorging myself on Chinese food.

Thomas came back inside, bringing a gust of cool, wet air with him. "Jules, I'm so glad you told me that. The Professor sounded lighter than he has in a few days, although it's a good-news/bad-news scenario."

"What's the bad news?"

"He finally got the coroner's report, and you'll never believe this. There were no nuts found in Evan's system. At all."

I sat up and untied my ponytail, letting my hair fall free. "Really?"

Thomas looked as shocked at the news as I felt. "That's what he said. Now we're back to trying to figure out what killed Evan."

"So it wasn't nuts?"

"Nope. The coroner listed anaphylactic shock as the cause of death, so Evan definitely had a reaction to something. The question is what. They're going to run some more tests."

"Does that change your investigation?"

Thomas sighed. "Who knows? This case has been weird all the way around."

He poured himself more wine. "Want me to top you off?"

I raised my hand for him to stop. "I'm fine, thanks. Tomorrow is going to be an early day for me, since I couldn't work tonight. I was freezing and so hungry. Thanks again for bringing dinner."

Thomas's eyes were searching. "Jules, I would do anything for you. You know that, right?"

"Right back at you." I tried to wink, but I'm sure my face must have looked contorted and silly, which was exactly what I was going for.

Running a callused finger along the rim of his wineglass, Thomas looked thoughtful for a moment. I sensed that he wanted the conversation to go deeper. We'd been dancing around talking about our past since I had returned home. When we broke up the summer after high school, I left for culinary school and never looked back. Not because I harbored any ill will toward Thomas, but because I was focused on moving forward and building a career and a new life for myself outside of the soft bubble of Ashland.

Growing up in Ashland had been idyllic in so many ways, from spending afternoons in Torte's lively kitchen to being surrounded by the creative energy of playwrights and actors. I know that my early experiences helped shape my approach to pastry. I had always thought I would stay in Ashland forever, despite the fact that I kept journals and sketches of the faraway places that visitors spoke of, that I dreamed of not just learning how to make French macarons but of actually working in a tiny French patisserie, where a surly chef would guide me step by step in the technique of crafting a light and airy macaron. Those thoughts were nothing more than childhood fancy, although on somewhat of a whim I did apply to culinary school in New York. I never thought I would be accepted to the prestigious school, let alone go. That all changed when Thomas broke up with me.

Thomas and I had grown up together and he had been by my side after my dad died. I don't know how I would have gotten through those first years without my father if it hadn't been for him. When he broke up with me it was a shock, a blow to my ego, and upset all of the plans that we had made. We were going to go to Southern Oregon University together where he would play football and I would hone my culinary skills. I would be able to continue to help Mom at Torte while I attended classes and had a built-in internship. The plan seemed infallible—until Thomas suggested that maybe we should take a break. He wanted to start college without any attachments so that he could focus on training and his course work.

I couldn't believe what I was hearing. Thomas was breaking up with me—and right before the start of the term no less. Suddenly, the envelope that I had hidden away congratulating me on my acceptance to culinary school felt like it was calling to me. After I dried my tears, I opened the letter again and without hesitation packed my bags and boarded a plane to New York a few weeks later. Mom was ecstatic that I had changed my mind, not because she wouldn't miss me, but because she wanted me to strike out on my own and experience the world while I was young.

"Juliet, go," she urged. "Your father wanted you to do this. Do you remember his favorite verse from *Romeo and Juliet*?"

I shook my head. My dad, like the Professor, had been a scholar of the Bard's work and could quote almost any line from his plays on command.

' "I never remember it exactly, but it's something

along the lines of, Do not swear by the moon, for she changes constantly, then your love would also change.' " She clasped her hand in mine. " 'Love changes, life changes, go follow your own moon, I know it will lead you to beautiful things.' "

Parting from her was sweet sorrow (as the Professor likes to say). We had grown even closer after losing my dad, but I followed her advice and went out in search of myself and my own adventures. If someone had told me back then that I would end up traveling to distant ports of call on a moonlit sea I wouldn't have believed it. But thanks to Thomas, Ashland became a fond memory of a place that I used to call home while I danced until midnight in the crowded streets of Madrid and swam in the sultry blue salty waters off the Moroccan coast. Life on the ship opened me up to flavors, tastes, colors, and textures that I didn't know I was missing. I became a pastry chef and a strong, confident version of myself aboard the cruise ship. If Thomas hadn't broken up with me, who knows where my path might have led. I held no trace of bitterness for our lovely and sweet past, quite the opposite—I owed him everything.

"Jules, where did you go?" Thomas's voice cut through my memories.

"What?" I shook my shoulders and planted my feet underneath me.

He chuckled. "You're spacing out again. Do you remember when you used to daydream in math class and Mr. Scott would toss an eraser at your desk?"

"Me? Daydream . . . never!" I grinned.

Thomas scoffed. "I believe the technical term we use in the police business is 'selective memory.' " He stared at his wineglass and cleared his throat. "Listen, I have to talk to you about something. I don't think that you're going to like what I have to say, but I have to say it."

My throat tightened. "Thomas, don't . . ." I started, but he sat up and held me off.

"No, Jules, I have to say this. I know that you know what I'm going to say and if I don't tell you how I really feel about you I'm never going to forgive myself. I let you go once and I'm not going to let that happen again."

"Wait, please." I did know what he was going to say, and I didn't want to hear it.

"Juliet, I've been in love with you since we were fifteen. There's never been anyone else. It's always been you."

"Thomas, stop. I'm married, remember?"

He closed his eyes and took a slow breath. "I know, Juliet, trust me. Seeing you with Carlos was painful, and I'm not trying to destroy your marriage or your happiness. I want you to be happy, whatever that means."

"But . . ."

"No, let me say this. I've been waiting ten years to say this to you. I love you, Juliet. You're the most incredible woman I've ever met. You're beautiful and kind, and you're so smart and witty, and don't even get me started on your baking."

I chuckled in hopes of changing the tone of the conversation. "That's your problem. You shouldn't eat my pastries. In fact, I should ban you from Torte. It's a real problem—Mom warned me about it when I decided to follow in the family business. She calls it a pastry crush. You should see the line of single men out the door when she bakes her sticky buns."

Thomas gave me a pained smile and shook his head. "Joke all you want, but I'm serious, Jules. I'm in love with you. I knew it the minute I saw you again. All those old feelings came flooding back. I can't believe I was such an idiot—why did I let you go?"

Keeping my tone sympathetic, I reached for his arm and placed my hand on his sleeve. "Thomas, letting me go was the best thing you ever did for me. Honestly, I'm so thankful that things happened the way they did."

He looked at my hand and then back to my eyes. His gaze was intense, and I wanted to pull away but didn't want to injure him further. "I'm glad you got to see the world too. It's not that. It's that I've waited for you here for ten years without even realizing that's what I was doing. No other woman could compare to you, and then when you came home it all became so clear."

I removed my hand. "Thomas, here's the thing, neither of us are the same. I've changed, and so have you. I think what you're feeling is normal—it's nostalgia. We had such a sweet and innocent relationship, friendship. I cherish those memories, but we can't go back in time."

Shaking his head, he exhaled and rested his head in his hands. "Juliet, we haven't changed that much. You're still the girl I fell in love with."

"But I'm not. I'm married. I love Carlos. I don't know where things are going with us, but I still love him, and I know you don't think so, but I am different. Really different. I'm not a girl anymore."

"Trust me, Jules, I *know* that you're not a girl, and whether you want to believe it or not, I'm in love with you right now at this very moment. The new you. The adult you. Not a childhood memory."

I didn't respond.

Thomas stood. His blue eyes were glassy but determined. "I'm not trying to make you uncomfortable or put you in a complicated situation. I just had to tell you for myself." He stacked our dishes. "I'm not going anywhere. Take all the time you need to figure things out with Carlos. I won't get in the way. If you're able to save your marriage, I'll stand by your side and support you in that, but if things don't work out and there's even a sliver of a chance for us, I'll wait another ten years. I'll wait a lifetime for you, Jules."

"I don't want you to wait for me, Thomas." I reached for his arm.

He positioned the plates in one hand and picked up the empty serving bowls with the other. "Don't say any more. I don't need you to answer me now, and I promise this is the last thing I'll say for the moment. We'll keep things strictly platonic, just friends. I feel better now that you know."

He walked into the kitchen and cleaned up the remnants of our dinner. I sat at the table, stunned. Had he really just professed his love for me?

After the kitchen was sparkling clean, Thomas put his coat on and gave me a wave. "See you tomorrow, Jules." He left without another word.

I couldn't believe that he thought he was still in love with me. It had to be nostalgia. I had suspected that he might have a lingering crush on me, but I never anticipated that he would be harboring such deep feelings. I should have listened to Mom, and Carlos, and Sterling, and Lance. Everyone around me had warned me that this was the case, but I'd blown them all off. Or maybe there was a small part of me that was flattered by his attention and enjoyed our familiar, easy banter. I didn't return his feelings, or at least I didn't think I did . . .

Emotions swirled in my head and stomach as I changed into pajamas and headed for bed. When I left Ashland, I left Thomas too. I couldn't remember a sleepless night on the ship when my thoughts had drifted to him. He was my first love, but he wasn't my last love.

I tossed and turned for hours, replaying every conversation that I'd had with Thomas since I had been home. Had I led him on? Could he have misinterpreted my friendly flirtation for something more? Despite his insistence that we hadn't changed that much, I knew that we had. We were both drastically different people than we were in high school and I was happy with who I had become. But I didn't want to break his heart.

Chapter Twenty-one

After a restless night of sleep, I woke up resolved to put the situation between Thomas and me on the back burner. With the Chocolate Fest wrapping up and our ovens being delivered later, the agenda for the day was packed with activity, which would hopefully serve as a welcome distraction from Thomas's revelation. I dressed quickly and headed for Torte. The rain had subsided overnight but its aftermath was visible everywhere. Muddy debris streaked the sidewalk and stacks of sand-bags lined doorways and front stoops. I hadn't seen an updated forecast but I hoped that no more water was predicted. If the plaza took another soaking like last night, we might all float away.

Tempering the chocolate for the last round of guests at the festival didn't take long. I worked at a lightning pace, not only because I had limited time, but because if I stayed focused on the task at hand my mind tended to wander less. The smell of melting chocolate and coffee permeated the air and perked me up. Within an hour I had the final round of tasting samples boxed up and ready to go.

Since the ovens weren't being installed until after lunch, I had given the team the morning off. With one final inspection of the bakeshop to make sure that installation would be as seamless as possible, I stacked the samples and locked the front door. When I returned later we would have shiny—and more importantly, functional—ovens. I felt like a kid at Christmas. The day couldn't go by fast enough in my opinion. Some people geek out over gadgets and the latest technology, but I geek out over baking equipment. I wasn't sure if that made me unique or slightly sad. Either way, I didn't care. Soon Torte would be working as smoothly as a buttered slice of bread again.

When I arrived at the hotel, I was surprised to see Sandi Kramer snapping photos of my wedding cake display. A professional photographer had constructed a temporary white background behind my cakes and focused two freestanding lights on either side of the cakescape.

"Hey," I said, greeting Sandi with a wave. "What's all this?"

Sandi snapped at the photographer. "Move that light. It's glaring on the cake. I don't like that reflection it's casting at all."

The photographer adjusted the light stand and waited for her approval. She stepped backward and made round circles of both her hands. She held them over her glasses like binoculars. "I want it to the left. Two inches."

She tapped her heel while he scooted the light to the left. "Nope, back just an inch. Not even an inch."

From my vantage point the cakes looked amazing. The lighting gave them a soft glow.

"Here?" the photographer asked, holding his camera in one hand.

Sandi squinted through her imaginary binoculars. "I guess it's going to have to do. The lighting in here is terrible. I don't think you're going to be able to use any of these shots. We might have to reshoot the whole thing later."

"It looks good to me," I said as I set the boxes on the opposite table.

"Maybe for Ashland, Oregon," Sandi scoffed, coming closer to me. "Remember, this feature is going in *Sweetened*. The world's premier pastry magazine."

I wanted to ask Sandi about Confections Couture, but I knew that I had to tread carefully. While she directed the photographer exactly where to focus his lens, I arranged the tasting samples and tried to think of a way to ask Sandi about the story she was planning to run on Evan without being too obvious.

"Are you featuring all of the chocolate vendors in your piece?" I asked.

Sandi scowled. "Goodness no. *Sweetened* only covers the best in the biz—pastry artists and couture chocolatiers." She glanced to the slushy booth. "Some of the vendors here are so juvenile. Chocolate slushies belong in the pages of *Mad* magazine. Not *Sweetened*."

I figured it would be best to keep the fact that I had devoured my chocolate slushy to myself. "Are you doing a feature on Evan?"

She blinked twice and then examined her candy-apple-red nails. "Why do you ask?"

"You mentioned couture chocolatiers. I thought you meant Evan."

"Evan Rowe is—was—a *has-been*. He had his time in the limelight, but I'm afraid his days of being the rock star of the chocolate world faded years ago."

"I wondered if you were going to write a tribute now that he's dead. I've seen that done for other chefs who've made a lasting contribution to the field."

Her body tensed, but she offered me a curt smile. "I write about who I want to write about. Period."

I could tell that she was holding back, and that cutting through her steel exterior would be as challenging as slicing through a rock-hard loaf of stale bread.

The photographer finished his photo shoot and packed up his camera. "I've got a lot to go on here," he said to Sandi. "Let me take a look at these on my laptop and touch them up a little. Then you can have a look, and if you don't like them we'll do another shoot before we fly out tonight."

Sandi brushed him off. "Fine, fine, but make it quick. We don't have all day."

Giving me a look as if to say "good luck," the photographer left with his gear. Sandi tilted her head to one side and stared at my cake. "You really do know your piping. I have to say, I haven't been this impressed with piping work for a long time."

"Thanks." I felt my cheeks warm at her compliment.

She focused her dartlike eyes on me. "Oh, I see. It's all clear now."

"What's all clear?"

"Why you're asking about the story I'm running on Evan."

"I thought you said you weren't running a story on him?"

"Well, I am." Her eyes were cold. "It's not a feature he would have liked, so it's probably for the best that he met such a tragic death."

"I don't understand."

"Ah, but I do. You're worried that I'm going to write a scathing review of Torte just like I did about Confections Couture. Let me assure you that you have nothing to worry about. You have hit your stride. Your cakes on the cover of *Sweetened* are going to make you a rapidly rising star in the world of pastry." She pointed a perfectly manicured finger at me. "A word of advice, though; be ready for what's about to happen. Your name is going to be spoken in every household across the country."

"I don't know about that." I swallowed. She had to be exaggerating. Maybe a cover feature in *Sweetened* was a bad idea. I wanted to grow Torte, but I didn't want to be inundated with calls from all over, especially when we weren't in a position to fill orders from outside of Ashland.

"I can make a chef and I can break a chef. Consider yourself fortunate that I've fallen for your charming designs. Mark my words, a month from now you can name your place and your price. Restaurants are going to be knocking down your door with offers. I suggest that you hold on tight and get ready for the ride of your life."

"But I . . ." I started to protest but Sandi waved her finger at me.

"Must go. I have to keep my eye on that man. I don't know how many times I've told him to stop with the soft focus. This is not 1980."

Without another word she went after the photographer. I couldn't believe how dismissive she'd been about Evan. Her words sent a shiver through my body. She could make a chef and break a chef. The implication of that reverberated through me. What if she had tried to "break" Evan through a bad review and decided to take it one step farther?

Sandi had risen to the top of my suspects list, and she had me regretting that I had agreed to a feature story. I was just getting settled in in Ashland, and I didn't want anything to do with being in the spotlight.

Chapter Twenty-two

When Mom arrived at our booth, she could tell that I was distracted. "You look stressed. Did you stay up too late last night?"

My cheeks felt hot as I shook my head and gave her a half-truth. "No. I came in early this morning to make the tasting samples." I omitted telling her about my dinner with Thomas. "The plaza was flooding."

"That's what Doug said. Is Torte okay?"

"It's fine." I watched as she struggled to unbutton her coat. "What about you? How are you feeling?"

"I'm fine, honey." She met my inquisitive gaze. "Really. My hands are cold, that's all." Tugging off her coat, she gave me a smile. "What's the scoop with the ovens? We're still on for them to arrive later this afternoon?"

"Yep. They e-mailed confirmation last night. Three o'clock."

"That should be great timing as things close up here. And you gave the kids the morning off?"

"Exactly. I told them to be in by two. I figure one of us can be down there and one of us can pack up here."

She leafed through our vendor packet. "The fest ends at four, but they're going to announce the award winners at three. You won't want to miss that."

I rolled my eyes. "Awards or ovens. I'm excited about ovens!"

"Oh, Juliet, you are your father's daughter. How many people your age would be excited about ovens?"

"I can think of a few pastry chefs who would share my excitement." I pretended to be defensive.

"Right." Mom grinned. "Don't let me keep you from your new toys. I'll stay here for the award announcements and to hand out any last samples. You go oversee the oven installation and then we can go out for a celebratory dinner tonight. I've already invited Doug and Thomas. I hope that's okay."

"Great." I busied myself with rearranging the handful of fliers we had left. Just great, I thought. Thomas wasn't on the top of my list of people whom I wanted to celebrate with tonight.

Mom didn't pick up on my tone, and the first guest arrived asking for a taste of our chocolate pasta. I tried not to dwell on how awkward things might be with Thomas as I drizzled warm chocolate sauce over the noodles. It wasn't my fault after all; if things were weird between us, that was on Thomas.

The crowd seemed thinner on the final day of the chocolate celebration. We had a steady stream of people stopping for tastes and to check out our cake display, but not the mob we had experienced yesterday. I kept watch on Mom as we worked side by side. She looked fine, but

I did notice her stretching her fingers under the table between handing out samples.

Around noon I heard the familiar ring of Lance's voice. "Darling, hello!" He pranced toward us wearing a three-piece chocolate-brown suit. "Do you like?" He posed. "I dressed for the occasion. Chocolate."

Mom kissed him on both cheeks. "Lance, you win my vote for best dressed in Ashland every day."

He returned her kisses and compliment. "Helen, you win my vote for most gracious. I tell everyone my other Helen has nothing on you."

"Your other Helen?" I asked.

"Helen Mirren, of course." Lance caught Mom's eye and gave her an exasperated look. "She has been at sea way too long, hasn't she?"

Mom laughed.

"Wait, you know Helen Mirren?"

Lance adjusted his dark chocolate tie. "Yes, darling. She and I did a production at the Globe years ago. She's absolutely lovely, but not quite as lovely as your mother."

"You're going to make me blush," Mom said. "Please don't stop, though."

Lance threw his head back and chuckled. "Never, Helen. Never." He put his hand to my cheek. "You definitely inherited this luscious skin from your mother."

I was used to Lance's over-the-top displays, but a young family walked up behind him and gave me a funny look. "Don't mind him, he doesn't bite," I joked.

Lance raised one eyebrow. "Depends on who's on the menu."

I punched him in the shoulder and held out a tray of

marzipans to the family. "Don't pay any attention to him. He's always dramatic."

"Drama is my business, darling." He held up a canvas bag with the OSF logo on it. "Speaking of drama, how do you feel about a little lunch?"

"How is lunch dramatic?"

He winked. "Just wait until you see what I have in store. You don't mind if I steal your darling daughter away for a few minutes, do you, Helen?"

Mom shook her head. "Not at all. She's all yours."

"But I haven't forgotten about you either." Lance removed a cardboard box from the bag and handed it to Mom. "Lunch is served."

"Thank you. You didn't need to do that," Mom protested.

"Tsk-tsk. It's nothing. You've been feeding me and the entire town for decades. The least I can do is bring you a token of my thanks while your kitchen is down."

Mom kissed him again. "Well, thank you. I appreciate it."

Lance extended his arm to me. "Shall we?"

I gave Mom a fleeting glance. Her face glowed with delight as she opened the lunch that Lance had delivered.

"Where are we going?" I asked Lance.

"Patience, patience. I've reserved the perfect spot for our tête-à-tête."

Arguing with him was futile. When Lance was on a mission like this there was no pushing him. He enjoyed the buildup of suspense too much. He guided me to the front lobby of the hotel and pointed to two plush wing chairs strategically placed in front of a marble fireplace.

"Ta-da! What do you think?"

"About what?"

"About this," he said with an exasperated sigh as he waved his hand in the direction of the fireplace. "I'll have you know that I had to work my magic to shoo away an elderly couple who appeared ready to camp out in front of the fireplace until their dying days."

"You kicked out an elderly couple?"

"Don't make it sound so ghastly. I offered them a backstage tour for their seats. I prefer to dine surrounded by beauty and ambiance, can you blame me?"

I considered telling him that I could blame him. I would have been just as content to eat lunch on one of the benches outside of the ballroom, but I knew that resisting his production would only fuel him on. "It is beautiful," I agreed, taking a seat in one of the soft chairs. "Doesn't it remind you of an Agatha Christie production?"

"I was thinking *Casablanca*."

A real wood fire crackled and popped behind an ornate silvery grate. Lance scooted his chair closer to mine and yanked a cloth napkin from his bag in one fluid motion. Flicking it in the air like a silk scarf that magicians use, he twirled it and placed it on my lap.

"Wow, that was impressive."

Lance cleared his throat. "I'm not done."

I threw my hands up in surrender. "Got it. Sorry."

He then proceeded to produce china with a delicate fleur-de-lis pattern and silverware.

"What's the occasion?" I asked, positioning the fancy plate on my lap.

Lance put his finger to his lips. "Just wait." He removed a bottle of champagne and two fluted glasses. As if on command, a hotel staff member appeared with a silver bucket of ice and uncorked the bottle of champagne.

"What is going on?" I repeated.

The staff member pulled a small end table between our chairs and set the bucket of champagne and bubbling glasses on it. Lance nodded his approval and the staff member scurried away. Raising his flute, he waited for me to raise mine, and then clinked our glasses.

"Darling, a toast is in order."

"A toast to what?"

"To you, of course." Lance raised his flute an inch higher and then took a sip of the champagne.

I watched the bubbles rise to the top of my glass. The champagne was a golden color with a peach scent. Effervescence hit my palate as I took a drink. "Why to me?"

"Rumor has it that you've scored the coveted cover of *Sweetened* magazine. Darling, that is a major coup."

The fizzy champagne had a sugary and fruity taste. I savored a sip as I studied Lance's face. He had a devilish grin as he watched my reaction. "How did you hear that?"

"Please. I have my sources."

"Your sources must work around the clock."

"Nonsense. Let's just say that my sources are everywhere." His eyes darted from side to side in a playful manner.

"Thanks for the celebratory toast, but to be honest with you I'm not sure how I feel about the feature. Sandi made it sound like once the magazine hits the shelves that I'm going to be inundated by job offers."

Lance topped off his glass. "You are. Absolutely. In fact, since you're gutting the kitchen you might consider adding a second phone line now."

"But I don't want job offers or a second phone line. I'm happy with the way things are at Torte. I don't want things to change."

Sipping his champagne with his pinkie in the air, Lance paused and considered my words. "That is the rub, isn't it?"

"What do you mean?"

"You come home in search of a change—a climactic change at that—you have it and now you don't want it."

"That doesn't even make sense."

"Of course it does, darling." Lance rested his glass on the table and removed two cardboard containers from his bag. "Lunch?"

"Sure. I'm starving." I opened the box and was immediately overcome by the intoxicating smell of seared beef and spices. Lance had brought us gyros wrapped in grilled pita bread and topped with tzatziki sauce, fresh tomatoes, feta, and grilled onions. The thick warm pitas had been slightly charred on the grill. I started to take a bite, but Lance grabbed my arm.

"Uh-uh, on your plate, darling. Let's continue our civilized lunch. To-go containers are so below our standards."

The gyro smelled so good that I would have eaten it

off the floor, but I agreed to Lance's request and tossed the cardboard container back in the bag. "Better?"

"Perfect. Go ahead. Eat." He circled his hand.

I bit into the steaming sandwich and my mouth practically cheered with pleasure. The meat had been sliced into thin strips and seasoned with paprika and maybe a hint of something slightly sweet like cinnamon or nutmeg. The balance of the sweet grilled onions with the salty cheese and acidic tomatoes was heavenly.

"This is so good," I said between bites.

Lance nodded. "I know. I have a guy."

"You have a guy?" I laughed. "A gyro guy?"

"Yes." Lance smirked. "Why, of course I have a gyro guy. Doesn't everyone?"

"Are you keeping him secret? Is he hiding out in the bowels of the theater or something?"

"Don't be so crass, Juliet. Anthony happens to be selective about his clients."

"Wait, Anthony as in the guy who runs the gyro cart up by campus?"

Lance scoffed. "I'm not at liberty to divulge my sources."

"Your gyro sources."

He couldn't maintain his composure and broke into a smile. "Perhaps."

I laughed and took another bite. "Well, tell your source that his gyro is absolutely delicious."

Lance raised his champagne flute. "Consider it done."

We devoured the savory gyros and drank our champagne as the fire's flames danced in front of us. I had to credit Lance with setting up a refined spontaneous lunch.

"I do have a juicy piece of news for you, but first I want you to dish on what happened with that little lovesick puppy-dog police officer friend of yours last night," Lance said, offering to refill my glass. I waved him off. Too much champagne and my head would be spinning, which wouldn't be good for overseeing the oven installation.

"What do you mean?" I gulped. How did Lance know about Thomas? He really wasn't kidding about having sources everywhere. I knew there was no way that Thomas would have said anything.

"Don't play coy with me. I saw you two sneaking off to your apartment together last night."

Great. I took a deep breath and carefully chose my words. Lance had a strange way of reading my tone and body language. It was probably due to all of the years that he'd spent in the theater. It was his job as artistic director to make playwrights' words come to life and to understand the nuances of speech—the ticks and pauses or movements—that said as much as the actual words.

"We weren't sneaking. We had dinner, that's all."

"And?"

"And what?"

Lance dabbed his chin with his napkin. "And he proclaimed his love for you?"

My mouth hung open. "How did you know?"

He shook his head. "The man has been following you around town since you returned home, offering you tokens of his affection in the form of flowers and drinking more coffee than any one human ever should. He's absolutely transparent."

I placed my empty plate on the table and rubbed my temples. "Do you really think so?"

Lance gave me a pained smile. "I'm afraid so."

"Is everyone talking about us?"

He hesitated for a brief second. "Not *everyone.*"

"Great." I ran my fingers through my hair.

Lance's voice turned compassionate. He lost his affected tone. "Don't worry about it. If anyone should be worried, it's Thomas. You're not chasing after him. He's chasing after you."

I felt slightly relieved at his perspective, but the last thing I wanted was to be the topic of gossip around town.

"Was it terrible?"

"Last night?"

Lance nodded.

"I don't know. I mean the thing is we've been friends forever. I'm so comfortable around him and I don't want that to change. Honestly, I don't think he's really in love with me. I think he's in love with the idea of being in love with me—some old memory of me. Not who I am now."

Shaking his head, Lance sighed and patted my knee. "Oh, darling, don't you wish."

"No, I'm serious. I get it. We grew up together and we had a great and innocent relationship. I think that's what he's holding on to."

"Hmm. Could be." Lance didn't sound convinced. "Doubtful, but I suppose there's an outside sliver of possibility there."

I didn't respond to that. "I just don't want things to be awkward between us."

"Then don't let them." Lance's matter-of-fact response struck a chord. "My advice is to continue onward as if nothing was ever said."

"That's not a bad idea, actually."

"I know. I'm brilliant. I keep reminding you of this fact, yet you ignore it."

"Thanks, Lance," I said with sincerity. "For lunch and for listening. It's helpful."

He waved me off and returned to his theater persona. "Wait, I'm not done with you yet. We haven't gotten to the juiciest piece of information."

Talking about Thomas had distracted me. "Right." I sat up. "What's your news?"

"It's about our New York diva, Sandi Kramer."

"What about her?"

Lance checked around us and then lowered his voice. "My sources tell me that Sandi had planned to run a scathing review of Confections Couture."

"I know," I blurted out without thinking.

"You know?" Lance gasped. "Have you been holding out on me? I thought we were a team."

"We are. I just found out."

"Well, did you know that she was bribing him?"

"What? No. How was she bribing him?"

Lance gave me a smug smile and folded his arms across his chest. "I have it on good authority that Ms. Kramer offered to kill the story if Evan paid up."

"Paid up?"

"Mmm-hmm." Lance ran his fingers along his clean-shaven chin. He had shaved off his goatee, and I was still getting used to him without facial hair. "In exchange for running a full-page color ad to the tune of one hundred and twenty-five thousand dollars, Sandi would shred the nasty review."

"Is that even legal?"

"Is anything in business legal?"

"So if Evan paid for the ad then Sandi wouldn't write the review, but if he didn't she would run it? That doesn't make sense, though. Wouldn't that give Evan a motive to kill her, not the other way around?"

Lance took a final sip of champagne and began to pack up our lunch dishes. "Money is always a motive for murder. Who knows? Perhaps Evan was planning to sound the whistle on Sandi's attempts at bribery. Forcing paid features wouldn't reflect well on the magazine. It could ruin her."

He had a point. I helped him pack up, and thanked him again for a fantastic lunch. "Don't give it a thought, it was my pleasure. But don't hold out on me. I want a full update on what you learn—if anything—today. Deal?"

"Deal," I promised.

Lance kissed both of my cheeks and strolled out of the hotel. My head spun, and not from drinking too much champagne, as I made my way back to the ballroom. Sandi had attempted to bribe Evan—for a lot of cash. The thing I couldn't figure out was why, and whether she had any motive in Evan's murder.

Chapter Twenty-three

"How was Lance?" Mom asked, giving me a knowing smile.

"As dramatic as ever," I replied. "You know Lance."

"Yes, I do." Mom gave each of the sauces a quick stir. "Lance appreciates your friendship. He needs a friend like you."

"Mom, Lance is friends with *everyone* in town."

She wrinkled her brow. "On the surface maybe, but being artistic director must be a lonely job sometimes."

I stretched a pair of latex gloves over my fingers. "Lonely? Everywhere we go people clamor to get a minute with Lance. He has groupies all over town."

"Exactly." Mom smiled knowingly. "Groupies aren't friends. It must be hard to always have to be 'on' and to know that everywhere he goes someone wants something from him."

"You're right. I guess I never thought of it like that."

Mom tasted the white chocolate sauce with the tip of her pinkie. "That's why he's lucky to have you. You don't want or need anything from him. That's the best kind of friend. I'm glad that the two of you have found each other."

"Am I that sad?" I laughed. "You make me sound like I'm desperate and friendless."

Mom swatted my hip with a hand towel. "Hardly. I didn't say anything of the sort. I'm glad you and Lance are friends. I think it's a good friendship for both of you." She rolled up the sleeve of her buttery turtleneck and tapped her watch. "It's almost oven time."

"Is it really?"

She nodded. "You should probably think about heading down to Torte soon."

"I feel like I've been zero help today."

"Hardly." She pointed to the tasting table. "Without your help we wouldn't have had anything to serve people this morning. It's been much slower today. Don't worry about me."

"New ovens!" I couldn't contain my excitement. Wrapping her in a hug, I squeezed her tight.

"I know. I can't wait to see it all put back together. This has been a long time coming. I was telling Doug that the last time we had an upgrade to the bakeshop like this was before your dad died."

"He would be so proud of what you've built, Mom."

Her eyes misted. "Of what *we've* built."

I kissed her on the top of the head. "What we're building. Onward."

At that moment I looked up and noticed that Sandi Kramer was standing at Howard's Sea Salt booth talking to Howard. Neither of them appeared to be enjoying their conversation.

"Hey, what do you know about *Sweetened*?" I asked Mom.

Mom shrugged. "Not much, other than what everyone knows—that it's the magazine in the world of pastry. Why?"

"No reason. She's going to feature Torte on the cover, which I guess is a good thing, but I get a weird vibe from her."

"Weird in what way?" Mom sounded concerned.

"I don't know. It's probably her harsh exterior, but I get the feeling that she likes to make and break careers. I don't want to be on the breaking end of that, but honestly, I'm not sure I want to be on the making end of it either. Sandi said we would be inundated with orders from all around the country when the feature goes live. We're not ready for that."

Mom looked thoughtful. "That could be true, but I don't think that *Sweetened*'s circulation is what it used to be."

"Really?" I watched Sandi lean closer to Howard and say something in his ear. From my vantage point I couldn't tell what she was saying, but by Howard's reaction I could tell that he wasn't pleased with her words. He jerked away from her and pointed to the doors, motioning for her to leave. Sandi held her ground. She folded her arms across her chest and continued her rant.

"Print magazines are struggling to stay relevant and current," Mom said, forcing me to tear my gaze away from Sandi and Howard. "Think of how many major publications have gone under or at least stopped producing print copies in favor of going online."

Mom was right. A number of my favorite foodie magazines had gone digital in recent years.

"According to what I've heard, *Sweetened* is in the same position. I think being on the cover will be great, but I don't think we need to worry about it skyrocketing us into a position as a leader in pastry either."

"You've heard that *Sweetened* is in danger of folding?" That would give Sandi a motive for murder. What if she needed Evan's cash to keep the magazine afloat? Maybe he refused and Sandi exacted her revenge.

"Nothing concrete, but there's been talk around town that the Chocolate Fest might be the magazine's last feature," Mom replied, giving me an inquisitive look. "Why are you so interested in *Sweetened*?"

"No reason," I lied. Grabbing my bag, I looped it over my shoulder. "I better get going. See you later for the big reveal!" I hurried away before Mom could ask me anything more. On my way to the front of the ballroom I stopped at Howard's booth. Sandi was gone. I wondered where she had disappeared to, and what she and Howard were discussing. Did he have the same suspicion that I did? Maybe he had accused Sandi of being involved in Evan's death.

"Sample?" Howard grunted without looking up as I passed his booth.

"I'm on my way out," I said, but then I stopped. My curiosity was piqued. Whether Howard would divulge anything to me was a long shot, but I had a few minutes before I needed to be at the bakeshop; it was worth a try. "Actually, on second thought, sure. I'll have a taste for the road."

Howard sliced a two-inch round chocolate truffle that

was topped with gorgeous red berries. "This is my Belgian chocolate truffle with pink peppercorn. Pretty simple recipe—butter, buttermilk, and pink peppercorn. That's going to give it a kick of spicy nutty flavor."

A glass bowl filled with the colorful beadlike berries sat in front of the truffles. I was familiar with pink peppercorns, which was a misnomer—the berry didn't belong in the peppercorn family. They were grown in Brazil and imported into the United States. The bright exotic berries had come onto the food scene in the 1980s and had become a favorite in fancy food shops and with chefs. I hadn't seen the fragrant and sweet berries paired with chocolate. Usually, they appeared in bottles of high-end vinegars and mustards.

I took the piece of truffle that Howard offered me. The Belgian chocolate was creamy with a nice tang from the buttermilk. The aromatic berries gave the truffle a sweet and citrusy finish. "This is delicious," I said to Howard.

"Thanks. I usually stick with salt, but I'm expanding my spice line to include imports like the peppercorns."

"I see why," I said, motioning to the bowl of berries. "May I?"

Howard shrugged. "Suit yourself."

I picked up the bowl and smelled the berries. I remember hearing something about them from a chef on the cruise ship, but what was it? A recipe? A special way to prepare them? I couldn't remember, but I knew it would come back to me.

"Is Sandi going to do a feature on your spice line for *Sweetened*?" I asked, hoping that Howard would take the bait.

"What?"

"I noticed that Sandi was talking to you a while ago; I wondered if she was going to do a write-up on your spice line."

"No." Howard shook his head and frowned. "That woman is a nightmare."

"Really, why?" I couldn't believe he was opening up so easily.

"Haven't you seen her clicking around in those fancy shoes? She thinks that because she's from New York and publishes a magazine that she's better than us little folk."

"Little folk, did she say that?"

"No, but I caught her drift. I don't want anything to do with that magazine of hers. It's pretentious and snobby. I do better with the sea."

"I feel you on that. By the way, I really enjoyed your presentation yesterday. The photos of the process of procuring salt from the sea were incredible. If you're ever up for a tagalong, I'd love to come watch you and your team in action sometime. I love getting firsthand experiences like that."

Howard gave me a slow smile. "You bet, but only because you're Helen's girl. Your mom and I go way back."

A group of people approached the booth, so I thanked Howard for the truffle and told him I would reach out about joining him on a sea salt excursion once the fest was over. My mind tried to process everything I'd learned as I walked to Torte. Sandi Kramer was up to something, that was certain. If she was in danger of losing the magazine that she'd spent decades building that could be a motive for murder. I still wondered what she and Howard had been arguing about. There was obviously no love lost between them, but why?

The pink peppercorn recipe was nagging me too. Once we had Torte put back together, I was going to have to dig through my stack of recipes from the ship and see if I could find it. The berries were so beautiful and had such a nice pop of heat. I was excited to experiment with them, but for the moment I was on a singular mission—new ovens!

Chapter Twenty-four

When I arrived at the bakeshop, Stephanie, Sterling, and Andy were all standing around the island drinking coffee.

"What's going on here, coffee break?" I teased.

"Hey, boss," Andy said, holding a ceramic mug up. "You're right on time. I told these two that you could probably smell the coffee brewing from the hotel."

"If it's your coffee, that's true." Hanging my coat on the back of a chair, I joined them in the kitchen. "Please tell me that you saved me some."

Andy placed his cup on the island and rolled his eyes at Sterling. "I told you so."

"You called it." Sterling stepped to the side and revealed a carafe of French press brewing on the countertop. "Andy wanted to start a pool to see how long it would take you to ask for a cup of coffee."

"My money was on two seconds." Andy winked.

"Am I that bad?" I asked, reaching for a cup.

"Yep," Andy and Sterling said in unison.

"Stephanie, a little help?" I pleaded.

Stephanie curled her top lip, which was coated in a purple lipstick that matched her violet hair. "You have a problem. You should get some help."

"Not you too?" I sighed and poured myself a cup of the French press. "I admit that I might have a slight tendency to drink too much coffee, but I don't care. I'm a pastry chef and I work in a bakeshop where we feature artisanal coffee, therefore it's my responsibility to our customers to make sure that I sample all our offerings, so we can bring them only the very best."

"You go ahead and tell yourself that story," Sterling said.

"Ouch." I pretended to stab myself in the heart and then took a big sip of the dark brew. "That's fine. I'll deal with harassment from my staff if it means I get this all to myself."

Andy adjusted the knit ski cap on his head. His shaggy auburn hair stuck out from the sides. "Hold up, you have to share. No one said anything about hoarding all the coffee."

"I could pull rank, you know? If we were on the ship, you would be my subordinates and I'd send you down to the bowels and make you fetch me a fresh scone to go with my coffee."

They all cracked up.

"Right, like that ever happened," Andy said. He turned to Sterling. "Can you imagine her ordering staff around? Now that is something I'd like to see."

"Hey, I'll have you know I ran a tight ship."

"Sure you did," Andy teased.

Sterling helped himself to a refill and offered the carafe to Stephanie. She declined.

"Any word from the installers yet?" I asked.

Stephanie slid a file across the counter to me. "Nope, but here's the final inventory list. We finished everything you asked."

I thumbed through the file. "This is great. Thanks for all of your hard work. Mom and I want to treat you to a celebratory dinner tonight."

"You don't have to do that, but if you want to I won't turn down a free meal." Andy rubbed his belly.

"Consider it one of the perks of the job," I said. "Let me grab the point-of-sale system. Hang on one sec." I headed for the office and came back with a twelve-by-twelve box that contained everything we needed for our new payment system. I couldn't believe how user-friendly and cost-effective the system was. The mobile system would allow us to swipe payments on a tablet or smartphone. We purchased an upgrade that included inventory management, kitchen ticketing, online ordering, and customer feedback.

I walked the team through a quick tutorial and tasked them with uploading the inventory lists and menus.

The delivery truck pulled up to the curb. We all raced to the windows to watch them unload the ovens. Andy and Sterling went out to help while Stephanie and I moved two tables in the front to clear a direct path to the kitchen. The installers hauled in two large crates and a toolbox. One of them had thick cable wrapped around his shoulder and wire cutters tucked into his back pocket.

"Are you Jules?" he asked, handing me an invoice. "You need to sign here, and then we'll get started removing the old equipment first."

I reviewed the order and signed the paperwork. "Everything looks good. Do you need anything from me and my team?"

"Nothing. We've got it under control. It should take us a couple hours and we'll be out of your hair."

"You don't need any extra muscles?" I pointed to Sterling and Andy.

"Nope." He patted his coworker's back. "Got all the muscle we need here."

"Great. The kitchen is all yours. I'll be in the office if you need me." I turned to Andy, Sterling, and Stephanie. "Go ahead and get started with entering the inventory and menus. I'm going to do the full tutorial. The beauty of the system is that we can have multiple devices connected, but you know that I'm not very tech savvy, so any input you have is welcome."

"We'll all help, Jules," Sterling said, taking the box from me.

I took my coffee into the office to go over the tutorial on my new tablet. The sound of hammers and drills reverberated through the bakeshop and made the floor beneath me vibrate. Scanning each item on the inventory sheet, I powered up the new tablet and began scrolling through our new ordering system. An automatic alert would pop up when we were running low on an item. Immediately, three alerts warned that we needed to order cinnamon, chocolate, and eggs soon.

The system was sleek and easy to use. It was going to save us hours of time. Next, I reviewed the instructions for our new point-of-sale system. It seemed equally simple. Sterling had already uploaded our menu, and set up categories for coffee, lunch, and pastry specials, as well as a custom order form and a ticketing system for our Sunday suppers. Torte was finally going to be up-to-date with the latest technology. I had a feeling our customers were going to appreciate the new system as well. Now they would be able to pay with their debit and credit cards with one swipe, or even by creating a Torte account that would flag them when they walked in the front door. We would simply click on their name and their order would be charged wirelessly.

I peered out into the dining room where Sterling, Stephanie, and Andy were huddled together at a grouping of tables that they had pushed together. There were inventory sheets spread out and Stephanie named each item as Sterling entered it on the tablet, and Andy doubled-checked it on his paper copy.

"You guys are lightning fast," I said, stretching. "I hadn't even gotten halfway through the demo when I got an alert that we're low on a few things."

"Technology, Jules." Sterling's penetrating blue eyes flashed. "Welcome to the new century."

"I know, I know, I'm hopeless." There was a knock on the front door. The owner of the vintage store waved at me. I walked over and let her in. Mom had arranged for her to come get the old cash register. She rolled in a hand truck. "Hi, Juliet, I hear I'm going to take this old clunker off your hands."

"Yes, you are the lucky winner of one very old cash register." I helped her lift it. It felt like it weighed a ton.

"Someone is going to snatch this up right away."

"Really? You think?"

"I guarantee it. They don't make them like this any-more," she said, as we both had to use all of our arm strength to position the register on the hand truck. Andy and Sterling jumped to help us lift the timeworn register.

"Because they make them like this now." I grinned and held up the thin tablet.

"You make an excellent point. Good thing I brought wheels." She tugged on the hand truck. "I told your mom that I would let her know when it sells and get you a commission check."

"Honestly, taking it off our hands is all I need."

"Just wait. You might be surprised what people will pay for vintage finds. I'll let you know when it sells."

I thanked her and watched her use both hands to cart the hand truck up the street. I also noticed Richard Lord walking in my direction. He was the last person I was in the mood to see. Richard runs the Merry Windsor, a Shakespearean-themed hotel, across the plaza. He appointed himself downtown's official king decades ago and has been desperately trying to rule his subjects ever since. Most of us have learned to ignore his ridiculous commands and his tendency to wear the most unflattering golf outfits. He had taken a special dislike to me since I'd returned home, in part because I had thwarted his attempt to take advantage of Mom's kindhearted nature and execute a hostile takeover of Torte. Fortunately, he failed, but he'd held it against me ever since.

The feeling was mutual. Richard Lord was off-putting and his self-important attitude was tiring. He caught my eye as he lumbered past Torte's front windows, but to my surprise he didn't stop at the front door, but rather turned at the corner in the direction of the basement property. What was he doing?

I checked in with the installers to make sure they

were still doing well and told the team I would be right back.

"We're almost done," Sterling replied, stacking the last inventory sheet. "Do you need anything else?"

"No." I grabbed my coat. "You all are amazing, see you for dinner tonight!" I ducked outside and peered around the corner. Sure enough, Richard stood at the top of the stairs to the basement entrance. He waited for a few minutes, looking impatient. Then a man in a cheap business suit appeared from the river walk.

"Hope you weren't waiting long, Richard. I got held up by some of the flooding up the hill."

"I have been waiting long, and I don't appreciate you wasting my valuable time," he grunted. His response summed him up perfectly. He couldn't have been waiting for more than two minutes, and his "valuable" time was usually spent ordering his staff around.

The man in the suit cleared his throat and sounded apologetic. "Understood. Here are all the specs—it needs work but could be a great space with the right owner. I have the key to the property if you want to come on down; we can have a look." They disappeared down the steps.

Richard Lord was interested in leasing the basement? There was no way I was going to let that happen. Flooding issues or not, Richard Lord could not lease part of Torte's building.

Chapter Twenty-five

I jogged back inside and went straight for my cell phone. Without a moment of hesitation, I punched in Rosalind's number. She picked up on the second ring.

"Rosalind, it's Jules. Let's do it!"

"You mean the property?"

"Yes! We want it."

"That's wonderful, but why the change of heart? I was under the impression after you saw the water damage the other day that you weren't sure that you were interested in moving forward."

"I wasn't, but now I am."

Her excitement came through on the line. "Wonderful. Absolutely wonderful. I'll submit the final application and let you know as soon as the committee makes its decision."

I thanked her and hung up. A wave of regret washed over me for not consulting Mom. While she had said it was ultimately my decision, we were a team and I had acted rashly. Hopefully, Mom would definitely agree with me that we couldn't let Richard Lord get his greedy hands on the property.

"Have a minute?" the installer called from the kitchen.

"Sure," I replied, sticking my phone back in my purse and hurrying to the kitchen. The ovens were installed and gleamed under the bright overhead lights. My throat caught, and I had to blink back a tear. Between the freshly painted walls, rearranged freestanding shelves, and the shiny ovens, the kitchen looked brand-new. "Wow! That was fast."

The installer tucked a pencil behind his ear. "Yeah, this was an easy job. I want to walk you through maintenance and everything before we take off." He proceeded to show me all of the additional features the ovens offered, like the adjustable and removable chrome-plated racks and a switch that automatically turned the fan and heating element off when the doors were opened. In addition to having functional ovens, the new models would fire up much more quickly than our old machines.

Once I was up to speed on all the bells and whistles, the installers gave me their card—the ovens were under warranty so on the off chance that anything went wrong, they would come out and make any necessary repairs. After they left I did a dance of joy around the island and touched all the buttons on the ovens. I couldn't wait to take them for a test-drive, but I needed to get back to Ashland Springs and help Mom pack up our booth. I knew there was no way I was sleeping tonight, so after dinner I planned to come back and try out the ovens before the Monday rush.

When I returned to the Chocolate Fest the organizers had already begun awarding winners in each category.

Mom waved me over and squeezed my arm. "How did it go?"

"They are in and ready for business."

"That was fast."

"I think those were my exact words to the guys who did the installation."

She started to ask me something else, but Chef Garrison spoke to the crowd. "Thank you all for making this the most successful Chocolate Festival in recent memory. Before we get to the winners—which I know you're all waiting to hear—I want to share some numbers with you." He took an index card that one of the other organizers handed him. "We had over three thousand people through the doors this year."

The crowd gasped.

He nodded enthusiastically. "That's right. Give yourselves a round of applause."

Everyone clapped. I spotted Bethany and Carter standing shoulder to shoulder near the Confections Couture booth. She gave me a friendly wave. Carter looked from her to me and then elbowed her in the waist. She dropped her hand and whipped her head toward the stage. That was odd. I wondered what was going on with the two of them, but Chef Garrison was revving up the crowd.

"Do you want to know how that equates to chocolate?" He waited for the crowd to settle down before continuing. "The chocolate numbers are pretty impressive too. By our count over one thousand pounds of chocolate were served this weekend. That's two and half million calories in chocolate."

"Time to get back to my morning runs," I whispered to Mom. "I think I sampled at least a pound on my own."

"Me too." Mom pinched her narrow waist.

"Now, what you've all been waiting for," Chef Garrison said, holding up a large envelope. "The results!" He ripped open the envelope and proceeded to announce the winners of the secondary awards. After each vendor took their chocolate trophies, he held up two envelopes. "And, for our final two awards. First, the People's Choice award goes to . . ." He slowly opened the envelope, peeked inside, and then announced, "Torte!"

Mom looked at me in shock. Her eyes were wide. "We won? Did he really just say Torte?"

"Yes!" I nodded. "Go, go up there," I said, pushing her toward the stage.

She beamed as she accepted the People's Choice award and started to leave, when Chef Garrison stopped her. "Wait a minute. We'll want to get a photo with you and the winner of the Best in Show." Mom caught my eye and beamed with delight as she cradled the trophy in her arms. I was thrilled for her; no one deserved recognition for their work more than Mom.

"Without any further delay, it is my pleasure to announce that this year's Best in Show winner is, drum roll, please . . ." Chef Garrison made a drumming sound on the podium before opening the last envelope. He looked at the certificate and then to Mom. "Torte!"

Mom's jaw dropped. I jumped up and down and cheered as loud as I could while the crowd applauded around me. Chef Garrison hugged her and a photographer snapped photos of her. We had won Best in Show and the People's Choice award. I couldn't believe it but soaked up every second of watching Mom have her moment of glory on the stage. People congratulated us as Mom and I walked in a daze back to our booth.

"We won? We really won? I still can't believe it." Mom handed me the chocolate trophies. "You are the one who should have gone up on stage to take these."

"No way. That was all for you. You've built Torte and made it is what is today. Torte wouldn't even exist if it weren't for you."

Mom grabbed me into a hug and we danced around the booth. "We won!" she finally squealed when she released me. "And we won because of *you*—don't even try to sneak out of taking credit."

Photographers from the Ashland and Medford newspapers snapped our picture, asking us each to hold one of the trophies and pose behind our wedding cake display. I directed their questions to Mom and stayed back, forcing her to answer. After our mini media blitz, the organizers came by to offer their congratulations again and informed us that the ballroom was being used for an evening wedding.

"Things went longer than we expected, and we need to set up for the wedding immediately. Go ahead and take anything you can now," she said. "Our maintenance team will take care of the rest. I've assigned one staff member to each vendor. All vendor items will be boxed and waiting for you in the storage area." She pointed to a team of staff members already tearing down the Chocolate Fest banners and wheeling in carts to stack tables and chairs. "The storage area is through the back doors and down the hall. If you want to access it from the alley, just stop by the reception desk and they'll give you a temporary key. You can come back this evening or tomorrow—whatever is most convenient for you."

"Guess we're off the hook from packing up." Mom grinned and stacked the empty pots of sauces in a cardboard box.

"We don't have that much stuff. All of our samples are gone. The big issue is going to be the wedding cakes. I can take one now, but we'll have to come back for the others."

"Leave them in the cake boxes. I think they'll be fine. Plus, this means we can go see Torte and have a double celebration tonight—new ovens and winners of the Chocolate Fest."

Grabbing as many supplies as we could, we packed one large cardboard box and the tiered cake. We left the rest for the hotel staff and headed out through a frenzy of activity. Half of the vendor tables near the front of the ballroom had already been disassembled and loaded onto carts. One staff member vacuumed while two others arranged round tables.

"They aren't wasting any time," Mom commented.

"I'm surprised that they would schedule events back-to-back like that. We weren't that late, were we?" I answered my own question as we stepped outside into darkness. "Maybe we were that late, what time is it?"

Mom hoisted the box of supplies. "I can't see my watch, but it has to be after five, maybe even six. We did go long. I wonder why they let that happen."

"Yeah, weird." I balanced the cake box as we walked to the bakeshop. "Mom, there's something I have to tell you."

"Uh-oh, that doesn't sound good."

"It's not bad, at least I hope you won't think it's bad."

She stopped and looked me straight in the eye. "Did something go wrong with the ovens? I thought you said installation was a breeze."

"No, it's not the ovens. Just wait, you'll see in a minute—they are amazing. I can't wait to test them out tonight. No, it's about the basement property."

"Okay." Mom gave me an expectant look.

"I called Rosalind this afternoon and told her that we want it."

"You did?"

I grimaced. "Are you mad? I didn't mean to do it without talking to you one more time, but I found out that Richard Lord is trying to get his hands on the space. I couldn't stomach the thought of having him anywhere near Torte, and before I even realized what I was doing I was dialing Rosalind's number. I'm really sorry."

"Richard Lord wants the property?" Mom's eyes were wide.

"Yeah."

She smiled. "I would have done the same thing, honey. If I wasn't holding this box, I would kiss you. Good work."

"You're sure?"

"Positive. We already talked about it—the brick oven, expanding our operations, all of it will be great. I know it's what you want. You know it too. Richard was simply the nudge you needed to make this happen."

"Mom, you're the best," I sighed as we continued down the street.

"Now we have three things to celebrate tonight. I can't wait."

Chapter Twenty-six

We made it to Torte and I forced her to wait outside while I put down the boxes and turned on the lights in the kitchen for the big reveal.

"Okay, are you ready for this? Close your eyes." I held her hand and led her inside.

"My heart is racing."

"It should be. You're going to love this." Positioning her next to the island, I stepped aside. "Go ahead, open your eyes."

She opened her eyes and gasped. Then she put her hand over her mouth as tears welled in her eyes.

"What do you think?"

"I love it." She blinked and wiped away tears. "It's even better than I imagined. The colors are so warm and bright and the ovens . . ." She walked closer to get a better look. "They're gorgeous. I don't even want to use them."

"That's exactly what I said when I saw them installed, but once you see everything they can do, you'll change your mind."

"I almost wouldn't recognize the space if I saw it in

a picture or something. You've done an amazing job pulling all this together, honey."

"It was a team effort." I clicked on the ovens and gave her a quick overview of all their features.

"What a day," Mom said, pulling up a stool. "I want to pinch myself. I can't believe how many good things have happened."

"And like I said before, I can't imagine anyone more deserving of good things. Do you want to see how the new ordering system works?"

"Yes." She started to stand.

"Don't get up. I'll bring it to you." I went to the office to grab the tablet. My notebook with the recipes I'd collected from my travels was sitting on the edge of the desk. I wanted to look through it later to see if I could find the pink peppercorns recipe that was evading my memory.

"Hey, have you ever used pink peppercorns?" I asked Mom, returning to the kitchen with the tablet.

"Pink peppercorn? Hmm. I don't think so, why?"

"Howard had me taste some on chocolate earlier today and it was fantastic. One of the sous chefs on the ship made a fettuccine with pink peppercorns that I fell in love with. I asked him for the recipe, and I'm sure I tucked it somewhere in my files. I want to dig it out and play around with it a little."

"That's my girl, always creating." Mom smiled.

I showed her how to use the ordering system and set up an account under my name to test the wireless payment option.

"It's so easy," Mom said when we finished. "This is going to speed up the front of the shop for sure."

"My thoughts exactly."

I glanced at the clock. "Hey, we better go change. We're both kind of a mess."

"Speak for yourself." She reached for a napkin and twirled it in the air. "I look like a queen."

Grabbing the napkin, I pulled her to her feet and steered her toward the door. We looped arms and walked to my apartment to change for dinner. Mom had brought a black velvet ankle-length skirt and white silk blouse. I let her change in the bathroom, while I dug through my closet. My wardrobe is pretty limited, since I spend most of my time in jeans and T-shirts. I decided on a knee-length black skirt that had a simple edge of black lace and a Spanish blue cashmere sweater. Carlos had bought it for me in Madrid. It felt like butter against my skin and brought out the blue in my eyes. I touched my lids with pale blue shadow and tucked antique bauble earrings into my ears.

Mom reached for my hands when I emerged from my bedroom. "You look lovely, honey."

"So do you." We spun in our skirts and headed back to the bakeshop.

A few minutes later the bell above the front door jingled, alerting us to the arrival of Thomas and the Professor. "Good evening, ladies." The Professor gave us both a bow.

Mom waved them both to the back. "Come see the kitchen."

Instead of his tweed jacket and corduroy pants the Professor wore a gray suit with a tie featuring busts of Shakespeare.

"You look dapper tonight," Mom said, greeting him with a kiss.

"A celebratory dinner calls for celebratory attire." The Professor ran his hand along his tie. "In honor of the occasion, I give you my tie. Alas, I couldn't find my cakes-and-ale tie, so the Bard's bust will have to suffice."

"It's quite festive." Mom touched his tie and then motioned to the ovens. "What do you think?"

The Professor examined the ovens as if he were studying a crime scene. He removed wire-framed glasses from his breast pocket and placed them on the tip of his nose, then he proceeded to scrutinize every dial and knob on the ovens. Thomas hung back. He was dressed for the occasion as well. Normally he was outfitted in his standard blue police uniform, but tonight he wore a pair of black dress pants, a crisp white shirt, and a red and blue striped tie. It had been a long time since I'd seen him out of uniform, and I had to admit that he looked good.

"Thomas, come in," Mom called to him. "You have to see this up close."

He hesitated, but then squared his shoulders and came toward us. "Hey, Jules," he said quietly as he passed me.

"Hey." I hoped my tone sounded friendly and light.

Mom gave me a funny look, but looped her arm through Thomas's and ushered him over to the ovens.

The Professor and Thomas were offering their praise when the door jingled again and Sterling, Stephanie, and Andy walked in. "The party can start now," Andy teased. I wasn't used to seeing the staff dressed up either.

Stephanie wore a black knee-length dress with black tights and black combat boots. Her hair was pulled back with a thick black headband, revealing crystal skull earrings in both ears. Andy's look was more all-American in his relaxed khakis and a shirt and tie. Sterling's transformation was the most impressive. He had abandoned his hoodie in favor of a gray dress shirt, black skinny jeans, Chuck Taylors, and a skinny black tie.

"Who are you?" Mom kidded as they all joined us in the kitchen for a better look at the finished product.

"Yeah, you look awesome," I agreed.

"We clean up nice." Sterling shrugged. His brilliant blue eyes were striking no matter what, but against his gray shirt they were incandescent.

"So does Torte," Andy piped in. "The ovens are killer. It looks money back here."

"Money?" Mom raised her brow.

"That's a good thing, Mrs. C." Andy winked.

"I figured." Mom clapped her hands together. She reached under the island and pulled out the chocolate trophies. "We won! Best in Show and People's Choice. Can you believe it?"

"That's awesome, Mrs. C." Andy reached for the trophy in her left hand. "That looks pretty tasty. You don't mind if I take a bite, do you?"

"Don't you dare, young man!" Mom grinned and clutched the trophies to her chest. "We are going to display these in the window until they bring us our real trophies. They're being engraved now."

"Congratulations," Thomas and Sterling said at the same time. The Professor gave Mom a tender smile and even Stephanie managed to grunt out a compliment.

Mom waved everyone off. "Thank you all for your tremendous work—we couldn't have done this without you. And, on that note, who's ready to celebrate?"

Everyone's hands shot up in the air. Mom laughed. "I think that's unanimous, let's go. Our table should be waiting for us."

Mom had made reservations at one of Ashland's most prestigious restaurants, Amuse Bouche, a French bistro with a rotating daily menu and gorgeous views of Lithia Creek. We made a merry party as we walked together down Main Street toward Lithia Park. Stars lit up the night sky, which I hoped was a sign that the rain was gone for good.

Amuse Bouche glowed with warm, yellow candlelight. The tables in its intimate dining room were adorned with white linens, crystal wineglasses, and gold-rimmed plates. I breathed in the intoxicating scent of searing meat and caramelizing onions.

"Whoa, this place is swanky, Mrs. C." Andy scanned the dining room and smoothed down his unruly hair.

"Only the best for the best staff on the planet," Mom said, squeezing his arm. "Your hair looks fine."

Andy chuckled. Sterling stood close to Stephanie and reached for her hand as the maître d' showed us to our table. Almost immediately after we took our places around the table our water glasses were filled and bottles of wine arrived. "White or red?" the waiter asked. I opted for red. Andy, who was to my right, chose cranberry sparkling cider.

There was an empty chair next to me with a place setting in front of it.

"Are we expecting someone else, Mom?"

As if on cue, Lance strolled inside. He stopped at two tables to greet theater patrons before arriving at ours. "I see I'm fashionably late as always," he said, taking the chair next to me.

"I didn't know you were coming," I said to him.

"Your mother invited me and I wouldn't miss it for the world." He held out his wineglass to the waiter. "White, please."

Under his breath to me, he added, "Not to mention that when your mother mentioned that Thomas was on the guest list, I knew I couldn't miss the opportunity to watch him drool over you."

I kicked him under the table. He clinked his glass to mine, and then leaned across the table where Thomas sat and toasted him. "Nice to see you again, Officer. They're giving you a break from patrolling Ashland's seedy streets."

Thomas laughed. "Something like that."

The Professor rose. He held out his crystal glass. "As the Bard would say, it is such a pleasure to be sharing this evening with all of you."

My heart pounded in my chest. Was he going to propose? I looked at Mom, who beamed up at him.

He nodded to each person seated at the table. "You've all been a part of Torte and our esteemed Helen's success." He paused and met Mom's eyes.

This was it! He was going to propose here—in front of everyone. I couldn't believe it. Did Mom know? I studied her face for any sign of anticipation, but although she looked happy and content her face didn't betray anything more.

"To Helen, and Torte." The Professor raised his glass. "Let us all eat, drink, and be merry!"

Everyone echoed his words and glasses clinked across the table. A wave of disappointment washed over me.

Lance narrowed his catlike eyes toward Thomas. "Do tell, what is the latest news in the investigation into Evan's death?"

Thomas looked at Mom and the Professor who were involved in their own conversation. "Nothing to tell. I wish there was."

"Juliet and I may be of service to you then, isn't that right, Juliet?"

"What?" I wrinkled my nose. What was Lance doing?

"Oh, yeah?" Thomas glanced at me. "Why's that?"

"I have no idea what he's talking about." I took a sip of my wine.

Lance made a tsking sound. "Darling, don't play coy with our friend here, you know exactly what I'm talking about. The *news* that we discussed earlier."

"What news?" Thomas's face shifted. He was all business. "If you know something that could be critical to the case you need to tell us."

I could tell from Lance's posture and the demure smile on his thin lips that he was loving this. "Do you mean Sandi?" I asked Lance.

"Of course I mean Sandi."

"Sandi Kramer the magazine editor?" Thomas asked. He had abandoned his wine and fumbled through his pockets for something. He pulled out his phone and waited for us to continue.

Lance looked at me.

"Fine, I will tell him." I glared at Lance. "Apparently, Sandi was trying to bribe Evan." I explained what I had learned earlier from Lance. Thomas typed on his phone as I spoke. When I finished he said something to the Professor and then excused himself. "I need to make a call. I'll be right back."

After he was out of earshot I punched Lance in the arm. "What was that all about? You were the one who learned about Sandi's blackmailing scheme. Why did you make me tell him?"

"Darling, I'm only trying to help you out, and it worked, if I do say so myself."

"What are you talking about?"

"Your little puppy dog." Lance pointed to the window where Thomas stood outside. "You needed something to break the tension between you two—it was positively palpable. Nothing breaks tension like murder. I believe you owe me a thanks."

I couldn't tell if Lance was kidding, but he was right. Once I had started to talk about the investigation, things felt much more normal between Thomas and me.

Lance folded his napkin in his lap as the chef arrived with the first course—sea scallops sautéed in butter. Mom offered another toast and we all dug into the food. Scallops can be very difficult to master. If overcooked, they have a tendency to become chewy and tough. These were cooked to perfection. The buttery sauce brought out their natural briny flavor. They burst in my mouth with a succulent and earthy taste.

"What do you think of them?" I asked Andy.

He chewed his scallop and swallowed before replying, "Good. Really good. If you're not going to finish that one, I'll happily take it off your plate. That goes for the whole meal."

I passed him my plate. "It's all yours."

"Score." Andy gave Sterling a high five as the next course arrived.

The chef explained how he had simmered leeks in chicken stock for hours for his signature pancetta and leek soup. The creamy soup was an excellent finish to the salty scallops. I knew from my years on the ships that chefs spend hours crafting a layered tasting menu. Each course was designed to complement the one before and after it. Tonight, we'd be experiencing five courses, so I was glad for Andy's offer to finish what I couldn't eat.

Wine and sparkling cider flowed along with a lively conversation about Torte's past and future while we ate. At one point, I sat back and drank it all in. Mom and I had built this together—not only was Torte a place I loved, but I loved these people too. This was my family.

Sometime after nine we finished the dessert course and stumbled outside with full bellies and rosy cheeks. Lance swayed a bit, although I couldn't tell if he was tipsy or still playing things up with Thomas. Everyone parted ways, and I considered going home and trying to sleep but I knew that it was futile. Despite the five-course meal and ample amounts of wine, I was wide awake and humming with energy.

The Amuse Bouche menu had inspired me, and I wanted to find that pink peppercorn recipe. I couldn't eat another bite, but I could do a little testing in the new ovens. I walked back to Torte and leafed through my notebook. Sure enough, the recipe for pink peppercorn fettuccini was near the back. It was written in the sous chef's messy scrawl with exact measurements and notes in the margins.

I read through the recipe, triggering a happy memory of a late-night dinner aboard the ship. Carlos usually cooked dinner for us after he finished his shift, but a few times a month he would hand the kitchen over to his staff. They would take turns creating dishes for Carlos, some of which ended up on the menu, like the pink peppercorn fettuccini. It was made with a creamy cheese sauce and topped with the bright berries.

The recipe looked straightforward. We had all the ingredients, except for pink peppercorns, but I could get those from Howard tomorrow. There was an asterisk at the bottom of the recipe with the word "WARNING" in all capital letters.

That's odd, I thought to myself as I read on.

Toxic? I flipped over the recipe and the chef's warning continued on the back. "Pink peppercorns are related to cashews. They can cause a severe—even deadly—reaction for people with a nut allergy."

I dropped the recipe on the floor.

Chapter Twenty-seven

Pink peppercorns were related to nuts? I read the warning twice just to make sure that I wasn't misreading it. Then I grabbed my phone and did a search for pink peppercorns online. I couldn't believe it. There were multiple cases of severe allergic reactions when people had consumed the bright berries. Many spice shops around the country had begun to include warning labels informing customers of the potentially life-threatening hazard associated with pink peppercorns.

One quote gave me pause: "Pink peppercorns are highly toxic and should be used in moderation. The FDA banned them temporarily in the 1980s."

My mind raced. Had Evan tasted Howard's pink peppercorn truffles? Maybe it had been an accident after all. Or maybe Howard had a motive for killing Evan, and found a devious way to make it happen.

I called Thomas, who didn't answer, so I left a message letting him know what I had discovered about the pink peppercorns. Then I called Lance. I'm not exactly sure why, maybe it was because of Mom's earlier comment about how we needed each other's friendship, or maybe it was because it felt like he authentically (in his weird Lance way) was trying to be helpful. He didn't answer either, so I left him the same message that I'd left for Thomas.

Pacing in front of the pastry case, I tried to decide what to do next. Why would Howard want Evan dead? What could his motivation be? I thought back to every conversation I'd had over the long weekend. Howard and Evan had partnered on their truffle line, pairing chocolate and salt to rave reviews and critical acclaim. Why would Howard want to end that?

A thought flashed in my head: what if Evan had wanted to end their business relationship? What had Carter said about Evan sourcing new vendors? Could Evan have been looking to replace Howard? He had hinted as much. I had assumed that Evan was going after new partnerships as a way to ensure that no one found out that he was losing his sense of taste, but what if there was more to it than that?

Torte's main phone line rang, making me jump and clutch my chest. Who was calling this late? I answered the phone on the third ring.

"Torte, Juliet speaking."

"Oh, Juliet, great, you're there. I'm calling from Ashland Springs and our hotel manager is nervous about your cakes. As vendors have been coming to pick up their things, they've almost been knocked over twice. Is there any chance you can come pick them up tonight?"

"Sure. I'll be right there." I hung up, thrilled to have

a distraction. What was taking Thomas and Lance so long to return my calls?

I pulled on my coat and hurried up to the hotel. The concierge pointed me to the storage area. I wasn't sure what we were going to do with the cakes anyway, maybe we could spray them with a preservative and display them in the windows. The hallway leading to the storage area was deserted, but I ran into Chef Garrison.

"Hi, good to see you, Jules." He greeted me with a hearty handshake. His chef's coat was pristine despite the fact that I knew he must have just finished overseeing dinner service.

"Great to see you too. I'm here for a cakes." I pointed to the storage room. "They had to push us out quickly for the wedding."

He nodded. "I know, we were booked solid tonight. My staff is about ready to strike between the five-course chocolate dinner I had them prepare and the wedding. With all of the guests here for the festival the hotel and my dining room have been booked solid all weekend."

"It's good to be busy this time of year though, right?"

"You can say that again." He gave me a thumbs-up. "Congratulations again on the win! I was pulling for you, and your mom of course, she's a pillar in the food community. We'll have to go grab drinks one night and do some collaboration. What do you say?"

"Absolutely. I'm in."

"See you later, good luck with your cakes." He started to walk down the hall, when I called to him to stop.

"Sorry. One quick question before you go."

"Sure, shoot."

"What do you know about pink peppercorns?"

"The spice?'

"Yeah."

"I haven't used them a lot. They scare me. I had a customer have a reaction to them once and, to be honest, after that I've steered away from them. Not worth the risk, you know?"

"You mean like an allergic reaction?"

He nodded. "Yes, pink peppercorns are a member of the cashew family. They are actually a type of tree nut. I never knew that until the customer started swelling up."

"I just learned the same thing."

"If you want my advice, I wouldn't recommend them in your pastries. Too much stress trying to make sure you let everyone know, you know?"

"Exactly."

"What did you want to know about them?"

"Oh, it's nothing," I lied. "I was thinking of experimenting with an old recipe, but when I read about its relation to nuts I wondered if that was something chefs knew."

He shrugged. "I doubt many of them do, but like I said, I don't think it's worth it. Sure the flavor is good, but it's not worth the risk of making someone sick, or worse."

Or worse indeed, I thought.

"Right, thanks."

"Drinks soon."

"For sure."

He continued down the hall. I turned and opened the storage room door. The room was dark, but when I stepped inside someone covered my mouth with their hand and tossed me up against the wall.

Chapter Twenty-eight

"What are you doing?" Howard's gruff voice sounded in my ear.

I tried to scream but he forced his hand tighter over my mouth. His nails pierced my chin. Panic began to build inside as my heart pummeled against my chest.

"You think you're so sneaky, but I heard every word you said."

I moved my lips but the only thing that came out was a muffled sound.

"Don't lie to me. I heard you talking about pink peppercorns right outside the door. You know too much."

I frantically tried to adjust my eyes to the pitch-black room by blinking them as fast as I could. I needed to get out of here and away from Howard.

"Stop moving. I need to think."

I wondered if I should try to scream. Howard had a tight hold of me and was strong—I'm sure it was thanks to all the time he spent in the ocean—but this was Ashland's busiest hotel. Someone would have to hear me, right? Or what about the other vendors? It was too dark to tell how much was left in the room.

It has to be close to ten on a Sunday night, who else would be coming to get their stuff now? I asked myself.

What would Thomas do in this situation? Probably try to keep Howard talking, and try to reason with him, but that was going to be difficult, considering that I couldn't open my mouth.

Howard pounded the wall behind us with his fist. "Damn."

I started. He yanked my hair back in one painful jerk. I winced in pain and tried again to get him to listen to me.

"I told you to be quiet. I need to think. You are a thorn in my side."

Hopefully, thinking was a good sign. At least he wasn't trying to take me out right here. Then again he had to be smart to come up with a plan to kill Evan with a spice that few people knew could be toxic.

Think, Jules.

At that moment my phone rang in my purse. This time Howard jumped at the sound and momentarily loosened his grip on me. I ducked out from underneath him and crawled on the floor.

"Hey! Where did you go?" Howard yelled.

My pulse quickened as I fumbled ahead blindly. All Howard had to do was flip on the lights and he would see me. He must be concerned that one of the hotel staff would notice the light on under the door.

I heard him take a heavy step and then crash into something and yelp. I figured he must be struggling to find his way in the dark.

I took the opportunity to get to my feet and silence my phone. The sound of things being hurled against the wall and floor crashed behind me. Was Howard having some kind of breakdown or was he coming after me? Either way all of the commotion was sure to attract the attention of a hotel worker. I let him rage on as I frantically tried to find somewhere to hide.

It was too dark.

At that moment voices sounded outside in the hall. I froze. Should I take the opportunity to scream or was there a chance Howard had a weapon? I didn't have a minute to decide, because the next thing I knew the door swung open, letting a crack of light into the crowded storage area.

Howard had opened it. He walked out and let the door slam shut behind him. I heard him say something to the hotel staff members. Then there was nothing but silence.

My heart beat so fast that I was having trouble catching my breath. I wasn't sure what to do next, but I knew that I wasn't staying in the storage room for one more minute. Keeping my hands in front of my face to guide me, I moved toward the door. I was almost there, when I tripped on something and landed in what felt suspiciously like cake.

I slipped as I tried to stand again, and fell on my back. The texture felt like chocolate frosting. I inched forward on my knees and ran my hand along the wall trying to find the door. I found it and tried the handle. My hand slipped. Had Howard locked me in or were my hands too sticky? I wiped them on my skirt and tried again. The door swung open and I fell forward into the hallway.

Now what? Howard could be getting away. I glanced at my hands as spots danced in front of my eyes. That was definitely chocolate frosting. I reached into my purse for my phone and punched in Thomas's number.

"Thomas, it's Jules. Howard just attacked me. I'm at Ashland Springs. You need to get here now!"

Next I called Lance; it felt like déjà vu. "Lance, Howard attacked me. I'm at the hotel. I'm going to see if I can get help. He's getting away. Get over here. I've called Thomas."

I scanned the hallway for any staff members. There was no one around. Then I noticed that the door to the back alley was propped open. Could Howard have gone that way? I ran to the door and, keeping my body safely inside, I glanced from side to side trying to see if there was any sign of Howard in the dimly lit alley.

The next thing I knew I felt a strong hand yank me outside. I kicked myself for not running to the front to get help.

"Gotcha." Howard's grasp on my arm was firm and cutting off circulation to my wrist. "Let's go, baker."

I tried to dig my heels into the ground, but they were coated in a layer of chocolate frosting. I slid forward as Howard yanked me along like a rag doll.

"Let's go. Move it. You're coming with me."

At least I could talk and more importantly try to keep him talking. "You're not going to get away with this, Howard. I've already called the police. They know it's you."

"Know what's me?"

"They know that you killed Evan."

"No one killed Evan. He had an accident."

"You knew that the pink peppercorns would send him into anaphylactic shock."

"Me? Ha. I'm nothing but a sea salt farmer. What do I know about fancy spices and stuff?"

"Look, I know that you killed Evan."

He tugged me farther down the alley. Where was he taking me?

"I didn't kill anyone. You've got no proof. Neither do the police."

"Then why are you taking me against my will? That's going to be proof right there."

"No one said anything about taking you against your will. The way I'll remember it is that you were dying to come watch how we get the salt out of the sea. You remember that conversation we had? A couple of my staff were there when you asked me if you could tag along sometime. It'll be too bad that you aren't a strong swimmer. Those ocean currents can be a killer. Bad riptides out on the coast."

He was evil.

"Howard, I've called the police. You're not going to get away with this."

For a minute I thought maybe I had gotten through, but he clutched my wrist even tighter, so tight that I thought it might break, and dragged me toward his van.

Chapter Twenty-nine

I had to get away now. I could not let Howard get me inside the van. The question was how. Screaming was futile at this point. I thought about Mom finding out that Howard had killed me. What would that do to her? Why had I been so rash?

Howard tightened his grip on me and stuffed his free hand into his pocket. He must be looking for his keys, I thought. This was my chance. I could kick him in the shins as hard as possible and try to make a run for it.

Suddenly, a whistling sound floated up the alleyway. I turned my head to see Lance stumbling toward us. He had a bottle of champagne in one hand and looked as if it were taking every effort to put one foot in front of the other. Whistling a tune I didn't recognize, he swayed toward us.

"Darling, what are you doing here?" His words slurred together as he spoke.

Howard shoved his nails so deep into my wrist I could feel him draw blood. I stood as still as possible.

"Hey, Lance, what are you doing?" I replied.

Lance sang the verse from a song I didn't know and waltzed toward us with the champagne bottle serving as his temporary partner. "Having a late-night cocktail, of course." His head rocked from side to side. "Shhh! Don't tell," he whispered in a yell, "but I use this as my watering hole sometimes."

My chance to escape had arrived in the form of a visibly drunk Lance. Not exactly ideal, but my position was looking much better than it had a few seconds ago.

Howard made a grunting sound under his breath.

Lance almost fell into me as he tried to kiss my cheek and missed. He tried with the second cheek and ended up kissing my hair. "You're so beautiful, Juliet. Isn't she beautiful?" he slurred to Howard. "She won't get on the stage for me. I've begged and begged and she won't do it. So much beauty wasted on pastry." The champagne bottle rocked from side to side as he spoke.

Howard looked disgusted, but I could tell he was biding his time until Lance continued on.

"Come have a drink with me." Lance tried to tug at my free arm, but Howard held his ground. I didn't want to become caught in a tug-of-war, so I pushed Lance off.

"I can't, it's late." I tried to catch his eye to give him a warning sign, but his eyes rolled back in his head.

"Oh, have a drink with your best friend," he pleaded.

I was about to protest again when Lance caught my eye. His eyes were bright and alert. He gave me a covert nod and motioned for me to duck. He wasn't drunk. Before I knew what he was planning, I ducked and he swung the champagne bottle at Howard's head and knocked him to the ground.

Howard landed with a thud and was out cold.

I threw my arms around Lance. "How did you do that?"

"Acting, darling," he said in a composed voice. "If I do say so myself, that was one of my best performances." He held up the bottle. "Drink?"

Police lights and sirens flashed on the side street below.

"How did you get here before the police?"

"I got your message."

"But how did you get here so fast?"

"I was having a drink here at the bar."

"What?"

"After our elegant dinner I needed a nightcap so I wandered up here for a glass of bubbly. Call it divine timing." He drank from the champagne bottle. I could see his hands trembling. For all his talk of drama, the reality of the danger we had just been in was starting to settle in.

"Thank you," I said with deepest sincerity.

He scoffed. "It's nothing, but does this mean you owe me? I wasn't kidding about the stage."

"No." I wrapped my arm around his. "It does mean that I'll walk you over to the police car. You've had a shock."

"Ah, the heroine saves the hero. Classic," Lance joked, but he didn't resist as we walked arm in arm toward Thomas's police car.

Thomas jumped out of the driver's seat as the lights lit up the back alleyway.

"He's over there." I pointed to where Howard lay on the ground.

Thomas stared at me. "Are you okay?"

"I'm fine." I nodded to Lance.

"Here, come sit," Thomas said, taking Lance's arm and walking around to the passenger side.

Lance sat without a word of protest. I stayed with him as Thomas, followed by three other police officers, ran toward Howard.

"Do you think I killed him?" Lance shuddered.

"No." I was fairly confident that was true.

"I mean, not that I care about that dastardly creature, but I wouldn't want someone's death on my hands. Imagine, I'd have to run around quoting, 'Out, damned spot' all the time."

I knew that joking was his way of coping with the situation, so I played along. "It would make for good theater, though. And imagine the headlines: 'Artistic Director Stages a Murder'."

"That doesn't even make sense."

"That's why I work in pastry." I grinned.

"Darling, you've ruined your beautiful outfit," Lance noted.

I glanced down at my sweater and skirt; they were both covered in frosting and spotted with blood.

The back door of the hotel opened and the Professor rushed out. Thomas filled him in as the ambulance arrived on the scene. Paramedics carted Howard off. By the time they finished working on him, he was awake, if not fully alert.

"See, he's fine," I assured Lance.

Lance let out a long breath. "Glad to hear it. What happened to my champagne?"

"I'll do you one better—how does a hot coffee sound?"

"Like something your mother would offer me."

"Exactly. Wait here, I'll be right back."

I stopped to tell Thomas I was going inside to get Lance a coffee. "Good idea. He didn't look so great," Thomas replied, as he snapped photos of Howard's van. "I never thought I'd see Lance shaken."

"Me either. You want anything?"

"No, I'm good. I will need to take your statement though, and Jules, I have to warn you that you're going to have to testify if Howard's case goes to trial."

"Testify?"

"Yeah, on both Evan's murder and Howard's attempted abduction of you." Thomas's voice caught for a moment.

I rubbed my wrist.

"Did he hurt you?"

I held out my arm and noticed that blood dripped from where Howard had grabbed me. "It's not bad."

Thomas gently rolled up the sleeve of my cashmere sweater and caressed my arm. "We'll have someone clean that up for you, but I'll need to take pictures of it first."

"Should I wait on the coffee?"

"Yeah. Hang on a second. I don't want you to wash your arm or go anywhere until I get photographic evidence. That will be critical to the DA's case, especially since right now Howard's attack on you is our entire case." Thomas went to grab a camera and first aid kit from his squad car. "Let's go inside. I want to make sure the lighting is okay for these photos."

We stepped into the hotel and he clicked what felt like a hundred shots of my arm. When he finished he whipped out a first aid kit and carefully cleaned and bandaged my cuts. "Jules," he said, his voice thick with emotion. "If anything had happened to you I don't know what I would have done."

"I'm fine."

He frowned. "I know, but I should have been here."

The Professor called for his help. I was relieved that our conversation didn't have to go any deeper, at least for the moment. The warmth of the hotel felt good, but the thought of having to testify against Howard didn't. I would have been fine if I never saw him again. Word must have spread among the staff because a number of employees came down the hall together. One of them noticed me. "Do you need help, miss?"

"Actually, yes. I need coffee for my friend. He's in a bit of a shock. Do you think someone could bring him some?"

"Of course. I'll go get some right now."

I thanked him and started toward the door when I heard a voice calling my name. I turned to see Sandi Kramer heading my way. A bellboy followed after her with a cart of expensive luggage. She adjusted her designer glasses and smoothed her wrinkle-free black tunic.

"You look like you've had a run-in with chocolate." She squinted behind the black-framed buglike glasses.

"It's been quite a night." I told her about Howard.

She didn't seem surprised. "Evan made as many enemies as he made friends in this business."

"What about you?" I figured I didn't have anything to lose at this point. "I heard that you were bribing Evan for a paid review."

She checked a silver watch on her wrist. "I'm almost

late for my flight, but no, that's not entirely true. I did offer him an exclusive advertising opportunity, but nothing more."

I wasn't sure if I believed her or not. "Hey, one last thing—I think I overheard you on the phone in the bathroom. Was that about Evan?"

"Jules, you surprise me and I like it." She scrunched her tight white curls. "You're more ruthless than your ethereal pastry face lets on. You'd do just fine in New York."

"Actually, I lived in New York when I was attending culinary school."

She snapped her fingers twice. "Excellent. And who knows what call you're talking about. My assistant has been driving me to drink. She cannot seem to make any decision without my approval. I've been on the phone with her nonstop since I arrived. The minute my plane lands, she's getting fired."

Sandi's phone buzzed. She threw her arms out in disgust. "Case in point." She waved the bellboy toward the lobby and answered her phone with a curt, "Now what?"

I returned outside where the Professor was taking Lance's statement. A hotel worker followed behind me. Not only had he brought a steaming hot coffee for Lance but he brought one for me and a tray for the entire police staff.

"I could practically kiss you," I said, taking the scalding cup from him. He grinned and went to deliver the rest of the drinks. I walked down to the police car with Lance's coffee. I was safe and so were the people I loved, and now I had coffee. Who could ask for more?

Chapter Thirty

Lance took the coffee from me with shaky hands.

"How are you holding up?" I asked. His face was drawn and the color of ice.

"Fine, darling." His voice quivered a bit. "A touch of real-world drama to use later on the stage."

I kneeled next to the police car. "Real-life drama isn't quite as fun, is it?"

Lance tried to smile. "Not at all."

The Professor, who was still sitting in the driver's seat, placed his hand on Lance's shoulder. "As Shakespeare wrote in *Henry VI,* you have now seen 'the gloomy shade of death.' It most certainly isn't appealing. It's understandable that you're overcome." His whimsical tie was loose around his neck and his suit jacket was slung around the headrest. "Juliet, a word?" He nodded to the hotel.

"Sure." As I stood, tiny lights flashed across my vision. Lance wasn't the only one affected by what had just happened. "Drink up. You'll feel better soon," I said to Lance, and followed the Professor to the hotel's back entrance.

When we stepped inside, the crowd of staff members jockeying for position dispersed. The Professor had a casual but at the same time commanding presence. He didn't need to speak or say a word, and everyone quickly returned to their work.

"How's Lance holding up?" I asked.

"He'll be fine, but I do believe he won't jest about sleuthing in the future." The Professor's brown eyes glinted.

"You knew about that?"

He tapped his ginger-colored beard. "It wasn't difficult to deduce. Lance is . . . how should I put it? Less than discreet?"

I couldn't help but laugh. "That's for sure."

"However, I must give him credit for springing into action. While I don't approve of his tactics, and would have preferred that he waited for us to arrive on the scene, his quick thinking may have saved your life. He must care about you." The Professor's kind eyes held a knowing gaze. Had he and Mom had a conversation about me and Lance?

"Funny, Mom said the same thing earlier."

"Your mother is a wise woman, Juliet." He opened his Moleskin notebook. "I digress, let's talk about you. Thomas says that you sustained an injury?"

I showed him my arm. "It's not bad. A few scratches and cuts."

He took a note. "And Thomas has photographic evidence, yes?"

"Yes. He got pictures and then bandaged me up."

The Professor studied my arm. "A fine job. I couldn't have done better myself." He sighed. "Now about Howard, I'll need you to start from the beginning."

I told the Professor everything that I had learned, from my early suspicions about Carter and Bethany, to Sandi's advertising blackmail, and then about pink peppercorns.

He took a quick inhale. "Pink peppercorns, you say? The Bard would be impressed. Ingenious if you think about it. Diabolical, but ingenious."

"Thomas said you were worried that this might have been the perfect crime."

He closed his notebook. "It looked that way. If it hadn't been for you, he might have gotten away with it. Again, let me stress, in no uncertain terms, that I do not approve of your methods but I am grateful that you cracked the case."

"Just like cracking eggs." The joke spilled from my lips before I could stop it.

The Professor chuckled. "Something like that."

"What I don't understand is why he came after me. He had crafted an almost infallible plan, why throw that all away by attacking me?"

" 'Time shall unfold what plighted cunning hides: Who covers faults, at last shame them derides.' "

"Shakespeare?"

"But of course"

I was used to the Professor quoting sonnets, but wished that sometimes he would speak in modern prose.

He must have read my mind. "What I've learned over the years, Juliet, is that killers often out themselves. Murder is a crime of passion, be it romantic or unrequited love, money, greed, or lust. That kind of passion and extreme emotion can never really be contained. Someone who appears smooth on the surface is bubbling with turmoil on the inside. In this line of work patience and diligence always pay off."

A hotel worker came by with more coffee and a basket of cheese Danish. I helped myself to a sweet Danish.

"I believe that is all I need from you for the moment. You're free to go, but we will be in touch in the coming days. Did Thomas inform you that you'll likely be called upon to testify?"

"He did," I said, taking a bite of the Danish.

"Shall we escort you home?"

"That's okay. I'm going to go find Lance. I have a feeling *he'll* need an escort."

The Professor gave me a small bow. "In that case, I bid you good night, fair Juliet."

I scarfed down the Danish in four bites. I couldn't believe I was hungry after the five-course meal, but I had a feeling the adrenaline pumping through my system had sped up my metabolism.

Lance was on his feet, leaning up against the police car. I took the fact that he was upright as a sign that he was doing better.

"Hey, I've been tasked with escorting you home."

He scoffed. "Please, I do not need an escort."

"It's either me or the police car. Take your pick."

Lance wrinkled his nose. "I'm not getting back in there. It smells like stale coffee and cheap doughnuts."

"Do stale doughnuts even smell?"

"Darling, they do and I promise it isn't pleasant."

Lance was definitely back to his old self. I tucked my arm through his. "I guess you're stuck with me then."

"I suppose you'll have to do. I have been stuck with worse." He shuddered for effect. At least I thought it was for effect. It might have also been due to the fact that we passed the ambulance and caught sight of Howard sitting on a gurney in the back. He shouted something at us.

"Let's go this way," I said, tugging Lance past the flashing lights and around the block.

"What did he say?"

"No idea. It sounded like nonsense to me, probably because you whacked him on the head."

Lance smiled. "All those years of blocking fight scenes on stage finally paid off." He noticed my arm. "Are you hurt?"

"It's nothing. Thomas stuck a couple bandages on, that's all."

"I bet Thomas stuck a couple of bandages on you," he said with an evil grin.

"You're about to lose your escort, sir."

Lance threw his free hand over his heart. "No, say it isn't so. I'll behave."

We walked past Torte and Lithia Park. I decided to change the subject and to keep Lance's mind off Howard. He lived outside of town and I didn't want him to drive home if he was still anxious.

"Hey, so did you have anything to do with the basement property?"

"Basement property? I have no idea what you're talking about." Lance winked.

"It *was* you! How did you know there was a hidden pizza oven down there?"

"I know everything about Ashland. *Everything.* Don't you forget it."

"Did you know that Richard Lord is also interested in the space?"

Lance sighed audibly. "Why do you think I sent Rosalind to you? We cannot let Richard get his hands on that space. Can you imagine? He'd install more of that hideous green carpet he's so enamored with."

"Well, thanks."

"Don't thank me. Thank the pastry gods. It's your destiny, darling."

We climbed the Shakespeare stairs that lead from the park up to the theater complex. Lance's car was parked on the street just up the hill from the bricks.

"Are you sure you're okay to drive?"

"I'm fine. Absolutely fine, unless that's a proposition, in which case, by all means please join me. I'm sure I have a pair of extra silk pajamas tucked in a drawer somewhere."

I punched him in the arm. "You're fine. See you later."

He started toward the car, then stopped and embraced me in a bone-crushing hug. It caught me off guard. I'd only seen Lance express real emotions a handful of times. "I'm glad we're both safe," he whispered in my ear and then let me go. He danced up the hill and before getting in his car he blew me a kiss. "Ta-ta!"

I watched him drive away and headed back down the hill to my apartment. I was glad too.

Chapter Thirty-one

The next morning was a mob scene at Torte. So much for testing out the new ovens and ordering system—we were slammed from the moment we opened the doors until long after the morning rush had passed. Our customers were eager for their fix after having Torte closed for the long weekend, and word had spread (as it always does in Ashland) about my run-in with Howard. Everyone wanted to know why Howard had killed Evan. I answered them honestly—their guess was as good as mine. The police were going through Howard's personal and business records. They would be able to determine a motive, as the Professor said, with some time and patience.

Mom pulled me away from the front counter, where I had been overseeing the payment system—it seemed to be running smoothly, and despite the crowd the line was moving quickly. "Honey, Sterling is doing great. Why don't we swap? My hands are bothering me this morning, I'll be a floater up here if you'll take over the dough for me."

"Thanks, Mom." I kissed her cheek knowing that her hands were a convenient excuse to rescue me from having to talk about Howard.

She bumped my hip. "Get going."

Stephanie was chomping on a wad of gum and twisting pretzel dough together. "These ovens rock."

"Aren't they amazing?" I washed my hands in the sink and assessed the list of pastries and cakes that needed to be baked. After being consumed with chocolate for weeks I was eager to take a break and try something new. I started on a hearty beer and cheese soup. Stephanie was handcrafting our doughy pretzel twists that she would generously butter and sprinkle with sea salt. They would go well with the soup for the lunch crowd.

I chopped yellow onions and sautéed them in butter. Then I shredded three kinds of cheese and found bottles of dark stout beer in the walk-in. I slowly whisked the cheese blend into the onions, allowing it to melt on low. Cheese can curdle and become chunky if it melts too quickly. Next I added glugs of the carbonated beer and chicken stock. I would let the soup simmer for a couple hours and add cream and fresh herbs before we served it.

With the soup bubbling on low, I started on lunch cookies. I creamed butter and sugar together with vanilla and eggs for a sugar-cookie base. The comforting scent of vanilla hit my nose as I shifted the mixer and added dry ingredients plus some sour cream to give the cookies a special tang. I scooped the dough onto cookie sheets and did a little dance before opening the new high-tech oven doors.

"You're pretty excited about the ovens, aren't you?" Stephanie said as she removed a tray of oatmeal bread.

"Can you blame me?"

She balanced the steaming bread tray with one hand and tapped her black fingernails on the oven door with other. "I'm kind of with you on this. It's awesome that the doors stay cool."

"Exactly." I placed my cookies on the middle baking rack and returned to the island to start on peanut butter jam cookies and cherry almond shortbread. Our customers in search of chocolate might be disappointed today, but they could deal with a chocolate-free menu for one day.

The new ovens baked my sugar cookies to a gorgeous golden color in less than seven minutes. Once they had cooled I broke one in half to taste it. The center was chewy and the edges slightly crisp. These were some of the best cookies I had ever seen. I frosted them with vanilla buttercream and added rainbow sprinkles to the top.

Sometime after nine Andy came back to the kitchen with a tray of coffees. "I meant to get back here sooner to let you try the special, but I've barely had a chance to breathe. You'd think Torte had been closed for years or something."

"What's your special?"

"I knew you all were on chocolate overload so I went a different direction today. I figured that everyone would be up for something more tropical after all this rain." He handed ceramic mugs to Stephanie and me. "Give it a try and let me know what you think."

Tropical? I'd never thought to pair tropical flavors in espresso. The coffee smelled slightly spicy and fruity. I took a sip and couldn't place the familiar flavor I was tasting.

Stephanie scrunched her heavily darkened eyes. "What's in this?"

Andy crossed his arms and smiled. "You'll have to guess, but no one has so far."

I looked at Stephanie and we both took another sip. "Pepper?"

Andy shook his head.

"Cinnamon?" Stephanie asked.

"Maybe." Andy's smile widened.

"It's something we know, right?" Stephanie stared at her mug.

"Oh, you know it." Andy grinned.

I racked my brain as I took another sip. "Is there even coffee in this? It tastes like tea to me."

Andy's jaw dropped. "Yeah, how did you guess?"

"Skills." I patted my back. "Remember, I'm a professionally trained chef," I teased.

Andy laughed. "I've got to hand it to you, boss, I didn't think anyone would get it."

"You've definitely succeeded in capturing a tropical flavor. I feel like my feet should be in warm white sand while I'm drinking this."

He blushed. "Thanks."

"What's in it?" Stephanie asked.

"Mango purée, a splash of fresh pineapple juice, and Oregon Chai. I foamed coconut milk instead of regular too."

I was impressed. Andy had a natural ability to strike

a balance between flavors. The Oregon Chai was a luscious blend of black tea, honey, and spices that reminded me of Thanksgiving. Paired with the creamy coconut milk and tropical fruits it hit all the right notes. I knew that our customers were going to love Andy's latest creation, and he was right—we all needed a comforting drink to remind us that spring would be here soon.

"This is amazing," I said to Andy. "Add it to the specials board."

"You got it, boss." Andy returned to the espresso bar and I finished the mango chai latte. He might be on to a new trend.

I returned to baking cookies and reveling in the speed and precision of the new ovens. The beer and cheese soup and pretzels sold out in the first hour of the lunch rush, and customers raved about Andy's creation. I wasn't sure if it was because they enjoyed the flavor combination or were more excited about the unique pairing.

Mom popped her head over the front counter and called to me, "Jules, do you have a minute? There's someone here to see you."

"Sure. One sec." I brushed flour from my hands and went to the dining room.

Bethany and Carter stood near the pastry case with a basket of brownies. They were both wearing the Unbeatable Brownie T-shirts. Bethany's was bright pink with the #Get In My Belly hashtag. Carter's was brown with the hashtag #EEEEATS.

"Hey, what's going on?" I asked.

Carter handed me a card and Bethany thrust the basket in my arms. "We wanted to say thank you," she said. "And I always say thank you with brownies."

Oh, no, more chocolate. To her, I smiled and took the basket. "I couldn't agree more, but why the thanks?"

Bethany looked to Carter. "I told him that I told you about him helping me and everything and how nice and supportive you've been to both of us. Some chefs aren't very nice to young chefs like us, but not you. You've been really nice, and then we heard what happened with Howard and we both felt terrible, so we just wanted to make sure that you knew we appreciated your help."

"Wow, thanks." I appreciated her praise. Many chefs had helped mold my career path and I was always happy to do the same. "What's up with the matching shirts?"

Bethany pointed to Carter's hashtag. "Isn't it great? I'm pink. He's chocolate. Carter's going to pair up with me."

"No more Confections Couture?" I asked Carter.

He shook his head. "It's too weird now that Evan is dead. I learned a lot that will hopefully help us grow the business." Carter glanced around the room. "I can't believe Howard killed Evan."

"Me neither."

His arms looked even scrawnier in the T-shirt. "You know, it makes sense. He came around Confections Couture a bunch and I saw him and Evan argue a few times, but I didn't think it was a big deal. Evan argued with everyone."

"Do you think he knew about Evan's GERD?"

"I doubt it, but maybe."

Bethany pointed to the line forming out the door. "You're busy. We better let you get back to work. Enjoy the brownies."

Carter gave her a look I couldn't decipher. Bethany

shook her head trying to discourage him, but Carter ignored her and stepped closer. "She wants to ask you something, but she's a chicken."

"What?"

Bethany blushed and looked at her feet. "I wondered if maybe you would be up for doing a post about Torte on my Instagram account, but I know you're totally busy and everything, so no pressure. I just thought it would be cool to share your cake artistry with my followers, you know? I mean, it would be good exposure for you. I have followers all around the world and depending on how I tag the post it could go viral. But really, it's no biggie if you're not up for it."

"Sure. What do I have to do?"

Her mouth hung open with delight and she caught Carter's eye. "I told you she would say yes," he said.

Bethany babbled even faster than usual as she explained that she would come back and take photos of our cakes and pastries. Then she would post them on her account and create hashtags about Torte. It sounded fine to me and it certainly couldn't hurt to have more exposure. Bethany proceeded to try and convince me to launch a Torte Instagram page. I promised that I would have Andy or Stephanie look into it.

We agreed to meet later in the week for the photo shoot. I thanked them for the brownies and brought the basket to the kitchen. "Brownie?"

Stephanie stuck out her tongue. "More chocolate? Oh, heck no."

"Hey, what do you know about Instagram?" I asked.

"For what?"

"Torte."

Stephanie thought for a minute and then nodded. "It could be good, actually. It's really visual and artistic. I could create an account and take some shots of the bake-shop and our products if you want."

Her tone was casual, but I could tell that she was interested in taking on the project. Stephanie had an eye for design. I always tasked her with updating our chalk-board menu and handwriting place cards for our Sunday suppers.

"Great. Go for it." I sighed as I looked at the basket of brownies.

If I didn't see another piece of chocolate for a week I would be fine. I knew exactly what to do with Bethany's brownies. I asked Stephanie to design a flier and assembled the brownies on a silver tray. Everyone who came in for the remainder of the day would get a free Unbeatable Brownie and Bethany would get a free plug for her new business.

Chapter Thirty-two

The next few days passed with ease. Torte's remodel had made things at the bakeshop even more efficient. Our customers loved the new payment system. Having everything on the tablets had sped up the line at the front counter, and freed up Sterling to help Andy prep drinks. The rain had finally stopped and the sun had begun to dry out Ashland's waterlogged streets and sidewalks.

When I commented on how much the puddle outside of the bakeshop had receded late one morning, Andy grinned. "You have me to thank for that, boss."

"Oh, really? And why is that?" I brushed flour from my apron.

"My tropical chai tea latte. It did the trick. I'm telling you, I have a direct link to the weather gods through my coffee."

I laughed. "Good to know. I'll have to remember that in a couple of months when we're all complaining about how hot it is."

"Speaking of the weather," Mom said from the pastry case where she was arranging rows of spring cupcakes with ladybugs, butterflies, and tulips. "I brought in that bag of gear for you guys to look through." She pointed to the office. "Andy, take a look and take anything you want. I won't be offended if it's not your style."

Andy grinned and pulled his apron to one side. "SOU gear is pretty much the only thing I wear, Mrs. C., so I'm sure it'll be cool."

"Sterling," Mom called to the kitchen where Sterling was assembling spring salads with lemon grilled chicken, cranberries, and hazelnuts. "Come take a look at the coats that I brought in when you have a minute."

"Will do," Sterling replied.

I smiled as I looked at the wall above the pastry case where Mom had framed our awards from the Chocolate Fest. It was hard to believe that only a week ago we'd been up to our ears in chocolate and mixed up in a murder.

At that moment, Thomas and the Professor passed by the front window. I waved as they walked toward the door. Mom hurried to open it for them and gave the Professor a warm embrace. They looked so happy and comfortable in each other's arms. It made me feel nostalgic for Carlos.

"Come in, come in," Mom said, breaking away and pulling both of them into the dining room.

"Good morning, Juliet." The Professor gave me a nod. "It smells heavenly in here as always."

"Would you like coffee?" Mom asked.

The Professor turned to Thomas. "I don't believe we'd ever turn down a mug of Torte's java, would we, Thomas?"

"No way."

Mom pointed to the pastry case. "Anything else? Stephanie and Juliet just finished these cupcakes. Aren't they adorable? We're all feeling ready for spring around here."

The Professor declined. "Indeed, they are quite artistic, but I must beg for a moment of your daughter's time." He tilted his head slightly and made eye contact with me. "Juliet, might we borrow you for a moment or two?"

"Oh, sure." I felt Thomas's eyes locked on me. "There's a booth open."

"Excellent." The Professor waited as I led the way to a booth by the window.

Mom delivered a tray of coffee with a carafe of cream and dish of sugar to the table. "Let me know if you need anything else." She eyed me with curiosity. I shrugged in response. Her guess was as good as mine about what the Professor wanted with me.

The Professor poured the bright roast into two cups. "Juliet?" He held a third cup in his hand. "Join us?"

"No, thanks." I waved him off. "I've been downing caffeine since before the sun was up."

"When has that ever stopped you?" Thomas raised one brow.

I was glad that he was teasing me. I hoped it was a sign that he'd taken my words to heart. "True, but if I don't cut myself off for a while I'll get the shakes and that's bad for business." I intentionally made my hands quiver.

Thomas laughed and a smile tugged on the Professor's face as he sipped his coffee.

"Ah, yes, as the Bard so eloquently wrote in *Antony and Cleopatra,* 'To business that we love we rise bedtime, and go to't with delight.' You have found such a business, have you not?"

I glanced around the dining room where families, students, and actors were gathered at tables and waiting for frothy drinks. Torte was buzzing with happy energy and the low hum of a mixer spinning in the kitchen. "I have."

"Alas, it is other business that finds us here this morning." The Professor rested his coffee mug on the table and removed a piece of paper from his breast pocket. He creased the paper flat and handed it to me. "Howard has yet to confess, and I'm afraid that it's likely that you'll be called to testify even if he changes his stance in the days to come."

I swallowed. "What does that mean? I've never had to testify before."

The Professor ran his fingers along his light gray and ginger scruff. "Yes, I'm aware of that fact. The issue is his attempted abduction of you. The district attorney is a dear friend of mine and will walk you through everything. I assure you, there's nothing to worry about."

I did feel reassured by the Professor's words. He had exuded a calming effect. "What did Howard say?"

The Professor furrowed his brow. "What motivates such ghastly acts?" He let out a long sigh and patted Thomas's shoulder. "Some days more than others I think that it's time I bid this work adieu."

So he was serious about retiring. I wondered if he and Mom had talked more about what was next for them.

"It seems that Evan and Howard had a falling-out. Evan found a new spice vendor and informed Howard of his intention to part ways. There's also some evidence that points to the fact that Howard wasn't actually pro-curing his salt from the sea."

"What?" I asked. "Where would he get the salt?"

The Professor frowned. "That's what we're looking into at the moment. One of his employees has come forward and confessed that they ordered salt from a big warehouse chain and packaged it as their own."

"Really?" I thought back to Howard's presentation at the Chocolate Festival and the photos of him and his team in thigh-high waders standing in the sea. "How could he do that?"

"My thoughts exactly," the Professor said with a small nod. "I believe that Evan realized the con. He wasn't partnering with an organic sea salt vendor but rather with an old coastal codger who was pulling a fast one. His expensive salts were nothing more than what you could buy at any grocery store."

"Wow."

Thomas interjected. "I've been pulling receipts from Costco and other discount warehouse chains. It looks like Howard bought salt in bulk and then packaged it in fancy bottles with some spices and stuff. He wasn't doing any of the real work to harvest salt from the ocean. That was all for show."

I couldn't believe it. How had Howard gotten away with that kind of deceit for so long? He must have gone to great lengths to conceal the fact that he was peddling table salt. Now it made much more sense why he had killed Evan. Evan wasn't just going to break up their partnership. He was going to expose the fact that Howard was a fraud. It made me feel even sorrier for Evan.

The Professor continued, "Howard claims that he had

no knowledge of Evan's intent, but we have witnesses who are prepared to testify to the contrary."

Thomas gulped his coffee. "Yeah, and so far Howard isn't budging on his story. He's saying that he had no idea that pink peppercorns could be dangerous—or deadly. We know that's a lie, but proving it is going to take some work."

"And that's where I come in?" I said in confirmation.

The Professor nodded. "Your testimony is going to be imperative for the success of the case. As I mentioned, some of Howard's staff members are going to testify as well, but the fact that Howard attacked you is going to be paramount to the DA's case." He tapped the paper that he had handed me. "The DA would like to arrange a meeting as soon as possible to go over details while they are still fresh in your head."

My body shivered at the thought of being trapped in the storage room with Howard. "Okay." I gulped back my fear.

"Juliet," the Professor said, leaning forward and placing his hand on my arm. "This will not be a pleasant experience. You'll have to face Howard in court, and I know how difficult that can be, but I assure you we will all be with you every step of the way."

I bit my tongue and looked around the bakeshop again. "I get it. I'll testify."

The Professor looked relieved. "Most excellent, thank you." He finished his coffee. "We must be off. Please let me know if there's anything that Thomas or I can do to be of service to you."

"I'll be fine," I said with more conviction than I felt. Testifying in court wasn't high on my list of things I wanted to do, but I couldn't let Howard walk free. I had a duty to Evan, to myself, and to Ashland.

They stood. The Professor gave me a small bow and Thomas winked. "Catch you later, Jules." He sounded like he was intentionally trying to be as casual as possible. As they left, Rosalind breezed in. She was wearing her custom handmade royal-purple Ashland shirt that read ASHLAND: SUCH STUFF AS DREAMS ARE MADE ON, and held a bundle of paperwork.

"Juliet, is your mother here?" she asked, not bothering to wait for the door to close behind her.

"She's in the kitchen."

Rosalind waved the papers with one aging hand. "Don't just stand there. Go get her. I have news!"

Before I could even turn in the direction of the kitchen Mom was by my side. I jumped back. "Where did you come from?"

"I saw Rosalind crossing the street," Mom said with a grin.

Rosalind thrust the papers at Mom. "Great news, ladies, the space is yours. It was a unanimous vote. The city council is thrilled to support Torte's expansion."

Mom yanked me toward her into a giant hug. We both shrieked with delight and rocked back and forth. Rosalind watched with a smile with the paperwork still in her outstretched hand.

"Sorry, Rosalind," Mom said, letting go of me and rushing over to hug Rosalind too. "Thank you!"

Rosalind looked genuinely happy, but then returned to her matter-of-fact businesslike manner. "I'm as excited as you are, but there is so much work to do. The inspector will be at the building tomorrow at noon.

You'll need to meet with the contractor immediately and figure out your budget. If you need to apply for any additional loan money, that application is due by the end of the week. Lance is arranging a press package in partnership with Southern Oregon University. Film students will be documenting the renovations for college credit, and their work will be submitted to the grant funders. We're planning an unveiling ceremony in July once all of the construction is finished. You'll be a part of that, of course."

Mom's eyes widened. "That is a lot of work."

"It's not a task for the lighthearted," Rosalind agreed. "Now, if you'll excuse me, I have more news to go share."

"Thank you again, for everything," I said as Rosalind turned toward the door.

She paused and smiled. "My pleasure, dear. You are Ashland's rising star."

With that she walked with an unsteady gait out the door and across the plaza. Mom grabbed my hand. "Are we really going to do this?"

"It sounds like it. Are you sure you're okay with this?"

She tucked her arm around my waist. "Are you kidding me, and miss a chance to watch Ashland's star rise to the top?"

I bumped her hip. We walked to the kitchen to celebrate with Andy, Sterling, and Stephanie.

There was so much work to do. I thumbed through the paperwork that Rosalind left us. Before we could start the expansion we had to pump all of the water out and install a new drainage system. The architect and city had approved our designs and building permits. As long as we didn't get a new storm anytime soon, demolition would begin in April and (fingers crossed) should be complete by June and the start of the busy season.

Mom and I pored over catalogs and paint swatches. Our enthusiasm was contagious. Customers, business owners who stopped by for afternoon treats, and Andy, Sterling, and Stephanie added their ideas. The kitchen was a flurry of excitement and activity for the rest of the day. Stephanie cleaned the whiteboard and created a graph for everyone's suggestions. Soon we had a running brainstorm list that included everything from selling gelato to wood-fired pizza.

Once everyone left for the night, I stayed late to review the paperwork more carefully. I poured myself a glass of wine, heated a bacon and cheddar biscuit in the microwave, and headed for the office. A stack of unopened mail and catalogs waited for me on the desk. As I went to move them to make room for the paperwork, I pushed aside the top one on the stack, assuming it was another cooking magazine. But a handwritten note from Sandi Kramer fell on the desk. I'd completely forgotten about *Sweetened* and Sandi's article.

"Jules, I hope you're pleased with the layout. I know I am. Here's an early look at the issue. Stop by and we'll have drinks the next time you're in New York."

My breath caught as I removed the mock-up cover. The photographer had managed to make my wedding cakes appear in focus while the background of the shot was fuzzy. They looked modern and elegant yet had a vintage touch. I'd never seen my work in print before and couldn't believe how beautiful they looked.

The headline read: "Torte, an Artisanal Pastry Shop with a Touch of Home."

A touch of home. That was it. Torte was my home and my home was about to expand. I wasn't sure that my heart could handle so much happiness.

Mom's Famous Chocolate Spice Cake
with Mocha Frosting

Ingredients:

 1½ cups flour
 1 cup sugar
 ½ teaspoon salt
 3 tablespoons cocoa powder
 1 teaspoon baking soda
 1 teaspoon cinnamon
 ½ teaspoon ginger
 ½ teaspoon nutmeg
 6 tablespoons vegetable oil
 1 teaspoon vinegar
 1 teaspoon vanilla
 1 cup water

Directions:

Preheat oven to 350 degrees. Sift flour, sugar, salt, cocoa powder, baking soda, cinnamon, ginger, and nutmeg into an 8×8 glass pan. Make three wells—pour oil in one, vinegar in another, and vanilla in the last well. Pour water over entire pan and mix with a fork. Bake for thirty-five to forty-five minutes. Allow to cool and frost with mocha frosting below.

Mocha Frosting

Ingredients:
  ½ cup butter
  6 tablespoons cocoa powder
  2¾ cups powdered sugar
  ½ teaspoon cinnamon
  ½ teaspoon allspice
  5 tablespoons of strong brewed coffee

Directions:
Whip butter in mixer. Sift cocoa powder, sugar, and spices together. Slowly alternate adding powdered mixture and coffee. Once incorporated, beat until creamy and fluffy. Spread generously on chocolate spice cake.

Meat Loaf Sandwich

Ingredients:
  6 sourdough or any other good crusty hoagie rolls
  1 pound ground beef
  ½ pound ground pork sausage
  ½ pound ground veal
  2 cloves of garlic

1 yellow onion
2 eggs
1 cup bread crumbs (Jules uses Italian-seasoned
   crumbs)
2 sprigs fresh rosemary
1 teaspoon salt
1 teaspoon pepper
Parmesan cheese

Sauce ingredients:
   2 tablespoons Worcestershire sauce
   ¼ cup barbecue sauce
   ½ cup ketchup

Directions:
Preheat oven to 350 degrees. Finely chop onion, garlic, and rosemary. Whisk Worcestershire, barbecue sauce, and ketchup in a small bowl and set aside. Knead meats together in a large mixing bowl by hand. Whisk eggs and work into meat. Add all other ingredients and a quarter of the sauce. Form into a loaf and place in a loaf pan. Coat the loaf with the remaining sauce. Bake for one hour. Allow the meat loaf to rest for ten to fifteen minutes. While the loaf is resting, toast hoagie rolls. Slice meat loaf into one-and-a-half-inch slices and place on roll. Sprinkle with Parmesan cheese and broil for just one to two minutes, until the cheese melts.

Chicken Apple Sausage Quiche

Ingredients:
  1 prepared pie crust
  4 eggs
  1 cup heavy cream or half-and-half
  4 chicken apple sausages
  1 cup grated Parmesan cheese
  1 cup grated Gruyère cheese
  Fresh chives

Directions:
Preheat oven to 350 degrees. Poke holes in bottom of unbaked prepared pie crust and set aside. Whisk eggs and heavy cream by hand for two minutes. Slowly incorporate cheese and diced chicken apple sausage. Pour mixture into pie crust and bake for one hour or until golden brown. Sprinkle with fresh chopped chives before serving.

Chocolate Pasta

Ingredients:
  2¾ cups flour
  ⅓ cup cocoa powder
  ⅓ cup powdered sugar
  3 eggs
  2 tablespoons chocolate syrup
  1 teaspoon almond extract

Directions:

Sift flour, sugar, and cocoa powder on a large cutting board. Make a well in the center and crack eggs into it. Then add syrup and almond extract. Mix in the center with a fork and then slowly begin adding flour mixture from the sides to form dough. Knead until smooth. Depending on the consistency, add more flour or a little water. Once completely kneaded, cover with plastic wrap and chill for one hour. Divide chilled dough into four equal portions. Use cocoa powder to flour a cutting board and roll the first portion into one long rectangle about a quarter of an inch thick. If you have a pasta maker, run the sheet through the machine. Otherwise, cut long fettucine-style strips and rest on a cookie tray. Repeat for the remaining three portions of dough. Once all of the noodles are complete, bring a pot of water to a slow, rolling boil. Add a dash of salt and boil noodles for two to three minutes. Serve with white chocolate sauce below.

White Chocolate Sauce

Ingredients:
   1 cup white chocolate
   ½ cup crème fraîche
   ½ teaspoon vanilla

Directions:

Melt white chocolate and crème fraîche on low heat, stirring frequently. Once the chocolate is melted add vanilla and pour over chocolate noodles immediately. Top the pasta with chopped pistachios and fresh berries.

Chocolate Truffles

Ingredients:
  12 ounces semisweet chocolate
  1¼ cups heavy cream
  1 teaspoon extract (play with flavor combinations—vanilla, orange, coconut, almond, etc.)
  Salt
  Toppings (play with flavor combinations—toasted coconut, sprinkles, cocoa powder, powdered sugar, etc.)

Directions:
Melt chocolate on low heat. Slowly whisk in heavy cream. Remove from heat once mixture is completely melted and add extract. Transfer to a glass or plastic bowl. Cover with plastic wrap and allow to cool for two to three hours. Use a melon scoop or large spoon to form chocolate into one-inch balls. Roll balls in topping(s). Use your fingers to make sure the entire ball is coated with the topping. Then place in an airtight container. Refrigerate. Truffles will keep for up to a week. Be sure to remove them from the refrigerator one hour prior to serving.

Mango Chai Latte

Andy's tropical tea creation made with spicy Oregon Chai will have you dreaming of sunny beaches and warm, blue seas.

Ingredients:
   3 oz chai tea mix (Andy uses Oregon Chai, but any
      black tea blend will work)
   1 cup coconut milk
   2 tablespoons mango purée
   1 teaspoon fresh pineapple juice

Directions:
Heat chai and steam the coconut milk. Mix the mango purée and pineapple juice in the bottom of your favorite coffee mug. Add steamed coconut milk and stir. Pour in chai tea. Can be served hot or over ice.

Read on for an excerpt from

A Crime of Passion Fruit

the next Bakeshop Mystery
from Ellie Alexander and St. Martin's Paperbacks!

They say that the heart is like the ocean; its rhythm shifting with the sand on the shore. My heart had found a steady rhythm in Ashland, Oregon, the quirky Shakespearean small town where I had grown up. It had been almost eight months since I had returned home to our family bakeshop Torte. And despite an occasional dull ache for the life that I had left behind there was no debate in my mind that I had made the right choice. My heart belonged in Ashland.

During my years working as a pastry chef on a luxurious cruise ship, I had forgotten how much I loved Ashland's Elizabethan charm, its lush parks, its eclectic shops and restaurants, and most importantly its warm and welcoming community. Tucked into the southernmost corner of Oregon, Ashland's sunny, mild climate, abundant recreation opportunities, and fairytale-like village attracted tourists from all over the world. Having seen many far-off places myself it was no surprise that people had discovered the town I loved.

This morning as I walked down the plaza past the

bubbling Lithia fountains and a troop of street perform-
ers who were dressed liked modern-day gypsies I
couldn't help but chuckle. They waved and played me a
spontaneous baking song on a harp and accordion. Only
in Ashland, I thought, as I took in the scent of the sulfur
water in the basin-like fountain. The water was piped
to the center of town from a rare, naturally occurring
mineral spring. A stop at the fountain was a must for
any tourist, not only because of the water's famed health
benefits but also because it tasted like rotten eggs.

I crossed the street and passed Puck's Pub, an old-
English style pub with a massive wooden door and
oversized wrought-iron handles. Torte, our family bakeshop, was located on the far corner of the plaza. I walked
along the tree-lined sidewalk. Magenta banners with
gold lions flapped in the breeze. Antique lampposts,
hanging baskets dripping with pink fuchsias, and collec-
tions of outdoor bistro tables filled the narrow passage-
way. Soon the plaza would be humming with tourists
grabbing a bite to eat or window shopping before the
afternoon matinee at the Oregon Shakespeare Festival,
but until the season officially launched, "gone fishing"
signs had been posted in storefront windows and only
a handful of locals lingered over leisurely lunches in
the late afternoon sun.

Torte's fire-engine-red awning sat like an anchor at
the end of the sidewalk. My mom and dad had started
the bakeshop when I was a young child, offering their
delectable sweets, savory pastries, and artisan coffee to
townsfolk and tourists. Torte was more than a bakeshop—
it was the heart of Ashland. That was thanks to Mom.
When my dad died she took the helm and had been

serving up home-style handcrafted food with a side of love ever since. She was part baker and part counselor. Her easy-going style and superb listening skills made strangers feel like family from the minute they stepped inside Torte's bright and cheery front door. Every touch and detail had been designed to make customers feel at home, from the chalkboard menu with a rotating Shakespearean quote and space for Torte's youngest patrons to display their artwork, to fresh cut flowers on each table, and its vibrant teal and red color palate.

Now it was my turn to continue her legacy. Not that she was going anywhere, but we were taking on a major renovation and I wanted to make sure that I was bearing the burden of our expansion plans.

Thanks to an art's foundation grant program that my friend and artistic director of the Oregon Shakespeare Festival, Lance, had helped us secure, we were about to double Torte's square footage. It wasn't exactly something we had planned on. Mom and I had discussed Torte's future many times since I'd been home, but mostly in passing. We had both been content with the bakeshop's slow and steady growth and had saved up enough cash to upgrade our ovens. That project alone had us both reveling in how much more productive we could be, but then when the opportunity arose to take over the property below us, neither of us could pass it up.

Real estate on Ashland's bustling plaza was always at a premium. If we didn't jump at the chance it could be years—or decades—before the opportunity might arise again. However, my goal since returning had been to encourage Mom to scale back. She'd been managing the busy shop for ten years without me. Part of the appeal of returning to home to Ashland was being able to relieve stress and take on more duties so that she didn't have to work so hard. I knew that she loved Torte, but I also knew that she was reaching a time in her life where she could travel and indulge in more leisurely activities. Without her gentle yet firm nudging I may never have followed my dream of going to culinary school, and I wanted to help her do the same. She and the Professor, the town's lead detective and resident Shakespeare aficionado, were getting closer and it was her turn to set sail and explore. I just hoped that she would allow herself the same freedom she had allowed me.

Expanding into the basement space had already turned out to be a bigger undertaking then either of us had initially imagined. The property had been abandoned for years. To make matters worse it had flooded numerous times, most recently after a monsoon hit downtown Ashland, leaving almost every business in plaza under inches of water. Our first task was to pump the basement and have a new drainage system installed. No work on renovations or breaking through to Torte's upstairs could begin until we fixed the water issue. The problem was that our fellow shop owners were in the same boat. In a town the size of Ashland there weren't enough contractors to go around. We were in a holding pattern until the construction crew finished other repairs along the plaza.

As I reached Torte's front door I pushed my worries about our basement plans aside. I had other pressing things on my mind—like tonight's Sunday Supper. We had started offering Sunday Suppers at the bakeshop as a way to supplement our income during the off-season and to showcase our cooking. Both Mom and I enjoyed cooking as much as baking, and Sunday Suppers allowed us to stretch our creativity. We served dinner family style to encourage guests to mingle and help build an even stronger sense of community. Thus far the suppers had been a hit. In fact they'd all been sellouts and we had a lengthy waiting list of guests who wanted to attend tonight. Yet another reason that expanding the bakeshop could be good for our bottom line. We simply didn't have enough space at the moment.

Although I had to admit that one of the reasons that demand for Sunday Suppers might be so high was thanks to my estranged husband, Carlos. He had been in town for a short stay and had entranced the town with his sultry Spanish accent and spicy tapas. His Latin-inspired feast had left the town hungry for more. With his succulent tapas still fresh in everyone's mind I had opted for a decidedly different cuisine for tonight's supper— Asian fusion.

"I'm back," I called, opening the door with my free hand and tucking the box of vegetables I picked up from the market under my other arm.

"It's about time, boss." Andy, Torte's resident barista, winked from behind the coffee bar. He pushed up the sleeves on his Southern Oregon University football sweatshirt. "We've been dying without you." In addition to handcrafting creamy lattes, Andy was a student and football star.

"Right." I laughed, scanning the dining room where a couple was sharing a slice of Mom's chocolate caramel cake at a booth in front of the windows and a student with headphones was nursing a coffee as she studied. "It looks pretty packed in here."

"I'm serious. We can't get anything done around here without our fearless leader." He gave me a half-salute and organized canisters of coffee beans.

I shook my head and passed by him. "Carry on. Just as you are." Torte's staff might be young but they were highly capable. Mom and I often commented on how lucky we were to find such hard-working and talented help.

Walking around the coffee bar, I entered Torte's open kitchen where Mom, Sterling, our young sous chef in training, and Stephanie, another part-time college student who had turned out to be an incredibly skilled baker, were working on the evening's dinner. Every time I entered the newly remodeled kitchen I had to smile. We had upgraded our old, clunky ovens with shiny modern beauties that not only sparkled but cranked out so much heat that we were still tinkering with finding the right settings. The team had painted the kitchen walls in an opaque teal about three shades lighter than the dining room. It gave the workspace a vivid feel and blended in with the cheery red and teal color scheme in the front.

"Juliet, did they have scallions?" Mom asked, whisking a sauce on the stove. Her chestnut hair was tucked behind her ears revealing a pair of coffee cup earrings.

I placed the box of veggies on the island and held up a bunch of scallions.

"Excellent!" She dipped her pinkie into the sauce and gave it taste. "I think that a nice bit of scallion will finish this off perfectly."

"You mean elevate," Sterling said from the opposite side of the island. His dark locks shaded one eye. He wore his apron around his waist with a dish towel tucked into it. It was a trick he had learned from Carlos. I could hear Carlos saying, "A chef must always have a towel, si? You do not need to use these pot holders." He would scoff at the silicon oven mitts we used. "These take too much time. A towel it is easy and quick and you can use it for so many things." Sterling had taken Carlos's words to heart.

"Elevate?" Mom wrinkled her brow.

"That's what the professional chefs say." Sterling pushed up the sleeves of his black hoodie, revealing his tattooed forearms and began kneading pork and spices in a large mixing bowl.

Mom grinned. "Well, I like the sound of that. I'm elevating my sauce. Very impressive."

"Since when do you pay attention to how professional chefs are talking?" I asked. Elevate wasn't a term I had ever heard Carlos use. He was much more provincial in his approach to food.

Stephanie, who as usual appeared uninterested in our kitchen banter, busied herself assembling strawberry tarts on tray and finishing each one with a sprig of fresh mint.

Sterling shrugged. "I've been watching a few cooking shows here and there. You know, for *research*."

He tried to sound casual but I knew exactly what he meant and by the looks of Stephanie's cheeks which matched the red strawberry tarts, I had a feeling I knew who he'd been watching cooking shows with. Stephanie was addicted to the Pastry Channel, especially the cooking competitions, which had surprised all of us. Her somewhat sullen attitude and Goth exterior didn't exactly match with cheesy culinary television. Which in my opinion just proves that the kitchen is the great equalizer. People of all walks of life connect over food. It's one of the many, many reasons that I love being a chef.

The attraction between Sterling and Stephanie had been apparent to everyone in the bakeshop, but as of yet neither of them had been public about whether they were or weren't a couple and I certainly wasn't going to ask.

Mom wiped her hands on her apron and joined me at the island. "That produce looks gorgeous." She ran her hand over a bunch of yellow peppers. I noticed that she wasn't wearing her wedding ring. Instead it hung from a simple gold chain around her neck. "Look at the color on these."

"I know." I nodded toward Sterling. "How is the pot sticker preparation coming along?"

"Good." Mom pointed to the pot she had left simmering on the stove. "The sauce is almost ready and as you can see Sterling is up to his elbows in the filling." To Sterling she added, "As soon as you're done incorporating the spices, I'll show you how to fill them."

My mouth watered at the thought of homemade pot stickers. At least once a month when I was growing up my dad would make an Asian-inspired feast which always included hand-rolled pot stickers. The flavorful dumplings were always my favorite. We were using his recipe tonight. In addition to the pot stickers, we planned to serve a noodle salad chock-full of cabbages, bean sprouts, julienned carrots, cilantro, and peppers, tossed in a tangy peanut sauce. For dessert we would add a touch of whimsy to the table with coconut and chocolate deep fried wantons.

"It's starting to smell amazing in here." I unpacked the rest of the vegetables and assembled piles of organic carrots and bunches of cilantro on bamboo cutting boards on the island.

Andy came into the back balancing a tray of coffees. As our resident coffee mixologist he was always experimenting with new drinks. No one ever complained about tasting one of Andy's creations. In fact usually we fought for position to be the first in line for a taste. "Hey, so I thought it might be cool to do a drink pairing with your wontons," he said, passing us each a cup. "Give this a try and let me know what you think."

I cradled the warm mug in my hands and inhaled the scent of Andy's drink. The creamy tea smelled fruity and fresh. I took a sip and immediately tasted a hint of pear mingled with just a touch of ginger. The balance of the spicy ginger and sweet pear was sinful.

"This is amazing," I said to Andy, taking another drink.

Sterling mumbled with his mouth full and gave Andy a thumbs up.

"What's in it?" Mom asked. "Pear?"

A smile tugged at Andy's boyish cheeks. He wore a baseball hat backwards making him look even younger. "That's right, Mrs. C. Asian Pear and a hint of fresh ginger. I used a custom blend of chai tea with coconut and almond milk. Do you like it?"

"I love it." Mom looked at me and widened her eyes. "He's done it again, hasn't he?"

"He has." I nodded enthusiastically.

Andy's shoulders swelled at the compliment. "I thought it might be unique."

"It's like we planned it," I said. "This will be great with our dessert wontons. You should add it to the specials board."

"Awesome." The door jingled and Andy hurried to the front to help the customer.

I was about to get started on chopping purple and yellow cabbage when my cell phone buzzed in the back pocket of my jeans. Not many people call me. Sadly I was way behind the digital trend after working on cruise ships for so many years, and practically everyone I knew in Ashland came to Torte at least once a day. Whenever my phone buzzed it always took me by surprise.

I rested the knife on the cutting board and pulled my phone from my pocket. My heart skipped a beat when Carlos's face flashed on the screen. Why was my husband calling me?

"Julieta, is that you?" Carlos's thick Spanish accent greeted me from somewhere halfway around the world. Carlos was the executive chef on the Amour of the Seas. It was fitting that the ship had been christened with a name like *amour*. The kitchen staff used to tease me, saying that Carlos was the love chef. He earned his nickname by showering me with luscious food, Spanish wine, and quoting poetry in my ear when he would pass me in the ship's long hallways. Why was he calling me now? He rarely called, and certainly not in the middle of the day.

"What's going on, Carlos? Where are you?" I asked, clutching the island to steady myself. Hearing his voice threw me off balance. After a brief stay in Ashland last month, Carlos had returned to the ship. I hadn't expected him to follow me to Ashland and was glad for our time together. I think we both had a chance to heal, but our future was shaky. As much as I loved him, and the chemistry between us was undeniable, we were worlds apart. Carlos was a vagabond at heart. He belonged to the sea. I belonged to Ashland.

"I am on the ship, mi querida." He paused for a moment. "I have a favor I must ask of you."

"Okay." I could hear the trepidation in my voice. Mom studied me. Her gingerbread eyes widened when I said Carlos's name. I held up my finger and waited for Carlos to continue.

"It is our pastry chef. He, how do you say it? He freaked out and quit."

"Why?" I glanced behind me. Sterling and Stephanie appeared to have everything in control, so I motioned to Mom and pointed to the window. She nodded while I hurried outside. Thankfully the sidewalk bistro table sat empty. I plopped down on an iron chair. "Why did he freak out?" I repeated.

"I do not know. Someone said he is angry because a customer complained that his flan it is no good." Carlos laughed. "I am with the customer. His flan was terrible."

I laughed too. "There's nothing worse than a bad flan."

"Si, si. It is not a real loss. No one liked this chef, but this is our problem. We have a new pastry chef coming from a sister ship, but he can't arrive for another week. He is already at sea."

"Okay." I stared at the tree above me. Its dainty green leaves quivered in the slight wind.

"Okay, so we want you to come."

"Me?!" I shouted. Then I regained my composure as a couple strolled past with a bag of Torte pastries. "I can't come on the ship. I'm working—at Torte. You know that."

"Si, I know, but it is only for a few days. We need someone and someone good to come help until the new chef comes. The staff they already know you. You know the ship. It will be easy for everyone and it makes the most sense."

"Carlos, I can't just leave Ashland and come back to the ship." A leaf floated down from the tree and landed on the table. I picked it up and ran my fingers along its spine.

"Only for five days. This is nothing. And they will pay you extra. Double pay."

"Double pay?" The cruise lines rarely offer bonuses or double pay.

"Si, double. And I talked to the captain about your mom." Carlos sounded smug, like he knew he had won.

"My mom?" I glanced into the kitchen window where Mom stood next to Sterling at the stove. "What about Mom?"

"I thought it would be so nice if you bring her along. And the Professor too. They could have a vacation here on the ship while you are baking, no?"

"A vacation?"

"Si. They can be my guests for free. No charge. They will each have a nice suite with a balcony and all expenses will be paid."

"Wow." I found myself at a momentary loss for words.

"It is a good cruise too. We will go to so many stunning locations, Julieta. You can show them the gorgeous white beaches, they can explore each port, and I will make you all such wonderful fresh food that you will never want to leave. What do you say?"

"I don't know what to say," I stuttered. "When? And how would it work with Mom?"

"I need you here in three days. You have your passport and you still have clearance, so it should be smooth and easy. The flights they can be arranged right away."

"Three days?" I ripped the leaf in half. That wasn't much time.

"Will you come?" I could hear the longing in his voice.

"I don't know." I hesitated and glanced inside again. "Let me think about it and I'll get back to you."

"Okay, but you must tell me soon. Otherwise we must continue to find someone else."

"Why don't you promote one of the sous chefs?"

"No, the captain will not allow it. There is too much drama. One of the sous chefs left with the head pastry chef and the others they are not liking the kitchen. It is a bad idea. You will be perfect because you will help things run smooth until the new chef comes."

"I don't know." I waivered. Mom deserved a vacation, but then again there was so much to do at Torte.

"You think about it. Talk to Helen and then you let me know, okay?"

"Okay." I agreed and clicked off the phone. When I returned to the kitchen Mom pounced on me. "Was that Carlos?" she whispered. "Is everything okay?" I tugged her by the shoulder toward an empty booth in the dining room. I didn't want to have this conversation in front of our staff.

I explained everything and she nodded along with relative calm until I got to the part about Carlos's invitation to her and the Professor. Her eyes lit up and I saw her body shift. She would never say it to me, but I could tell that she was excited about the idea.

"Would you have any interest in going?" I asked, carefully.

She tried to keep her face neutral but I could see the glimmer in her eyes when she said, "No, I mean that's a wonderful and generous offer from Carlos, but I wouldn't want to put you in the middle of something like that or make things awkward for you."

"I'm not worried about that. I'm worried about leaving Torte. We have so much going on right now, with the expansion."

Mom leaned her head from side to side and looked thoughtful for a moment. "True, but we're in a holding pattern for a while and it's only five days right? I think the kids could handle things for a while, don't you?"

I nudged her in her petite waist. "You want to go, don't you?"

She shrugged and smiled wider. "I have to admit the thought of lounging by the pool with a good book and tropical drink is very appealing. It's been a stressful winter."

"Done. I'll call Carlos back right now."

"No, honey, wait. You don't need to do this for me."

"I'm not. You're right. A free trip for you, double pay for me, and there's nothing we can do here until they get the basement pumped out. Let's do it. Five days in paradise. What could possibly go wrong?"

Famous last words.